THE BLUE DEVIL

DEVIL

Melynda Beth Skinner

ZEBRA BOOKS

KENSINGTON PUBLISHING CORP.

http://www.zebrabooks.com

For Barry, my love

ZEBRA BOOKS are published by

Kensington Publishing Corp.
850 Third Avenue
New York, NY 10022

All Kensington titles, imprints and distributed lines are available at special quantity discounts for bulk purchases for sales promotion, premiums, fund-raising, educational or institutional use.

Special book excerpts or customized printings can also be created to fit specific needs. For details, write or phone the office of the Kensington Special Sales Manager: Kensington Publishing Corp., 850 Third Avenue, New York, NY 10022. Attn. Special Sales Department. Phone: 1-800-221-2647.

Zebra and the Z logo Reg. U.S. Pat. & TM Off.

First Printing: August 2001
10 9 8 7 6 5 4 3 2 1

Printed in the United States of America

"Nigel, allow me to introduce Miss Kitty Davidson."

Nigel?! A toll of warning clanged in Kathryn's head. That name . . . that voice . . . no, it could not be! Kathryn looked up and her mouth dropped open.

The devil was staring back at her.

A mixture of surprise, amusement, and suspicion marched across the sharp planes of his handsome face as he towered over her. As she watched, his grin turned from amused to sardonic. The wispy seeds of recognition swept over his features, and Kathryn felt herself blanch. If he identified her as Titania, poor Aunt Ophelia truly would be ruined. Blackshire would expose Kathryn to Lady Marchman without delay, and Ophelia's diary would never be rescued from her clutches. Then, if whatever secret it contained did not entirely ruin Aunt Ophelia, the story of Kathryn's shocking masquerade as one of Lady Marchman's students would— for Kathryn had no doubt Blackshire would delight in maliciously telling the tale, were he to discover that it had been she who had witnessed his attack upon Lydia.

That it had been she dressed as the fairy at the masquerade.

That it had been she who had swatted his rump with her wand.

That it had been she who had delivered him that insolent, malicious, and very public cut direct.

And that it had been she who had melted into his arms and kissed him like a strumpet at twilight. . . .

BOOK YOUR PLACE ON OUR WEBSITE AND MAKE THE READING CONNECTION!

We've created a customized website just for our very special readers, where you can get the inside scoop on everything that's going on with Zebra, Pinnacle and Kensington books.

When you come online, you'll have the exciting opportunity to:

- View covers of upcoming books
- Read sample chapters
- Learn about our future publishing schedule (listed by publication month *and author*)
- Find out when your favorite authors will be visiting a city near you
- Search for and order backlist books from our online catalog
- Check out author bios and background information
- Send e-mail to your favorite authors
- Meet the Kensington staff online
- Join us in weekly chats with authors, readers and other guests
- Get writing guidelines
- AND MUCH MORE!

Visit our website at
http://www.zebrabooks.com

Chapter One

London, England
1815

The tired old coach pulled into Grosvenor Square seven hours late, just after one-o'-the-clock, its lamps glowing weakly in the foggy darkness. Swearing and mumbling, its driver maneuvred the vehicle and its single passenger among a throng of other equipages, whose brilliantly liveried coachmen tossed catcalls and the odd apple core after the ancient coach as it passed.

Inside, Kathryn St. David groaned. The Square was a crush of splendid, black-lacquered coaches and magnificent matched teams. Surely Great-Aunt Ophelia wouldn't have thrown a ball for her on the very night she was to arrive in London!

Kathryn moved the curtain aside to peer at the enormous, marble-fronted mansions which lined the square, then squeezed her eyes shut and sagged back against the thread-bare squabs of her parents' coach. It had been a mistake to come here. Kathryn didn't belong here among the elegant *ton.* Why, only yesterday she'd been romping over the hills, where she'd managed to fall into a brook, returning home sodden and laughing.

She supposed the grandeur before her should not have surprised her. Palin House was Great-Aunt Ophelia's chosen home, after all, and wasn't everything about Ophelia grand? Everything large sums of money could have an effect upon, at least? Unfortunately, no amount of money could turn back the hands of time. Kathryn was two-and-twenty, and nothing could change that, not even the formidable Ophelia.

But Auntie *had* insisted she could work some sort of miracle upon Kathryn's looks. It wasn't appearing long-in-the-tooth that plagued Kathryn, but just the opposite. To her unending disgust, she didn't look a day past fifteen. Slender as a wisp and short of stature, she possessed a childishly rounded, heart-shaped face crowned with tight, blond curls. And she didn't have much in the way of curves to which a dampened petticoat might cling! Yet in spite of Kathryn's advanced age and diminutive size, Ophelia had promised her a London Season with ballrooms full of handsome young suitors, all eager for Kathryn to toss them a crumb of notice. According to Auntie, Kathryn would be lucky to escape the avalanche of vellum invitations she would soon have. Ophelia foretold anonymous odes writ to her niece's eyes, desperate pleas for the grant of a dance, tender love letters from sincere beaux—as well as deliciously improper missives from beaux not so sincere, which Kathryn would certainly not acknowledge, though there would be no harm in the reading. Ophelia vowed Kathryn would have a flock of dashing, wealthy gentlemen vying for her hand by summer's end.

Kathryn did not see how that was possible. Yet neither did she concur with her parents' projections. They had abandoned London long ago, rejecting its perfidy and politics for the slow honesty of the country the year Kathryn was born. Stubbornly hoping she would find her heart's desire there, they had thus far resisted allowing her a Season in

London. But even they had to admit that two-and-twenty maidenhood was cause for alarm. Desperate circumstances required desperate measures. And so, they sent her on her way under a shower of warnings: London was full of handsome young demons eager to steal her innocence. They would swoop down upon Kathryn, and she would be forced to flee for home. She would be lucky to escape London with her life—to say nothing of her virtue—intact.

Fortunately, both of those improbable scenarios—her parents' and Auntie's—sounded quite exhilarating to Kathryn. And since good sense told her reality would fall somewhere between the two, she had been eager to see for herself what London had to offer.

Until now.

As her coachman pressed forward and Kathryn peered around the curtain, she identified the dignified lines of Palin House, disconcertingly aglow. Music and laughter wafted from its glittering windows, while bejeweled, bemasqued guests overflowed onto its lawns and even into the Square. In Auntie's typically daring style, she'd chosen to give a masqued ball. Kathryn looked down at the front of her dusty brown kerseymere traveling costume. Even in the gloom, she could see the dark stains of blackberry jam left there when the coach had done battle with an enormous pothole and lost. The lurch broke a wheel as well as the crock of preserves Kathryn's mother had packed for her noonday meal. She'd washed as best she could, but even if she'd been able to get all of the jam out, the dust and the wrinkles would still be there now. An idea hit Kathryn. Perhaps she could attend the masque as an urchin!

Looking out at the gaily colored costumes of the ladies who floated across Auntie's lawns, Kathryn's customary optimism deserted her. She might be a country mouse, but even she knew making an entrance dressed like this, much less as an urchin, would be a disaster.

The coach lurched to a halt. "We're 'ere, love!" John called, and the carriage swayed precariously as he swung down from his box. Panic rose within Kathryn, and she would have urged John to turn the coach and head for home, but for one supremely logical thought. Even if she never appeared in anything better than what she was dressed in at this moment, her chances of finding a husband here in London were still far better than finding one back home in tiny, distressingly underpopulated Heathford. There, she could dress like a princess at court every day, and it wouldn't matter. No man could take notice of her where there were no men at all! Besides, if she left London now, Great-Aunt Ophelia would be disappointed as well as hurt. But perhaps she'd be doing Ophelia a favor in the long run, for no matter what Auntie said, finding a husband for Kathryn wasn't going to be easy. And Kathryn's arrival in this state was about to make the task much more difficult.

She tugged her gloves on tighter, girding herself for the ordeal to come, but when the driver yanked open the door, which squeaked on its rusty iron hinges, she froze.

"John!" Kathryn cried. "Please, close the door. I am not ready." John scowled, his bushy gray brows meeting in the center, but he complied without comment. "And, pray," she added, motioning at the outsides of the coach, "put out the lamps." This instruction brought a muttered string of unintelligible complaint, but John did as he was told while Kathryn wrapped her brown wool cloak about her and raised its hood before tapping on the door.

John opened the door again and peered inside. "You 'iding from someone?" he asked.

"No."

He ignored her. "Don't blame ye. I'd 'ide too, if'n I could." He swabbed ineffectually with his handkerchief at a blob of apple pulp that clung to the side of the coach.

"John . . . perhaps you've got something there."

"Got what? I don't have nothing 'cept a mess of a 'anky!" He held up the offending square of cotton.

"No, no. What I mean to say is that you've a splendid idea."

"I 'ave?"

"Yes."

"About what, may I ask?"

"Hiding."

"'Iding?"

Kathryn smiled and nodded. "Kindly escort me to the back door, John."

"The *back* door?"

"You do know the way? You were here with Mama and Papa years ago."

John grumbled. "'Ow could I forget that? Wish I *could* forget. But who could forget 'Er Majesty? The old dragon!" He spat in the direction of the house, forgetting his manners, and Kathryn stifled a grin. John's ire for her great-aunt was legendary—and so normal that it was comical. He hooked his thumb toward the house. "The 'ag. O' course I mind the way. Just ain't fittin', that's all, you bein' family. What's got into you, miss? Walkin' in the back door like you was a servant!"

Kathryn smiled and looped her arm through his. "Well, John, you must admit that I am not exactly dressed for the occasion."

"Nothing wrong with 'ow you're dressed." What John lacked in polish he made up for in loyalty. "Why, you'd put any o' them Town pugs in there to shame, you would. Your 'air is like spun gold, and you've a wisp of a figure, beggin' your pardon, and your eyes are like the biggest, shiniest blue shoe buttons a body ever saw, and . . . and 'your lips are like a red, red rose,'" he misquoted Mr. Robert Burns.

Kathryn smiled fondly and patted his arm. "The back door, if you please, my old friend."

There were actually several back doors to the enormous house. Kathryn wasn't quite sure which to choose, but John seemed to know just the one, after Kathryn explained what she had in mind. The narrow entrance he took her to led directly to a set of cramped back stairs. There, John parted company with Kathryn and left to see to the team and coach.

Kathryn stood listening on the first landing. The house hummed with activity, but the servants were busy either in the kitchen or ballroom, and the back stairs were empty. She ascended to the third floor and walked briskly down the main hall, looking for her bedchamber. It was easy to spot. The door was ajar, and as soon as she entered, she saw that the coals on the hearth were banked and glowing, providing some heat, but very little light. She made for the bedside table, where a candle would be, but in the darkness she kicked a heavy oak washstand, doing an injury to one of her littlest toes. She stifled a howl. Curse these flimsy slippers! They were not good for traveling. Kathryn would have much preferred her own thick leather walking boots, but her mother would not hear of her taking the ugly things to London.

She plunked down on the bed and reached for her foot. She didn't think she had broken it, but it was throbbing, and it was obvious it would be sore for quite some time.

She looked about her. The room was appointed in a lavish style, with touches of gilt and silver here and there and rich scarlet hangings and a scarlet brocade counterpane on the bed. An ornately carved clothespress stood empty in the corner, awaiting the contents of her trunk.

Limping a little, she placed the candle on the sill to signal John as to her location, wishing he would appear instantly, though she knew it would be a good hour before he had the coach and horses settled to his satisfaction.

The hall echoed with muted revelry from below. She knew nothing she could pull from her baggage was fancy enough to wear to the ball. Auntie would be perturbed when Kathryn came down dressed in her Sunday sarcenet, but the old lady would just have to smile and endure. It was Ophelia's own fault, after all. Giving a ball tonight, of all nights—what had she been thinking? Kathryn slumped down onto a royal blue velvet-covered settee and massaged her neck. All she wanted was a hot bath and eight hours of stillness. The bone-jarring journey had felt much longer than it was—even before the back wheel had fallen off the poor old coach.

As Kathryn sat, gingerly rubbing her heels over the thick, red, blue, and cream Aubusson carpet, the voices carrying faintly up from the ballroom seemed to grow louder. Her eyes narrowed, and her gaze darted to the door just as a lady's laughter trilled in echoes down the hallway.

Someone was coming.

A thought suddenly occurred to her. What if Auntie had overnight guests? What if this were not Kathryn's chamber at all? What if it belonged to the approaching lady instead?

She doused the candle, her heart hammering in her chest. She couldn't close the outer door now without taking a chance on being seen. Her pulse pounded in her ears. What if she were found lurking about someone else's bedchamber?

At home in Heathford, it would be shrugged off ... but not in London. Auntie had warned that in Town Kathryn could well find herself ostracised for the smallest of infractions.

She must not appear, even for the briefest instant, outside without an escort. She must not take her shoes off in the park to wiggle her toes in the grass. She must not use her fan for cooling herself lest she send some unintended signal to a gentleman. She must always accept and taste the dainties offered her at tea, but she must never finish them. She must never agree to dance more than twice in one evening with any gentleman. She must never ride astride no matter what she was wearing ... and for heaven's sake, she must never wear anything which would render her capable of riding astride!

The list of rules was endless.

Kathryn wanted very much to please Great-Aunt Ophelia, and so she would do her best to remember all she'd been told. Poor Ophelia had hopes of convincing the *ton* Kathryn was a catch, a desirable and demure debutante, a Diamond of the First Water.

Kathryn knew the scheme was doomed from the start. She was a hoyden, a diamond of the *last* water. No *tonnish* man would take one such as herself to wife. Not even Ophelia could accomplish that sort of social *coup*, but it would be a shame to dash the lady's hopes so soon by being caught in someone else's bedchamber, and now there was only one way to be certain she would not be seen.

Kathryn hastily ducked into the clothespress as the lady's unintelligible chatter progressed down the hallway. She was being a pea-goose, she told herself, for the lady would no doubt pass by unawares. Kathryn's diminutive stature allowed her to stand erect in the clothespress, and she felt a little silly standing there—until the lady stopped—right in front of Kathryn's chamber door.

"It seems we have arrived, darling," the woman's voice cooed.

Darling? There were two of them!

"What game are you playing, Lydia?" a masculine voice queried.

"Oh, look . . . someone has left this door ajar. Do you think a servant is in there?" The lady gasped—rather dramatically, Kathryn thought. "Or perhaps a thief? Perhaps you should go in there and see, before we proceed."

"Lydia . . ." the man's voice warned.

"I assure you I am playing no game!"

The gentleman sighed and pushed open Kathryn's door, just missing the soft click the door of the clothespress made as it closed behind Kathryn. "See? No one here," he said.

Kathryn pressed her face as close as she dared to the front interior of the clothespress and peered through the high keyhole. She saw a tall figure pass in front of her, and then the room went black as the outer door was shut behind the two. She could see nothing, but she knew the couple stood scant inches in front of her.

"Yes, darling, it seems you are correct. No one here but us. Alone."

"Lydia!" He sighed.

With a start, Kathryn realized she was about to witness a . . . a *liaison!* Oh, heavens, if she thought it a wrinkle to be discovered lurking in someone's room, how much worse would it be to be found lurking in someone's clothespress as they . . . they . . . *liaisoned?*

Kathryn could do nothing but stand and listen for a chance to slip away. Perhaps they might become so . . . involved that she could escape without their knowledge. The room was large, and as they moved away—toward the bed, no doubt!—their voices became difficult to discern. She thought she heard the bed creaking. Then the man raised his voice. He seemed to be passionately angry.

Or just passionate, perhaps.

A maiden she might be, but Kathryn was not ignorant in the ways of love. She had seen the horses and other animals on her father's estate mating many times. The act of love was always violent, and it was often hard to tell if a pair were courting or fighting. In fact, Kathryn had made up her mind long ago that she wanted no part of it. Marriage seemed pleasant. Her parents were happy. But what one had to go through to get children must be horrible. After all, even her parents, who loved each other, had only been able to endure the rigors of having one child, Kathryn herself.

Listening now to the muffled, angry-sounding voices of this couple, Kathryn's resolve strengthened. No. She would ask Ophelia to find her a husband who definitely did not want children. Perhaps Ophelia could find a widower with a liking for windswept country hills, one who already had an heir.

After a few moments, the couple seemed quite distracted. She could hear struggling and grunting and then something which sounded like ripping cloth. Now was her chance. She slipped deftly from the clothespress and raced in what she thought was the direction of the outer door—only to smash into the cheval glass, reinjuring her already throbbing toe. The pain was intense, and Kathryn cried out. "Owee-me . . . owee-me . . . owee-meeeee!" It was the pain chant she'd invented while still in the nursery, and it had always been reserved for the most grievous of injuries.

Behind her, the woman cried out. "Who is there? Blackshire! We are not alone!"

Kathryn wildly groped for the door and flung it open, flooding the room with light from the hall sconces. She ran blindly, looking for a place to hide until she came upon a darkened, shadowy alcove where stood a large, ornate statue carved in the shape of a satyr. There was just barely enough room for Kathryn to squeeze behind it.

The lady appeared first. She rushed past Kathryn's hiding place, crying and holding the ripped bodice of her white muslin gown to her chest with one delicate hand. Why, she was younger than Kathryn by a margin of at least five years! She was dressed as Artemis, and a small diamond-studded archer's bow, entangled in her long, brown curls, swung wildly across her shoulder as she ran. But Kathryn had no time to further contemplate her appearance or her tender years, for the gentleman emerged from the room, calling after her.

"Lydia!" he hissed. "Lydia, you must not be seen in that state. Come back here—at once!"

But Lydia did not heed him. She ran headlong down the hall sobbing instead, and disappeared around a corner. Kathryn was stunned. It seemed she'd been mistaken. Poor Lydia had not been the participant of a tryst. No. The dear girl had been sorely used. Taken advantage of. Compromised unwillingly!

Kathryn turned to deliver a set-down to the man—who was certainly *not* a gentleman—but her breath caught in her throat as his gaze swiveled in her direction, and she shrank back into the dark alcove. The beast's eyes were black as midnight, and the sconce light seemed to flash and glint across them as though they were made of obsidian. Hard they were, hard and cold. Kathryn sensed the man was angry beyond measure, and she was gripped with a sudden, paralyzing fear.

Her intended scolding stuck, nearly forgotten, in her throat as the man drew from the pocket of his trousers a blue satin demi-mask and tied it over his eyes. Kathryn blinked. If he thought to conceal his identity and escape the house, she decided with satisfaction he wasn't going to be very successful. His thick, dark hair was unfashionably long, and, even without the uncommon style, he'd hardly be difficult to spot across a crowded ballroom, for he was tall and broad-shouldered. In fact, he looked quite strong. Quite strong and quite able to overpower a lone female, Kathryn realized. She wondered how poor Lydia had escaped.

Would Kathryn herself be so lucky, if the need arose?

Softly, the man swore, and the tenor of his voice surprised her. Silken, and strangely warm, it did not match his harsh expression but soothed itself around Kathryn's senses like a whispered promise. A sudden, ridiculous desire to hear him sing overtook her, and she had to suppress a giggle of rising panic.

Would anyone hear her if she screamed? The walls of her alcove pressed in on her. What had seemed a sanctuary before now seemed a trap. She fought down an urge to run and tried instead to memorize every detail of the devil before her to tell the authorities later. Maybe she could be of some help to poor Lydia yet.

Kathryn noted for the first time what the blackguard was wearing. He was dressed as a highwayman, in a flowing, white linen shirt laced loosely up the front. His throat was wrapped with apparent carelessness in an azure silk kerchief. Kathryn couldn't help staring at the shocking triangle of browned skin he'd boldly allowed to show below the knot of blue silk. His chest was covered with dark, springy looking curls, and Kathryn was fascinated. Her eyes followed the solid column of his torso downward almost of their own will. His black trousers, indecently tight about his muscled legs, ended in a pair of soft, low boots, very much like the ones Kathryn had left back in Heathford. Clenched in one fist, he held a black cape lined in rich blue satin, and as

Kathryn watched, he swept it into the air and fastened the clasp at his Adam's apple, the material swirling around his massive shoulders. The clasp sparkled with the unmistakable glint of a large sapphire.

Kathryn swallowed, her eyes fixed once more on that triangle of skin. She thought she detected a pulsing there, where his blood beat through his veins. She could not look away. Had it been the same for Lydia? Is that how he had fascinated her? Was that triangle of skin all he had bared to the poor girl?

And what had he done to her in that darkened bed-chamber?

The devil swore again, and she remembered the muffled sounds she'd heard from within the clothespress. He must have been using that silken voice to seduce Lydia. Kathryn imagined how it would be, hearing that soft voice whispering endearments near her own tilted ear, and she shivered. It was a barely perceptible movement, but the demon's gaze swept her end of the hallway once more as though he'd sensed her presence. She willed herself to stop breathing. He stood motionless, listening, and then, finally, he turned and disappeared like an apparition into the gloom at the other end of the hallway.

Kathryn stood transfixed, staring after him. The corridor seemed to spark with the electricity of his presence. Tiny hairs that had prickled with goose bumps on her arms and down her back gradually subsided, and Kathryn remembered to breathe.

Emerging from her hiding place, she understood how poor Lydia had been lured to such ruin. The man was more than charismatic. His eyes were hypnotic, his voice enchanting. He was exciting. Enticing. Way too much temptation for a flower of tender years and experience such as dear Lydia.

Fortunately, Kathryn was beyond the age where rakes such as Lydia's tormentor held any real power over her. Though her experience with the manly portion of the population was admittedly lacking, she was still a sensible, cautious, worldly-wise two-and-twenty. Why, she had hardly a blush left in her! Certainly, she was incapable of tumbling into the trap Lydia had fallen into. Wasn't she?

Her hands were shaking, and she dreaded going back to that bedchamber. On impulse, she decided to wait in another room. By Town schedules, the ball was just getting started, and she'd most likely be safe there for several hours anyway. John would be finished with the horses soon. Quickly, she opened the last of the doors in this hall of lady's chambers. Stepping in, she gasped. Then, immediately, she heaved a sigh, for Kathryn knew instantly that *this* bedchamber—and no other—was the one Auntie intended for her.

There on the dressing table stood an enormous bouquet of violets, her favorite flower. The other rooms on this floor had been decorated sumptuously in golds, crimsons, and blues, with no expense spared. But this room, though equally beautiful, was not the same. The bed and windows bore counterpanes and draperies of deep, liquid purple exactly matching the shade of the violets, while the rest of the room was decorated in shades of palest lavender and cream. No gaudy gilt moldings or flocked wallpaper spoiled its simplicity. Kathryn looked up and wondered at the magnificent high ceiling. It was painted in *trompe l'oeil* to look like a blue summer sky, complete with puffy white clouds and a bird flying high above. The entire effect was lovely.

It seemed she was home.

Kathryn turned the key in the lock behind her, lit a candle, and set it in the window to await the arrival of John and her clothing, but there was no need of them, for Auntie had already provided a costume for the masqued ball. On the bed lay an exquisite gown of sheerest white silk. Beside it lay a wreath for the hair fashioned of violets and the palest yellow roses. Eyes wide, Kathryn examined the creations. The gown was sewn with tiny faceted silver beads that sparkled even in this pale candlelight. It was stunning, and Kathryn smiled.

Ducking into the small dressing room, Kathryn made

efficient use of the water basin and some soft linen toweling before donning the gown. She fluffed her short blond curls with her fingers, settled the wreath of flowers on her head, and finally marveled at the effect in the cheval glass. The magnificent gown fit reasonably well, and Kathryn wondered how Ophelia had accomplished that. Admiring her image, she remembered the fairy character Titania from *A Midsummer Night's Dream,* which Ophelia had taken Kathryn to see when a traveling company had passed through Heathford some years before. Kathryn had openly admired the gown the actress wore, and it was obvious Auntie had ordered this gown to be made similar to that one.

A box on the bed held matching silver gloves and slippers, a delicate lace reticule, a white satin-and-silver lace mask, and at the very bottom . . . sparkly silver wings and a wand! Kathryn tipped her head back and chuckled. Then, remembering Ophelia's admonition that ladies of the *ton* did not laugh out loud, she clapped her hand over her mouth. Lifting the filmy gauze wings out of the box, Kathryn twirled about the room, and then she noticed the diamond-studded coronet waiting for her on the dressing table.

Diamond-studded, just like Lydia's bow.

Her feet stilled. How could she have forgotten the girl's plight? Or the man responsible, the rotter? Outrage surged through her. Would he have the audacity to appear in the ballroom after what he'd done?

Poor Lydia certainly could *not* appear below, not with her dress torn and her hair wildly askew. No. Everyone would see her chaperon was otherwise occupied, and dear sweet Lydia would be ruined instantly.

Spoiled. Sullied. Done for.

And the shameless despoiler, meanwhile, would no doubt return to the ball with impunity. Perhaps he would try to deny he'd had any part in the unpleasantness. Perhaps he was someone of importance, someone who could ruin Lydia with a single word. Perhaps he would attempt to place the blame elsewhere and implicate some unsuspecting young man to save his own reputation. Then two lives would be ruined, for, even if they wed, Lydia and her young man would both be cast from Polite Society. Well! Kathryn was not about to let that happen.

She snatched up the wings and other accessories and hastily finished dressing. Since dear, innocent Lydia could not defend herself, Kathryn was honor-bound to come to the sweet flower's aid!

Chapter Two

The sweet flower, meanwhile, was much too busy to be concerned over what was being said about her in the ballroom. Having slipped the grasp of her elderly duenna, the Honorable Lydia Grantham was making the most of the resulting opportunity. Though the delectable but tiresome marquis had been reluctant to act the part which his highwayman costume suggested, Lydia found that the handsome thing dressed as a stable boy, whose company she was enjoying, felt no such reluctance.

In fact, he was behaving exactly as a stable boy could be expected to—which was not at all surprising, since he *was* a stable boy.

Lydia was very glad her hair matched the color of the straw in which they were rolling. Her duenna was old and dotty, to be sure, but she was not as blind as Lydia could wish.

While Lydia was doing her best to attract the attention of the opposite gender in the stables, inside the ballroom, Nigel Moorhaven, Marquis of Blackshire, was doing his best to avoid it. Though Nigel's title was not the loftiest to be found at Ophelia Palin's ball that evening, his wealth was superlative. All the scheming mamas had their eyes on the marquis. He would not be likely to spend his bride's dowry before the ink on the betrothal documents was dry, for all six of his estates had smooth plaster and intact roofs. Blackshire steered well clear of dun territory, and it was well known he was not in dire need of a dowry.

The trouble was, the marquis didn't seem to be in need of a wife, either.

At nine-and-twenty he had never shown the slightest inclination toward making any commitment. Blushing Diamonds waited behind every fluttering, inviting fan, but the marquis remained enticingly, stubbornly single. He was obviously quite out of reach—which of course made him all the more attractive to the mamas and their daughters.

Consequently, the marquis was always up to his cravat in a mire of unwanted attention. If a miss were not swooning conveniently at his feet, she was tripping in front of him and genuinely needing his assistance—usually because she hadn't yet learned the art of batting her eyelashes and walking at the same time.

It was really quite embarrassing.

Nigel had hoped to avoid that sort of foolishness at Ophelia Palin's ball this evening. Masquerades were not considered proper for young ladies just coming out, and Ophelia's balls were notorious for being a bit fast anyway; one never knew what to expect, as she always pulled some outrageous stunt. Thus, Nigel had thought tonight's company would be composed of only the more seasoned of the ladies, but word of his acceptance must have got out. Ophelia herself had probably spread the news, the dear old vixen, for she wished to see him wed, and if it were known Nigel was to attend, then nothing could keep the ambitious mamas at bay.

Not that Nigel would have declined Ophelia's invitation, had he known. He couldn't stay away. He always tried to attend Ophelia's balls. She made no pretense of indifference; he was a great favorite of hers. She often said she wished

to be forty years younger, and Nigel loved to bring the roses
to her cheeks by flirting with the old spinster.

Everyone in London had been trying to beg an invitation
to this particular ball for weeks. It was rumored Ophelia
planned to display a fabulous treasure beyond value. The old
lady was rich as Croesus, and everyone had been speculating
about what she would produce. As of yet the treasure had
not been brought out, and anticipation was high, but Nigel
now wished he'd gone to his club instead.

That silly chit Lydia Grantham had surely caused him
trouble.

Nigel had fought on the Continent with Lydia's uncle,
and as a favor to him Nigel had escorted the girl to several
entertainments as a way of boosting her status among the
bachelors of the *ton*. But Nigel knew that Miss Grantham,
an heiress, had not the slightest need or desire to wed,
for she enjoyed the single state too much, and her sweet-
tempered, elderly duenna, a distant relation, had not the
slightest idea that Lydia's frequent absences from the ballrooms of London were not excursions into the refreshment
rooms at all, but excursions into linen closets, darkened
coaches, and hothouses. Nigel's one evening at the opera
with Lydia had been interrupted by one such foray, a trip
to the ladies' retiring room—or so Lydia told Nigel. But
when she had not returned in a half hour and her chaperon
was snoring softly at the rear of the box, Nigel had gone in
search of Miss Grantham himself. Fortunately, he'd found
her before anyone else had.

She was in the arms of the occupant of the next box, a
wet-behind-the-ears young man who, Nigel believed, had
just come down on his first holiday from Oxford. Nigel
quickly sent the lad on his quaking way and led Lydia
back to her chair, with her duenna—and the rest of Polite
Society—none the wiser.

During the second act, Lydia flagged down an usher.

This time, at least, the two were safely concealed behind
the velvet curtain at the back of Nigel's own private box.

Nigel patiently let the tryst go on until the participants forgot themselves and the rather enthusiastic sound of their kisses threatened to make its way to the ears of the surrounding patrons.

Nigel tipped the usher lavishly and sent him on his way as well.

Lydia apologized immediately and proceeded to ruin his cravat with her tears. He wasn't offended, was he? It wasn't that he wasn't charming and handsome and ... and rich . . . .

No, Nigel had thought dryly. She was too busy with the eager young lads around her to form a *tendre* for him! He was certain he knew her mind, though she was too well-bred to speak it: the barely nubile Lydia simply thought Nigel too old.

And he couldn't agree more! Nigel didn't have the heart to tell her he wasn't really interested in her, either. He merely instructed her to be more cautious in the future. She was a sweet girl in spite of her ... taste for adventure. A harmless and intelligent creature, Lydia was, and she was also, surprisingly, quite shy.

Ever since that night at the opera, she had worshipped him with her eyes. She was not the only female who looked at him in that way, but ever since the opera she had been the only female who could do so without making him feel like a plum pudding displayed before a crowd of starving urchins.

So it was that when Lydia had said she was in trouble and asked for his help this evening, like a gallant knight Nigel followed her without question. Now, he cursed himself. He was not a gallant knight. He was a foolish, gullible knight.

He had been wrong. Lydia apparently did not consider him too old for her. Oh, he had been correct about one thing; she was shy—but only with him. Unfortunately for them both, where he was concerned she'd managed to overcome her shyness that evening.

Nigel frowned and made his way through the crush of

people at the perimeter of the ballroom. Weaving his way among milky alabaster statuary and lavish red rose-and-ivy-swags, he headed for the front stairs, which led down to the street entrance. The musicians started into a lively country dance, and the scent of the roses and beeswax perfumed the air. The huge room was so brightly lit that the dancers turning figures on the gleaming pink marble floor did not throw shadows. Ophelia had spared no expense.

It was a lovely setting—for his betrothal announcement, he thought sourly. For that's what would happen if Lydia were foolish enough to appear in the ballroom. Upstairs, she'd ripped the bodice of her gown away, dramatically offering herself to him. If she appeared in the ballroom in that condition, she would be questioned about her obvious ravishment. If she refused to answer, she would be ruined. And if she uttered Blackshire's name, his honor would be destroyed. Either way, Nigel's honor would demand that he offer for her. He could only hope that if anyone did catch a glimpse of her dishevelment, that she would concoct some clever lie.

But was Lydia clever enough?

Nigel snorted and shook his head, drawing curious looks from those nearby. After what had just happened upstairs, he wasn't so sure. Until now, Nigel had thought Lydia was a sensible girl, but was she sensible enough?

And there was another thought nagging him. Someone at Ophelia's ball—some female, judging by the timbre of her howl of pain—knew he'd been with Lydia Grantham, unescorted, in that bedchamber upstairs. In the confusion, he'd rashly assumed she was a servant. Though a servant's gossip might be bandied about, it would not be taken seriously. But now it occurred to Nigel that their witness might not be a servant.

"Blackshire. I say, old man, did you swallow a fly?" The speaker, portly Sir Henry Bartling, poked Nigel in the ribs with his elbow. "You've the most sour expression. I daresay

I would not be so morose if *my* name appeared on every lady's dance card.''

Sir Henry was correct. Nigel's name *was* penciled in on many a lady's dance card, and leaving now would offend every last one of them. Allowing his witness to stand alone on the periphery whilst she should have been seen dancing with the Marquis of Blackshire was not the thing. He could not leave abruptly without making it seem as though he were giving someone the cut, something he could not afford to do.

''Is that your trouble?'' Sir Henry asked with an inebriated slur. ''Too much feminine attention, perhaps? Have the ladies tired you out?'' He laughed loudly at his own jest.

Nigel sidled around another blow aimed at his ribs and looked at Sir Henry sharply. Had the news of his ''tryst'' with Lydia already spread? No, Nigel decided. Sir Henry would not be so bold—or so subtle, in his condition. Nigel dismissed Sir Henry with a polite nod. He was bound to stay until the ball was over.

He hoped Lydia had the sense to have left. He strode purposefully toward the card room and peeked in, confirming for himself what everyone at the ball must already know— that Lydia's duenna was there. The sleepy old lady had nodded off while engaged in a game of whist and was snoozing in the card room as usual. Hell and blast! Where was Lydia?

Nigel swore under his breath and made his way to a post near the main stairs, from which he could keep an eye on all three entrances to the grand ballroom. He leaned with studied casualness against an elaborate Corinthian column, his shoulders tense and his eyes watchful.

If Lydia were bold enough—or silly enough—to enter the ballroom dressed as she was, he would see her immediately. *Everyone* would see her immediately. If he could reach her before she opened her delicate little mouth, perhaps he could still save them both from her folly.

He left his post only long enough to dance with each

partner to whom he was already promised. He took a chance
on offending a few of the ladies by not fetching them refresh-
ments when they hinted their throats were parched after their
turn on the floor, but he hoped the effect was mitigated by
the fact that he was equally inattentive to every lady. He
knew that unless he angered a matron it did not signify, and
none of *them* seemed to mind very much. Still, several of
the unmarried ladies looked him daggers when he abruptly
returned to his column after he'd danced with them.

He was going to throttle Lydia.

It was during one such trip to his sentry place that the
fairy queen entered the room. Nigel overshot his column
and nearly bumped into an arbor, so entranced was he. She
was shockingly, hauntingly beautiful. Who was she? He was
sure he'd never seen her before.

She was very petite, and she floated down the stairs in a
filmy gauze creation, sparkling in the candlelight like a
silvery crescent moon on the water. Her face was mostly
covered in a three-quarter mask, rather than the more common demi-mask, with only her lips and chin showing. Her
delicately lavish mouth was bow-shaped and her chin was
slightly pointed. He imagined the mask she wore concealed
a heart-shaped face. He was suddenly eager for supper,
though it had nothing to do with hunger. It was when the
guests would unmask themselves as usual.

He watched the fairy queen in hungry fascination. Her
eyes and her body expressed hesitance. She was unsure of
herself as she entered the room, and he wondered why.

As she came closer, he could see a hint of her eyes'
color—a fine sky blue. A wreath of violets and pale yellow
roses circled her mass of glossy blond curls.

Instantly, an image of himself ridding her of the flowers
and combing his fingers through those glorious tresses
gripped Nigel, and without thinking he started through the
crowd toward her. She had stopped on the very fringe of
the ballroom and was looking about her as though searching
for someone, but no man emerged from the crowd to take

her arm. Nigel silently thanked Ophelia Palin. A masquerade was the only time when a gentleman could approach a lady without first being introduced. He would go and introduce himself to his fairy queen. Then, he could . . .

Nigel stopped moving. *His* fairy queen?

If he'd be offering for Lydia Grantham, it would not do to be seen paying court to another lady tonight. He would be better off introducing himself to the marble column next to him! The dire nature of his situation slammed home. It was rendered all the more untenable by a personal code of ethics unusual to a man of the *ton*. Nigel Moorhaven considered marriage vows sacred, and once he made his own, he would not violate them, even if his marchioness were Lydia, who would most assuredly not view her own vows with any seriousness.

Nigel enjoyed women, but he had never dallied with a married woman. Whenever he had been tempted to do so, a memory beat down the impulse, a memory so painful and so strong it seemed freshly made, though he had been but a little boy of five years at the time.

It was at his mother's funeral. There had been several hundred mourners, and Nigel had known almost none of them. His father stood straight and unyielding. In pain himself, he was heedless of his young son's distress. Nigel felt alone.

And then a lady gathered him into her lap.

Like his father, she was a good twenty years older than his mother. She had dark brown hair streaked with gray, and lines at the corners of her mouth.

He remembered burying his face in the black crepe of her dress and crying. It was the first time he'd cried since his mama had died. The lady crooned softly to him and rocked him until his sobs subsided, and then she gently set him on his feet and walked away. Nigel had been so pitifully grateful. For years, he had worshipped the memory of her soft eyes and tender hands. But then, when Nigel had already reached his majority, he learned the woman had been his father's mistress for years before his mother's death.

He couldn't understand how another woman's presence could lend his father comfort at his wife's own funeral. How could he dishonor her memory so? From the day he found out about his father's mistress, Nigel had never spoken to his father again. When a man and woman wed, they spoke promises to each other. Promises to love and honor. Nigel had not plan to marry until he could speak those words with conviction.

He sighed and took one last, longing look at the fairy queen, at her wand, wings, and cloud of curls, savoring what might be his symbolic last look at the freedom of choice.

Just then, the fairy queen's eyes lit for the barest moment on him. Then, inexplicably, they returned, and she rested her gaze with his. Nigel was delighted and then stunned, for the look she leveled on him was one of malevolence.

Pure rage.

So, of course, Nigel smiled at her.

She had to have mistaken him for someone else; he'd done nothing to provoke such a reaction. It would be easy enough to mix up identities at a masquerade, especially if one were new to Town. Nigel couldn't let the moment pass. What the devil? It couldn't hurt to introduce himself to her. *If* he managed somehow to get out of the tangle Lydia had spun, and *if* the fairy queen were unmarried, then the introduction may turn out to be quite ... agreeable, he thought while allowing his eyes to glide over her lithe form.

Her gaze never wavered as she watched him advance toward her. Her eyes were stunningly beautiful in her anger, and Nigel couldn't help wondering how much more beautiful they would be drugged with satisfied passion. He had just gained her side and was feeling a warm glow that had nothing to do with the thousand beeswax candles that illumined the huge room, when Lydia appeared.

Nigel felt, rather than saw, her enter. The entire ballroom surged with a wave of shock as heads turned one after the other toward the open glass doors where Lydia stood, eerily haloed by the flambeaux on the terrace behind her. She was a mess. It was worse than he'd imagined. Not only were Lydia's bodice torn and her hair down, but her face was smudged with tears. She looked lonely and frightened. Guilt washed over him; her shame was really his fault. He was a covert operative for the Home Office, by Jove! He should have known better than to allow her to trick him that way. Nigel coldly noted the censuring looks the guests were shooting Lydia's way. She was being tried and convicted right then and there. There was not a drawing room in London that would receive her after this.

He could not let her stand alone.

Squaring his shoulders, he took a last look at the fairy queen and then turned away, wishing she truly were a fairy and could do magic to change what had happened that evening. If she could only wave her sparkling wand and—

Just then, she did.

The wand made square, swift contact with his backside. Nigel spun around, and the fairy queen neatly stepped around him on her way to Lydia's side, where she stood, almost challengingly, staring back at him. Nigel almost groaned aloud. The two must be acquainted.

And her assault on his now-stinging backside had been intentional!

Obviously, Lydia had already told the fairy some version of what had transpired upstairs. But Nigel had no opportunity to ponder it further, since Lydia caught sight of him at that moment.

"Blackshire!" she cried, capturing the eyes of every goggling guest. Nigel noted more than one head bobbing in his direction, including the ancient dowager Countess Rangnor, who whispered near him, "I knew it had to be Blackshire. Randy fellow—lucky gel!"

The dowager wasn't the only one with an audible comment. Into the shocked silence, the fairy queen interjected her own venom.

"Lydia was having such fun until the cur got rough!"

The entire assemblage gasped, and a chill like a hundred-year winter pervaded Nigel's spine. Not only had the fairy queen just announced Lydia was willingly compromised, but she was also implying Blackshire had attacked the silly girl! Perhaps Lydia really saw it that way. He *had* firmly grasped her shoulders to put her aside . . .

She must have embroidered the tale when she told it to her friend, the fairy. And that spelled matrimonial doom for Nigel, judging by the disconcertingly public and determined way the fairy queen projected her voice across the room. Lydia, for her part, stood in mute silence, staring open-mouthed at the fairy queen.

But then something extraordinary happened.

The fairy turned to him and placed a dramatic hand over her suddenly wrinkled brow.

"Oh, my Lord Blackshire! You were correct," she said, loudly enough for the entire ballroom to hear—which was not surprising, as one could have heard the wind stir a dandelion's fluff at that moment. "That dog *was* vicious." The fairy's eyebrow crooked pointedly a fraction of an inch before she continued. "Lydia and I should never have attempted to feed the mongrel. But we just couldn't help ourselves; it was so piteously starved." She slipped her arm around the other young woman. "Isn't that so, Lydia?"

Lydia's mouth hung open and she said nothing for the space of two heartbeats. Then Nigel could have sworn he saw the fairy give Lydia a nudge in her side.

Lydia stammered. "I . . . well . . . yes. Yes, that is so. Uh . . . we were feeding the dog some scraps we procured from the kitchen and—"

"And our supply was most distressingly inadequate," the fairy supplied, "so I left to ask Cook for more." She looked at Lydia.

"Yes," Lydia agreed, attempting without much finesse to go along with the faradiddle. "Yes, and . . . and then the scraps were . . . gone?'' Her voice trailed off into a question as she looked back at the fairy, their heads nodding in unison.

The fairy nodded emphatically. ''All gone. Eaten. Completely depleted. That's when the cur turned on you!'' the fairy finished. Almost as an afterthought, she drew one dainty hand to her mouth in a surprisingly convincing display of shock.

''Yes,'' Lydia agreed, with more confidence in her voice now. ''It bit me.''

''*Nearly* bit you, you mean. Thank goodness only the bodice of your gown was torn and not your very flesh!''

''Oh my, yes! It *nearly* bit me, and I . . . I had to scramble over the terrace wall just now to escape! I even lost my diamond bow.'' Lydia-as-Artemis sniffled convincingly and even wiped a tear away from her cheek.

Nigel was impressed.

The fairy smiled. ''There, there, Lydia. No harm done.'' She turned to Nigel. ''My Lord Blackshire, I take full responsibility. It was I who persuaded Lydia to accompany me on a quest to relieve the poor mongrel's suffering. It was I who refused to listen when you tried to convince us our actions were foolish.''

''Yes,'' Lydia agreed, ''and I know it was most foolish of me to follow when you went off to find our chaperones. But I so wanted to help that poor, starving creature! I pursued you hoping to divert you from your errand, for if you had been successful in finding my duenna, she would have insisted I abandon this folly, of course, but at the time I really did not see how feeding the unfortunate beast could hurt. I do apologize for disregarding your wise counsel. Will you not forgive me?''

As she stood there, a bit of stable-straw fell from her hair. It spiraled and fluttered slowly to the floor, and Nigel crooked an eyebrow at Lydia. Without taking her eyes from him, Lydia neatly covered the straw with one silver slipper.

The barest hint of a mischievous smile danced in Lydia's eyes. Nigel fought down a chuckle. ''Do not think twice about it, Miss Grantham. I assure you it is nothing. I am only relieved you are uninjured.''

A strangled sound came from the doorway as Lydia's duenna entered the room and spied her charge's disheveled appearance. Lydia's smile bloomed, and she moved toward the old woman. "Well, I must remember that what seems a good idea at the time is not always so. I am too impulsive by half." Coming abreast of Nigel, she paused. "Wouldn't *you* say so, my lord?"

Nigel nodded, her meaning clear. Sweeping his highwayman's cloak from his broad shoulders, he offered it to her. As its blue satin lining settled over Lydia, the guests turned away, and the dancing resumed. The tale was outrageous, but there was a disappointing lack of proof of any indiscretion, and the matter was therefore settled in their minds. They all set about the task of finding some other scandal to discuss on the morrow. Lydia departed.

Nigel turned to the fairy to express his gratitude, but she was already moving in the opposite direction. What a clever, generous woman!

"God's blood!" Mr. Jeremy Scott appeared at Nigel's elbow. "That was a near miss. I was afraid you were caught in the parson's mousetrap that time, my friend." Nigel and Jeremy had fought together in the army. He was a trusted friend.

Nigel's eyes followed the fairy queen as she approached Ophelia Palin. "There are worse fates than marrying Lydia Grantham," he said.

Jeremy's eyebrows rose. "Thinking of getting married?"

"No. Just thinking."

"Please . . . *do* think on it. Put yourself out of your lovelorn misery."

Nigel grunted. When his body had received that last fateful bullet, Jeremy had stayed by him in a filthy field hospital for a fortnight. Out of his head with delirium, Nigel told Jeremy things he'd barely admitted to himself. Jeremy knew

Nigel would not willingly marry for anything but love—or honor.

Jeremy prodded him. "You're almost thirty, for God's sake. Isn't it time you secured the blessings of your bloody title and fortune to your bloody fortunate descendants?"

"You know I don't give a damn about continuing the line. I just want a loving wife."

Jeremy nodded the way Lydia had gone. "As you said, you could do worse. Why not marry Miss Grantham? She's beautiful, intelligent, wealthy. Come, old man, what is she lacking?"

Nigel considered for a moment and then chuckled. "What she lacks is a good aim, my friend." He clapped his friend on the shoulder. "A good aim and a willingness to use it."

The younger man, who had not witnessed the fairy's unconventional use of her magic wand, scowled at Nigel's enigmatic answer. "What the deuce is that supposed to mean?" the younger man demanded.

Nigel only smiled and shrugged, then cocked his feathered hat to one side and took his leave. Whistling to the music, a bad habit he'd picked up as a Hussar while in Spain, Nigel went in search of his fairy queen.

He found her standing on the small dais at the end of the room, beside their hostess, who sat enthroned on a tall, carved-stone chair. Ophelia was smiling fondly up at her and holding her hand. As he watched, the fairy bent and kissed the old woman's cheek. Obviously, theirs was a close acquaintance. Nigel's smile broadened, for his status as a great favorite of Ophelia's could be nothing but an asset to his current objective.

As he approached, Ophelia was listening to her companion speak, but when she spied Nigel, she motioned for the fairy queen to be silent. "Come here, dear boy, and meet Titania. Titania, this is the Marq—umm . . . the Highwayman."

Nigel was sure Ophelia had not suffered a slip of the tongue. The sly dame had just given the fairy notice that he was a marquis. Nigel relaxed and decided he would ask her to dance the Sir Roger de Coverley with him at the end of the ball. He almost never danced the Roger de Coverley. As the last dance of any formal evening, it was a sign of excessive fondness between those who stepped out for it together, so Nigel avoided it. Being seen dancing the Roger de Coverley with the Marquis of Blackshire would be a major social coup for Titania, he thought, and he smiled benevolently up at her. It was just what a girl making her debut needed to clinch her status. He looked forward to her expression of delight. "My fairy queen," he said, sweeping into a low bow and cocking his head to grin up at her.

"Yours?" Her brow rose insolently into her cloud of shining curls. "Humph! I hardly think so."

Nigel nearly fell over.

Chapter Three

Kathryn's eyes widened, and she stared at her aunt with disbelief. " 'Dear boy' my—"

"Titania!" Aunt Ophelia interrupted her and tapped the devil's sleeve familiarly with her fan. "Perhaps you should come back later, dear—er ... boy." She finished lamely, smiling wanly at the man.

What was his name? Kathryn tried to remember. Blackshire? Yes, that was what Lydia had called him. Blackshire. And Kathryn hadn't missed her aunt's bit of social subterfuge; he was a marquis. The Marquis of Blackshire. That made it all the worse. To think a man in so high a station would ... oh! Kathryn couldn't even think straight, she was so outraged.

"Madam," she addressed her aunt, "you obviously do not know this man. He is—"

"Titania is a bit ... dyspeptic," Ophelia interrupted her again.

"Not anymore," Kathryn denied smoothly.

"And she is suffering from a ... megrim" Ophelia went on as though Kathryn had not spoken.

"I am recovered!" Kathryn glared at her aunt.

"She is overwarm."

"I feel fine." Really, Auntie didn't know the man's true colors if she thought to pair her off with him! She clenched her fist tightly around her wand and slapped it smartly against her open palm, hoping to show Blackshire that her "indisposition" had not deprived her of the adroit use of her hands.

Ophelia went on. "She was just about to retire to her— er . . . to one of my rooms to lie down."

"I think that is best," the marquis said with apparent solicitude. "It wouldn't do to have such a . . . delicate young lady staying up beyond a reasonable hour."

Delicate? Young? The truth of the situation hit her between the eyes. The beast must think she was as young and green as his previous victim. That explained his solicitous application for an introduction.

"I am quite healthy, I assure you, and though I may look as though I just stepped from the nursery, it is many years since I had a regularly enforced bedtime, and I am—"

"Months!" Ophelia blurted. "She means many months. Don't you?" She said, turning a little too urgently toward Kathryn.

Kathryn suppressed a sigh. "—and I am staying."

"Why, I am glad to hear it, my lady," said Blackshire. "If you should leave now, the ballroom would pale considerably."

Kathryn knew any fool could see she was angry with him, and the Marquis of Blackshire was clearly no fool. Those shadowy, obsidian eyes of his were deep wells of the keenest intelligence. He had only one reason to continue this maddening conversation: he was toying with her, like a barn cat with an hour-old chick.

The cat's eyes glittered. "These maladies have a way of making one believe they have gone and then returning without warning." He lifted Kathryn's hand as though to feel her pulse. She snatched her hand away, and Blackshire smiled. "But it seems, dear Mrs. Palin, that fair Titania has experienced a most brilliant recovery."

"Yes . . . quite," Ophelia agreed dryly. "Quite extraordinary, that is!" she amended and smiled nervously over at Kathryn.

Poor Auntie. She was transparent as a summer sky. It was obvious to Kathryn—as it was to the marquis, she was sure—that Ophelia was trying desperately to push the two of them together. When Blackshire had approached the dais, Kathryn had only just greeted her aunt, who sat stunned and blinking beneath her bejeweled purple turban, speechless, for once, at her grand-niece's surprise arrival and startling performance with Lydia Grantham. Kathryn hadn't had time to tell her about what she'd seen and heard upstairs, and she knew Ophelia was distressed by her niece's apparent lack of manners toward Blackshire, but Kathryn would not, under any circumstances, do the pretty for *him*.

The marquis persisted. "Since my lady is so favorably recovered, may I have the pleasure of the next dance?"

Kathryn put her hand up to her head as dramatically as she could, wilting like a morning glory at noontide. "I find I am quite fatigued at the moment. I could not possibly dance . . ."—she hesitated the barest fraction of a second—"with you."

Blackshire only nodded his head and bowed, first to her and then to her aunt. "My ladies," he said softly and then walked away.

"Are you mad?" Ophelia whispered. "Do you know who that was? He is the—"

"The Marquis of Blackshire. Yes, I know, Auntie."

"Lord take us, you *are* mad!"

"I am quite sane, I assure you, but I do owe you an explanation."

"I daresay! And how *do* you know his name? I only let slip his rank."

"Auntie . . ." She patted Ophelia's shoulder and smiled. "I know perfectly well you let nothing slip."

"Answer my question, gel, and none of your impertinence!" Ophelia said severely, but she returned the pat and
the smile.

"Well, I was upstairs just after I arrived, when Blackshire
and—"

Ophelia shushed her. "Later, dearling. There are some
introductions to be made." She nodded toward a group of
three young men dressed similarly in pirate costumes. They
were approaching the dais with obvious intent.

"My lady." The first bowed over Kathryn's hand, an
enormous *faux* golden earring hanging low over his clean-
shaven jaw.

"My queen." The second took her other hand and brushed
his *faux-mustached* lips over her fingers.

"My angel." The third dropped down to one knee, drew
his *faux* cutlass from his leather waistband, and held it to
his throat. "I would rather die if you will not grant me the
honor of the very next dance." His comrades scowled at
his bold approach.

Kathryn laughed—softly, as Ophelia had taught her. "I
cannot let you ruin the pristine floor with a pool of blood,
now can I?" she said. "I shall be delighted to dance with
you." After having petitioned places on her dance card for
themselves, the other pirates moved off.

Kathryn had not missed her aunt's small intake of air as
she accepted the pirate's offer of a waltz. She knew her
acceptance of this dance so soon after her refusal of Blackshire's offer was tantamount to the cut direct, and she was not
sorry, as that, after all, had been her intention. In fact, the
only thing she regretted was that no one but her aunt would
know of it.

As she stepped out onto the floor with the young gentleman, Blackshire, at the edge of the ballroom, was already
leading out another lady. Upon seeing Kathryn and her pirate
sweep onto the floor, the blackguard stopped cold and
watched her, his partner trying her best to look as though

the delay were her idea as she fussed with her fan and reticule.

His expression held neither reproach nor malice. It was simply cold. Unfeeling. Glacial. She shivered. She certainly did not need a fan this evening, for Blackshire's stare was enough to freeze the blood. She thought of poor Lydia and longed to shatter his icy composure. Perhaps an audience for her rudeness was what was needed.

As the pirate swept Kathryn past Blackshire and his companion, Kathryn suddenly said gaily, as if in answer to her partner, "La, I am not at all too tired to dance with pirates— only with highwaymen." She flicked a glance at the marquis, whose expression remained irritatingly impassive, but several of those nearby wore shocked expressions.

This time, the cut direct was public knowledge.

She smiled and dismissed the demon from her mind.

Kathryn loved to dance, and the waltz was an especial favorite. Her parents did not believe in the waltz's inherent impropriety, so in Heathford she had been allowed to dance it, unmarried or no. She knew the steps well. Unfortunately, however, the pirate did not. The complicated steps were enough to occupy his brain without the added confusion of Kathryn's last cryptic statement. The confused fellow faltered at her words and lost his way, blundering onto Kathryn's satin-slippered feet and trodding on her swollen toe.

"Oweeee-*me!*" The unladylike pain chant slipped out before Kathryn could think to stop it.

Her eyes darted to Blackshire, who froze and swiveled his gaze in her direction. He'd heard her silly, childish pain chant once before. Her heart pounded in her chest as she hobbled off the floor, assisted by the crimson-faced pirate, who beat a hasty retreat on the excuse of procuring her some lemonade. She couldn't take her eyes from Blackshire's.

A spark of certain knowledge passed between them.

You were the one upstairs.

You know I was the one upstairs.

He squared his shoulders and started toward her, weaving

determinedly through the throng of ball guests, and never taking his eyes from hers. His strong features were determined, ruthless. He did not yet know who she was, but Kathryn held little doubt he intended to find out one way or another. She could not allow him to reach her.

Rising, she winced with pain, but fear drove her through the dreadful crush and past the open terrace doors. Then she ran.

Nigel went after her, his mind full of questions he meant to answer. The fairy queen was his witness. She'd been hiding in that room upstairs, the room Lydia had lured him to. Had she been there by prearrangement with Lydia? Was she to have served as a witness to Lydia's ruination? Had Lydia been trying to force him into marriage? If that was so, then why had her friend the fairy so cleverly saved Lydia's reputation with the story she concocted about feeding the mongrel kitchen scraps? And if she hadn't been in that pitch black bedchamber by prior arrangement with Lydia, why *had* she been there? One thing was certain: Nigel wanted to know her name now more than ever.

The clumsy lad who had stepped on his fair partner's foot was still stammering an apology to her back. Nigel was amazed when she, in a voice designed to carry, declared that *she* was the clumsy one. That it was *she* who had forgotten the step and twisted her ankle in the process. And her pirate, the puppy, was all too relieved to agree. Her care for the senseless pirate's sensibilities was admirable, and Nigel shook his head in wonder, for she was not what one expected from a young lady making her debut. She was . . . different.

But "different" did not begin to describe her.

Her cloud of blond curls shone in the candlelight as she fled through the tall terrace doors. Her gown swirled lightly about her feet, and her iridescent wings fluttered gently over her narrow back. She looked like an angel, but heaven—and now Nigel—knew that, in spite of her cleverness, her kindness, and her gallantry, she was not.

She was a hell-spawned imp with a magic wand she knew how to use. A hell-spawned imp Nigel ached to take into his arms.

He'd kiss the devil right out of her.

He was not surprised to see that by the time he gained the terrace she wasn't there. There were two sets of steps leading down and away, one that led toward the gardens at the side and back of Palin House, and one that led to the front of the house and the Square.

The gaslit square and the terrace flambeaux were soon far behind him, and darkness enveloped the garden. Then the half-moon peeked from behind its curtain of thick clouds, and in the weak illumination Nigel caught a slight movement at the base of a chestnut tree. But he had no time to investigate for the fairy emerged from between two hedgerows and gasped.

"You! Wh—what are you doing here?" she demanded. Her hands fluttered to her mask once more, and Nigel saw them trembling violently.

"I am out for a moonlight stroll," he plainly lied. "Might I ask you the same?"

"Why," she said, pulling her gloves on tighter, "like you, I am out for a moonlight stroll in the garden."

Nigel shook his head. "There is little moonlight. You were not strolling. You were hurrying."

"You are mistaken, my lord. I was not hurrying."

"You were running. Fortunately I am faster," he said, "or I should never have had the chance to speak with you alone."

She crossed her arms. "That seems to be the theme of the evening. 'Speaking' with unaccompanied young ladies. Tell me, my lord, do all such meetings end with the young woman running from you?"

Her words stunned him to silence. She did not understand. She thought Nigel had *attacked* Lydia!

"What you witnessed upstairs, it was not what it seemed to be. It was . . . it was a misunderstanding."

"Is that what they are calling it these days? A misunderstanding?"

"You must believe me. I don't know what Lydia told you, but—"

"She told me nothing. We are not acquainted."

"But you were in the room waiting for—"

"For someone else. I was there waiting for someone else."

Nigel's pulse quickened. She hadn't been waiting in that darkened bedchamber for Lydia, she'd been waiting there for *someone else*. A man? Who else? He felt a hot, quick stab of jealousy and immediately the thought of wooing her away from her lover gripped him. Nigel made no effort to hide the quick, passionate direction his thoughts took him. He allowed his angular face to slide into what he knew was an expression of blatant desire, playful speculation, and obvious invitation.

He was not disappointed.

He watched as her exposed skin flamed crimson, from the bottom edge of her silvery mask on down, over the smooth flesh of throat and her chest, where it curved and disappeared into her low *décolletage*.

He nodded in the direction of the stableyard. "Is your carriage back there? Is it in need of repair? Come," he said, not waiting for her to answer. "I shall accompany you." He proffered his arm. She might have her family's crest emblazoned on her carriage. And if not, then a guinea applied to her footman's palm would probably serve Nigel's purposes just as well.

"No," she declined. "My driver has parked my carriage in the Square. I am merely strolling the gardens before returning to the ball."

"That is odd, for when you emerged from the hedgerows just now, you appeared to be trying to escape something. Or someone."

Her eyes narrowed, and for a moment she appeared to be

ready to acquiesce, but at the last moment, her eyes hardened and she said, "I am taking a walk, I tell you."

"Alone? What will your chaperon say?"

"If you think me a child because I am small of stature, then you are much mistaken. I assure you I am old enough to make my own decisions—"

Good, Nigel thought.

"—and I am not afraid of being alone in the dark. Or of anything else," she added, though the tremor in her voice belied her bold assertion. She was afraid, all right. But she wasn't afraid of being alone, she was afraid of being alone with *the Marquis of Blackshire.*

Nigel frowned. Devil take it! He was not the scoundrel she thought he was, but how could he convince her of that without telling her *exactly* what had happened in that bedchamber upstairs and how he'd come to be there? For that he would not do. He would not besmirch Lydia's reputation no matter how richly the miserable chit deserved it.

"How fares your foot?" he asked in a show of solicitude.

"What foot?" She pasted an unconvincing look of bemusement on her face.

"The one at the end of your leg. The one your pirate swain crushed under his clumsy feet."

"What pirate?"

Nigel put his hands on his hips and waited for a different answer.

She coughed. "Oh. That pirate. Yes, well . . . I am certain you are in error once more. I . . . that is to say, he . . . he was such an accomplished dancer, so light on his feet that I'm not certain his feet ever touched floor. Much less my foot."

"Then why did you howl?"

"Howl?"

"Yes, I heard you quite clearly." He crossed his arms over his chest and spread his feet, blocking her exit from the hedgerow. "Twice in one evening, in fact."

"I do not know what you are about, my lord. I am—"

"You are lying."

She scowled at him again. "And you are a demon."

"A devil, actually." Nigel threw her a wry grin. "But then, that does nothing to reform your opinion of me, does it?"

"Is *that* why you have pursued and detained me, to secure my goodwill? For if that is true, then I assure you your purpose is destined for failure. My opinion of you is firm, and we can have nothing to say to each other."

"Perhaps you have nothing to say to me, but I have something I wish you to hear."

"Then you shall have to write me a letter."

"Fine. Tell me your name and direction, and I will post one with all haste."

She stamped her foot and winced, then tried to slip past him, but Nigel blocked her way.

"Stand aside!" she ordered.

"Not until you listen to what I have to say."

Her eyes blazed her fury. "I shall call for help. I shall scream. I shall—"

"You shall be married," he interrupted her.

"I—what did you say?"

"You shall be married," he repeated, "to me. For that is what will be required of us if you scream and bring the entire ballroom running to us."

"We would not be expected to marry were I resisting you when they arrived." She looked smug.

He could have sworn that in spite of her genuine ire the imp was enjoying their verbal sparring. Her remarkable blue eyes shone with intelligent defiance, her creamy complexion glowed with a rosy fire, her bosom swelled rhythmically with the rapidity of her agitated breathing. She feared him. Yet she faced him like a truly worthy adversary. She had a wildness about her, an almost reckless impulsivity Nigel was at once repelled by and drawn to. He felt like a man about to go over a falls. A rushing sense of dread swept him onward.

Why was he prolonging this interview? He'd come out here to learn who she was, to discover her motives, and if at all possible, to convince her that what she'd seen upstairs had not been what she'd *thought* she'd seen. Why was he not confronting her more forcefully? Why was he playing this cat-and-mouse game with her?

He knew the answer all too well. He was enjoying himself. He did not want their verbal sparring to end. He did not want to part company with her just yet.

What he wanted was to kiss her.

And unless his masculine instincts were seriously in error, his fairy queen was feeling the same attraction. The current between the two of them was palpable. He was close enough to see the pupils of her eyes, outlined in gold, expanding and contracting as her gaze left his eyes to land for a fleeting moment on his mouth, then on the triangle of bare chest he'd allowed to show as part of his highwayman's costume. Nigel smiled. Despise him she may, but Nigel was absolutely certain she felt the pull of the current between them. She was fighting it, in fact.

And Nigel wasn't about to offer her any help.

He stepped even closer, narrowing the distance between them to mere inches. "Crying out for help may not be your best course of action at this time," he said.

Her breathing shallowed out, and her color deepened. "Oh?" she managed. Her eyes flicked to his lips again.

"Yes," he said softly. "You see, screaming is quite impossible when one's mouth is busy with other pursuits." He bent his head toward hers.

She didn't move. Their lips were almost touching when she said, "Was this your strategy with Lydia? Fascinate her with a kiss? Entrance her so that she would not scream when you . . . you—"

Nigel dropped his arms to his side. "What happened upstairs was not what you think it was."

"Oh, come now. I did not fall off the turnip cart yesterday.

You honestly think I'll believe you did not lure Lydia
upstairs to—m—''

"No. I don't expect you to believe it, but that is exactly
what I am saying. It was a terrible misunderstanding. I don't
know what Lydia told you, but—"

"You do not listen, my lord. Lydia and I are not
acquainted. Or at least we were not, until tonight. I suppose
we still are not, for she doesn't know my name, and she left
right after I—that is, right after we . . .''

"Right after you saved her reputation, you mean."

She shook her head. "My role in this does not signify.
All that matters is that Lydia is gone, and she does not know
who I am.''

"That makes two of us."

"You shall find out who I am at the unmasking," she
said.

Nigel watched her pulse leaping in her throat, and she
swallowed reflexively and looked away. She was lying.

"So," he said, taking a step forward, "you intend to stay
at the ball through supper? You're not trying to escape the
unmasking?''

She rolled her eyes skyward. "How many times must I
tell you? I am only taking a stroll—a brisk stroll—about
the garden. The crush of people makes the ballroom uncom-
fortably warm.''

"It is warm outside, too." Nigel moved forward again,
and she stepped back.

"You jest! All signs point to a late frost. It is freezing
out here.''

"Nay, my lady." Nigel, having succeeded in backing her
into the tall hedge, focused his eyes on her perfect, bow-
shaped lips. "In fact, I think we are in for a thaw, for I feel
warm all over.''

"You are trying to seduce me!''

"Is it working?''

Her eyes widened, and for once she was speechless. Nigel
knew the reason, too: a part of her wanted him to seduce

her. It was the perfect moment to kiss her. The perfect time to let nature take its course.

Unfortunately, at that moment, nature *did* take its course.

There was another scuffling movement at the base of the tree. And then a flash of white as a cat pounced, missing its prey by a whisker. A small bird, only partially fledged, had fallen and was hopping about the ground, frantically searching for a way back to the safety of its nest. Nigel and the fairy moved at the same time, scaring the poor cat, which jumped to safety under the hedge. Nigel bent, gently caught the brown, fluffy baby, and stretched to place it on a lower branch from where it could rejoin its nest-mates.

"There you are, little fellow. Go find your parents. They'll be worried." The fledgling chirruped as though it understood and disappeared into the dark canopy above. Nigel turned around.

She was staring at him, mouth open.

"What? What have I done now?" he asked irritably.

She shook her head, put one hand on her hip, and used the other to point into the tree. "What was that?"

He glanced upward. "A robin."

"You put him back in his tree!" It was an accusation.

"What else should I have done? What did you expect me to do with it? Let the cat take it?"

She swallowed reflexively. "I don't know . . . I . . . I . . ."

Nigel saw her hesitation and knew she was trying to figure out how a man who could ravish a young woman against her will one moment might be the same man saving baby birds from neighborhood cats the next. The facts warred with her assumptions. Her desire warred with her logic. She was even more unsure of herself and her feelings than she had been before.

Nigel didn't feel a moment of remorse for taking advantage of her moment of unsureness.

He pulled her into his arms and took her mouth in a kiss that was at once gentle and demanding, slow and insistent. He kissed her as though they had all the time in the world.

He kissed her as though he couldn't wait another moment to possess her.

It was his best effort. It was the kiss women had betrayed their countries for.

She froze at first, but Nigel's persistent attentions soon rendered her pliable. Her mouth gave way to softness and she sighed, yielding to the desire coursing between them. She wound her fingers through his hair and kissed him back, matching his movements with surprising enthusiasm.

Nigel's hand moved over her narrow waist, up across her shoulders and the smooth skin at her neck. Meeting the mask she still wore, he fingered it a moment. He was going to take it off her himself, of course. He still couldn't trust her to—

"Meowwww!" Nature interfered again, as something furry rubbed against his leg and then against hers. "Plurrt?" the cat said, looking up at them both expectantly.

"She's skinny as a fence post," the fairy said. "You did her out of her dinner, you know," she said, casting a glare up at Nigel. She looked back down at the cat. "My, aren't you a pretty one?" she told the cat. "Such unusual markings, all white except for here on your belly—" As her hand moved under the creature's black-furred underside, it stilled. "Oh, no . . . you've got kittens! You poor creature." She looked up at Nigel again. "She would have taken that bird to her kittens, you know. I wonder where they are. They can't be too far away. If we find them, we can ask the cook for some scraps or a dish of milk."

Without waiting for Nigel's assent, she started casting about for the litter, looking under shrubberies and behind statuary. Nigel looked down at the cat, who licked her paw once and walked over to the hedgerow where she'd taken refuge before. She paused a moment to look up at him, flick her tail, and meow before ducking underneath.

Nigel chuckled. "I think I found them."

The fairy approached and Nigel pointed. "Well," she

said, "what are you waiting for? Get down there and see if that's where she has hidden her kittens."

"The ground is muddy. My valet will have an apoplexy."

"Would you rather I ruin my gown?"

Nigel sighed again and knelt in the mud. Poking his upper half under and into the prickly hedgerow and suppressing the string of oaths that came easily to mind, he finally located the nest with its tumbling mass of kittens. "Well," he said, backing out and wiping off his hands, I found them. Five, maybe six of them. I'm sure their mama would appreciate a little help—" He looked up.

The fairy was gone. He knew enough not to bother charging into the stableyard or back into the ballroom. She wouldn't be there. She had more sense than that. A lot more.

"Bloody, blasted hell and back."

"Prow?" The cat sat next to him.

"Yes." Nigel told her. "She's run away, and I don't know her name, and it's all your fault." The cat rubbed up against him, and Nigel patted her absently. She had a collar of sorts, a dirty, matted bit of string tied crudely. It was much too small for her. If the collar didn't tell him she'd been someone's pet, her calm acceptance of his presence did. She was too friendly to be wild, too thin and dirty to belong to someone now. "Well, I suppose I owe you a meal." He pulled the drawstring from his cape and tied it to her makeshift collar. "I'll take this off once we're safely arrived at my town house. Don't look at me like that. Your babies are invited too." Nigel went back under the hedgerow and extracted the kittens from their nest, then wrapped them and their mama securely in his cape.

His valet was going to have *two* apoplexies.

"Feeling better, I see," Ophelia said cynically the next morning as Kathryn entered the breakfast room, limping a little after dawn.

"Much," she lied. She really felt awful. She hadn't slept much, and when she had, she'd dreamed of *him*. To make matters worse, her foot was throbbing. She'd ridden in Hyde Park this morning, and she'd had a devilish time dismounting. "You are up early," she told her great-aunt, changing the subject.

"No, I am merely late in getting to bed. Really, Kathryn, you must attempt to keep Town hours." She coughed. "Your sudden disappearance caused quite a stir last night—especially since Blackshire followed you out into the garden."

"Oh?" Kathryn asked, alarmed that someone might have followed them and witnessed her encounter with Blackshire. Her behavior had been deplorable. Distressing. Disastrous.

Well . . . almost disastrous.

One more second, and Blackshire would have had her mask off. And at the time she hadn't cared one whit! What had come over her? Oh, she knew exactly what had come over her. And so did he.

Ophelia waved her fork in the air. "When you slipped away, I was surrounded by a crowd of dashing young hopefuls. A great number of people heard you insult Blackshire, and those who did not hear it directly heard *of* it within seconds." She waved her fork some more. "You did not *see* Blackshire on the way to that back door, did you? It was obvious he was following you."

"I hurried, Auntie," Kathryn averred. "I got to the back door as fast as was possible."

"Too bad. I rather hoped he'd find you. You are the only female ever known to rebuff the Marquis of Blackshire's advances, you know, and a man like that cannot resist a challenge."

Is that what Kathryn was to him? A challenge?

"Of course, you've no real chance with him. You had none even before you insulted him, though that's not meant as a discredit to your looks or pretty manners, my dear. No chit has any chance with Blackshire this Season, methinks. But I congratulate you, nonetheless, for the cut you dealt him has secured the fascination of the entire *ton*. You are an instant success."

"Not me, Auntie. Titania."

"One and the same."

"Perhaps so," Kathryn allowed, "but that does not signify, for you must promise not to reveal Titania's identity to anyone."

It was already a quarter of eight. By now, Lydia would have been besieged by a flurry of inquiry regarding her "friend," the fairy Titania, and Kathryn had no way of knowing what tales Lydia would tell regarding their imaginary acquaintance. She couldn't risk ruining Lydia's deception with the revelation of her true identity.

Kathryn turned to Ophelia. "No one must ever know Kathryn St. David appeared at your masque as Titania."

Ophelia started to protest vigorously, but she stopped, midsentence. Clapping her mouth shut, she waggled a conspiratorial eyebrow at Kathryn. "Aha! I see. You sly gel. You've got your cap set at Blackshire after all!"

"No, I—"

"O-ho!" Ophelia held up her palm. "Do not deny it! What other reason could you have for holding Titania's true identity secret?" She clicked her teeth together. "That's my gel! Can't set your sights too high, I say." The lady plunked down her fork. "Very well. I shan't utter a word to Blackshire or anyone else. Your secret is safe with me—until your betrothal. Then I shall let the matter slip, and it won't matter to whom you are wed; you'll still be the Toast of all London. Oh! And what if you manage to bring Blackshire himself up to scratch? Wouldn't that be amusing?" Her eyes glazed over and she stared, unfocused.

Leaving Auntie to her pleasant speculations, Kathryn pulled off her riding gloves and helped herself to the steaming plates of food at the sideboard. As she was riding in the park that morning, she had done some thinking of her own.

She had no reason to be ashamed of her behavior. Kissing the Marquis of Blackshire had been unavoidable. He was powerfully attractive, and he was an expert at seduction. Armed with a perfect physique, a charming smile, and an excellent brain, he wielded a potent ability to fix a young lady's regard. Or any lady's regard, judging from Ophelia's overt fondness for the man. Kathryn couldn't be blamed for allowing him to kiss her last night. He was wicked. He'd even used that poor baby bird to confuse her.

Thank goodness she'd escaped him when she had!

She had no desire to marry Blackshire, of course, but she couldn't tell Auntie the reason why. Ophelia was fond of the man, and since Lydia was none the worse for the experience, Kathryn would not relate the sordid tale of the marquis and Lydia to her great-aunt. She could not see what good exposing him as a licentious despoiler of innocents would do, and it might cause poor Auntie distress. No. She had best try to forget the matter entirely—except when Blackshire was near, and then Kathryn would be on her guard.

It did not signify now, anyway. Blackshire would never know Kathryn St. David had been involved in the matter in any way.

The sun had been up only an hour, and the garden outside the open window was alive with birdsong. Kathryn broke off a piece of biscuit and tossed it onto the granite-pebbled pathway. Auntie's eyes refocused, and she examined Kathryn's worn riding habit with distaste. "Egads, have you been out riding in that?"

Kathryn laughed. "Do not fret, Auntie. It is not the hour to be seen in Rotten Row. John and I were the only ones there."

"John? I did not know I had a groom named John . . . or is he a footman?"

"No, I meant John from back home in Heathford."

Aunt looked as though the sausages on her plate had just come to life and begun squirming around on her plate. "Surely you do not mean that . . . that *ruffian* employed by your parents?"

"The very same!" John said cheerfully from the doorway. He strolled jauntily into the breakfast room, took off his cap, and mopped back a lock of thick, gray hair. Handsome even in old age, John was a friendly and sincere man, and Kathryn had often wondered why he'd never married. He plucked a sausage and a biscuit from the sideboard as he went past, then plopped down onto a chair next to Kathryn. " 'Ow're you doing, you old dragon?'' He smiled at Ophelia.

"The servants eat in the kitchen," Ophelia said.

"I'm sure they do," John said around a large bite of sausage, "but I ain't a servant."

"Poppycock! Out!" Ophelia pointed toward the door. "Out!" she ordered again, but John just sat there grinning at Kathryn.

"The dragon ain't changed a lick, I see," he said. "What's the matter, old girl, run out o' little children to breakfast on?" He smiled over at Ophelia and smacked his lips maliciously.

"Humph!" Auntie got up and sailed out the door.

John laughed. "I ain't seen 'er that mad in years. Think I'll go needle 'er some more."

Kathryn chuckled. "Have a care, John! Sometimes, dragons breathe fire."

The two of them, Ophelia and John, had been swapping venomous insults for years, and Kathryn was not truly alarmed. John strode from the room, a sausage in his hand, and Kathryn was left alone. She was soon lost in thought.

Here she was on the morning of her first full day of her Season and she'd already had an adventure! If she could save herself and another young lady from the clutches of a rake, what couldn't she do? Perhaps finding a husband to love wasn't out of the question after all. Dismissing the Marquis of Blackshire from her mind, Kathryn positively brimmed with optimism.

What was next? By all accounts, an endless whirl of balls, routs, operas, ballets, picnics, and balloon ascensions . . . shopping, fittings, and more fittings . . . silks, sprigged muslins, and fine lawns . . . invitations, love letters, and odes writ to her eyelashes . . . Heaven! Kathryn sighed with satisfaction, clapped her hands together, and then hugged herself. She could hardly contain her excitement.

Just then, the mantel clock struck ten, and Ophelia hurtled back into the room. Her cheeks were stained with tears, and she sniffled as she dismissed the footman with a wave.

"Dear Auntie! Whatever is the matter?"

"Oh, Kathryn," she wailed, "we are ruined!"

Chapter Four

Ophelia plunged her hand into the pocket of her voluminous purple morning gown and rummaged through its contents. "Oh, where is that blasted vinaigrette when I need it?" Two folded squares of white handkerchief linen flew from her hand and fluttered to the carpeted floor, punctuating her indignant complaint, and Kathryn's spine wilted in relief.

If Great-Aunt truly needed the vinaigrette to ward off a swoon, she would not be so robust in her search for the pungent little sachet. No, Auntie was just being a little theatrical, that was all. Thank goodness!

Another square of linen flew into the air. Landing unnoticed on top of Ophelia's chartreuse-and-lavender-striped turban, it hung there precariously as Ophelia's head bobbed. Kathryn suppressed a chuckle and stood. "Auntie, 'ruin' obviously means something quite different to you than it does to me," she said, placing her napkin on the table. "What is the matter? To which ball have we not been invited? Which *modiste* has closed her shop?" Kathryn asked, unable to keep from smiling just a little.

To her shock, Ophelia rounded on her with an angry

expression. "The time for frivolity was last night, my gel, and I hope you enjoyed it, for it will be the last taste you get of it! We are in genuine trouble here. I am not being overly dramatic."

Kathryn winced. "I'm sorry, ma'am." She sat down numbly. Aunt Ophelia had never uttered a single sharp word to Kathryn before. "I meant no disrespect."

Instantly, Ophelia looked contrite. "Oh, I'm sorry, dearling," she said miserably and gave up her search for the elusive vinaigrette. She patted her niece's shoulder and kissed the top of her head before lowering herself into the chair next to Kathryn's.

"Dear Auntie, whatever has happened?" Kathryn asked, though her hands trembled in her lap as the swirling vision of Blackshire returned to bedevil her.

In answer, Ophelia moaned and a sigh of torment issued from the old lady's lips. Kathryn was alarmed, for her aunt suddenly looked quite frail and tired.

"I've done us in, I'm afraid, Kathryn. I've made a horrible blunder." She closed her eyes for a few moments. "I left my diary at Baroness Marchman's School for Young Ladies," she explained at last. "I stopped there the day before yesterday on my way back from Bath, and—"

"But, Aunt, I thought you and Lady Marchman were bitter enemies."

"We are."

"Then why did you pay her a social call?"

In spite of her real distress, Ophelia smiled. "I acquired a little trinket in Bath—a gift from a friend," she said coyly, "a very handsome friend. The ring belonged to his mama. Very old, it is ... a family heirloom, in fact, the principal stone of which is fabled to have once belonged to Queen Matilda, who chose to bestow it upon the first Duke of—"

"Yes, yes. But the diary, Auntie." Kathryn shifted impatiently. "How came the diary to be at Lady Marchman's?"

"I had to go and show it to her."

"You shared the contents of your diary with Lady Marchman?"

"No, no, the ring. I had to show Agnes the ring."

"Ah!" Kathryn nodded her understanding. "What you mean is you had to wave the ring in front of her nose, don't you, Auntie?"

Ophelia dimpled. "Well, of course. I couldn't very well parade the gift-giver in front of Agnes's nose. Lord Arborough was not well enough to make the trip."

"Lord Arborough! Is he not the one you told me about? If what you said is accurate, Auntie, Arborough is too feeble to make it to the grave!"

Ophelia's dimples grew deeper. "There! You see? I was *forced* into visiting Agnes." Ophelia fanned her fingers and waggled them, admiring the fiery sparkle of the huge cluster of diamonds on her finger, but then her face fell. "Oh . . . I forget myself. This rightfully belongs to you."

"To me?"

"Yes," Ophelia said sadly. "If only I hadn't visited Lady Marchman! When she finishes announcing the contents of my diary all over town, I'll be cast from Polite Society. And you, my dear, will never be allowed to enter society at all. You will be shunned. No decent man will have you, and every woman will pretend she doesn't know who you are. So you see? You have already paid dearly for the ring, for you bought it with your reputation. We must both leave London for Heathford at once." She took the enormous ring off and placed it carefully on the table, then pushed it toward Kathryn before laying her forehead on the tabletop and sobbing. "I'm so sorry, my dear . . . so very sorry."

The orange and yellow turban came loose and rolled onto the floor, revealing a decidedly untidy mop of thin, snow white hair. Ophelia didn't make a move to recover the thing, and Kathryn's heart swelled with concern. "What is this terrible secret contained in your diary, Auntie?"

"It is awful. Shameful. Do not ask me to speak of it."

Kathryn rose and enfolded her aunt in a fierce hug, knowing not what to say at a time such as this. Instead of attempting to comfort Ophelia with words, Kathryn smoothed her white hair with gentle strokes and listened patiently to the old woman's muffled sobs.

Kathryn felt like joining Ophelia for a good cry. Returning to Heathford was the last thing she wished for. But it wouldn't do to have both of them blubbering into the table-cloth. Besides, Auntie had so much more at stake than she did. Heathford was a much larger step down in the world for Ophelia than it was for Kathryn, and Kathryn knew any pity she had should be directed at her aunt rather than toward herself. So Kathryn took a few deep, steadying breaths, tried not to think of satin and silks—and tried even harder not to think of her few suitors back home—and waited patiently for Ophelia's tears to subside.

After a while, Auntie slowed to a sniffle, raised her head, and stared blankly at the pineapple that crowned the center-piece on the breakfast table.

"It is so unjust," she said. "I have had my fill of every-thing, but you've not had your first taste yet." Kathryn knew the old woman was not speaking of the pineapple. Scooping up a square of linen from the floor, she gave it to Ophelia, who buried her face in it and waved her hand absently, shooing Kathryn away.

Just then, a sparrow landed on the windowsill, drawing Kathryn's attention. He chirruped a greeting and then flitted through the open window to the sideboard. Hopping among the laden dishes, he examined each one until he found the plate of biscuits. Choosing one wedged underneath the others at the bottom of the pile, he plucked at it gingerly until he had broken off a largish piece. And then, in a flash of vivid brown and white, the little thief was gone.

Kathryn turned to Ophelia, a delighted smile on her face, but Ophelia's eyes were still pressed firmly into her napkin. Kathryn's smile faded, and she gazed out the window, wish-ing she could help her aunt somehow.

"I did not want to leave my diary unattended in the

coach," Ophelia explained. "Too risky, you see, and it was too big for my reticule, so I tucked it under my arm and took it in with me. I know I didn't have it when I left. The only place it could be is on the divan in Agnes's salon. Well . . . it is probably more accurate to say it is *in* the divan. It must have slipped out of her sight between those gauche, fuchsia brocade elephant mattresses she calls cushions.''

With concealed amusement, Kathryn eyed Ophelia's own turban and voluminous spangled morning gown of magenta and orange silk trimmed with rose-dyed feathers. Though the cut of the gown was of the latest style, and the quality of the fabric was peerless, the entire effect was well beyond what one could charitably term "gauche." Ophelia's comment was a case of the pot calling the kettle black.

No one could miss Ophelia's personal style; it did not make a gentle impression. Her style reached out and slapped all who made her acquaintance. But after a moment's conversation with the grand old woman, it was impossible for anyone to find her outrageous ensembles remarkable in any way. They suited her. What else would Ophelia Palin wear to breakfast but spangled magenta and orange?

Ophelia snapped her napkin indignantly at the table. "Yes. I am sure that is what happened to my diary. It slipped out of sight. Lady Marchman mustn't even know it is there yet—'else the secret it contains would no longer be secret. When she does discover the blasted diary, I'll wager not an hour will pass before the news of it reaches Palin House.''

"Then there is no time to lose. We must do something.''

"Yes. You are right, my dear. We must leave London for Heathford immediately.''

That wasn't exactly what Kathryn had in mind. The trouble was Kathryn didn't have any better plan. She thought leaving London and waiting for doom to fall was silly. It was not in her nature to give up so easily. But how was the diary to be recovered, even if they stayed?

Ophelia waved her hand expansively and continued. "The scandal will blow over more quickly if I am not in Town when it breaks, and if you are not present then perhaps when I am dead and buried you shall return to Town and the *ton* will accept you. Thank goodness we did not announce your identity last night when—Bendleson!'' she interrupted herself, summoning her butler. Her tone of voice was shrill, and the middle-aged butler appeared with startling speed. As he came through the door, he passed Richard the footman, who was standing sentry just outside the closed breakfast room door. The two men traded significant, worried looks as Bendleson entered the room.

"You require assistance, madam?"

"We are retiring to the country. We travel to the estate of my grand-niece's parents, Squire St. David, and his wife," Ophelia instructed him. "See to it everything is made ready."

"Very well, madam. When do you wish to depart?"

"Within the hour."

"Holy mother of—!" Kathryn heard the footman exclaim just on the other side of the door and then his footfalls as he bounded off down the hall. Bendleson opened his mouth and then snapped it shut. "Very well, madam." He bowed slightly and exited sedately. Though the butler's voice and visible demeanor betrayed no great sense of urgency, as soon as the door had closed behind him his footfalls instantly increased to a most undignified pace, their staccato rhythm echoing down the marble-floored hallway.

Poor Bendleson. Leaving in under an hour? Impossible! But the harried butler hadn't offered a syllable's resistance, and Kathryn had no doubt the carriages would be waiting for them, fully laden and ready for the journey to her parents' estate in under an hour.

Ophelia tossed her napkin aside and stood up, appearing to Kathryn like Wellington about to go into battle. "Go upstairs and change, my dear. Ladies do not wear riding habits in carriages. The carriages will be ready at the stroke of the hour. For once, dearling, you must not tarry."

Oh Lord! If Kathryn could not devise some course of

action right then, Auntie would whisk herself away upstairs to prepare for their journey, and Kathryn would find them both ensconced on a misery-bound carriage within the hour. She couldn't let that happen.

A movement in the young chestnut at the far end of the small courtyard garden caught her eye: the sparrow in its nest. The little fellow had taken the biscuit to his babies, and Kathryn could see their tiny beaks waving frantically above the rim of the nest. The little thief had stolen for his children.

Suddenly, Kathryn's hand stilled on the pineapple. If a tiny bird could be a daring thief for his family, why couldn't she? "Auntie," she said, "where exactly did you leave the diary?"

"I told you. On that outlandish excuse for a divan in Agnes Marchman's salon. But what has that to do with anything?"

Kathryn's mind was too busy to answer that question right away. Somehow, from the swirling cloud of panic that threatened to engulf her good sense, a plan had coalesced.

It was daring. It was dangerous. It was outrageous. And it was almost certain to fail. But it was the only way.

Kathryn took Ophelia's bony hand in her own and rubbed it reassuringly. "Listen, Auntie . . ."

As she explained, the muffled shouts and footfalls of Ophelia's harried servants sounded throughout the house. Kathryn hoped they wouldn't be too upset to learn their efforts had been for nothing.

Chapter Five

The day had turned rainy and cold, and the fading light of late afternoon lent an eerie cast to the gray stone façade of Baroness Marchman's School for Young Ladies. Kathryn alighted from the hackney coach and paid the driver, then hurried up the worn brick steps.

She stood shivering against the cold in a brown, simply cut cloak, a thin garment borrowed for the occasion from a housemaid of Ophelia's. The cloak, which actually belonged to the maid's younger sister, fit Kathryn's small form reasonably well, as did the rest of the ensemble. Underneath it, she wore a plain, worn blue dress of outmoded style. Thick black woolen stockings, home-made mittens, and low, stained leather boots, which were made exactly the same for both left foot and right, completed the costume.

At first, Kathryn had tried on the maid's clothes, but they had been too big, and she'd been forced to endure the humiliation of fitting into a much younger sister's attire. Though Kathryn was well past the first blush of womanhood, with her lithe build and round face she could easily pass for a child of fourteen. She'd always considered it a nuisance.

She was passed over for the next customer in line at the market fairs or pinched on the cheek by her friend's visiting aunties. Even more troublesome was that her looks effectively prevented her from attracting the serious attention of any handsome travelers who happened to pass through her village.

She never thought she'd find a use for being mistaken for a child. For once, though, Kathryn was grateful for her looks. For this occasion, she'd enhanced her youthful appearance as much as possible. Her short, curly locks were gathered into two childish pigtails and tied with two lengths of bedraggled, blue satin ribbon. Another span of ribbon was employed as a sash about her waist. The three large bows swayed and bounced gently as she moved. She pinched two girlish roses into her cheeks and took a deep breath, which steamed into a cloud of vapor when she exhaled forcefully, trying to calm her skittering insides. The cold ride over had done nothing to stem the tide of a growing anxiety. As omens went, freezing rain in March was not reassuring.

The wet brass knocker chilled her fingers even through the wool of her mittens, and she quickly tucked them back under the cloak. Waiting for the door to be answered, she noted the smoke curling out of the school's chimney and inhaled the sweet, dusky scent of oak. Oak! The mighty English Navy was built of oak, and there wasn't much available to burn. Lady Marchman's School must be exclusive indeed to be able to afford it. Kathryn stamped her foot, which felt like a block of ice. Blast, what was taking so long? Couldn't Lady Marchman afford a butler as well?

Finally, the tall, green-painted door opened. A slender, severe-looking young woman stood over the jamb, barring Kathryn's passage. Her white-blond hair was pulled tightly into a knot at the nape of her neck and covered with a starched lace cap. She wasn't much older than Kathryn. Her eyes surveyed Kathryn's borrowed clothes, and Kathryn stared up at her with purposefully wide eyes, shifting a little to make her bows bounce. She crossed her fingers behind her back in childish supplication for good measure.

"May I help you, moppet?"

Moppet? Kathryn stifled a delighted shiver of triumph. She was a *moppet!* Her deception was successful. But the diary was still inside—and Kathryn was still *outside.* The woman's voice was colored with sympathy, but her tone indicated that helping Kathryn was last on a long list of tasks she needed to accomplish.

"Yes, ma'am." She pulled from her pocket a carefully rumpled letter—sealed with wax and impressed with one of the intricate fobs that hung at the ends of Palin House's bell pulls—and held it up like a shield in front of her. "I . . . I'm supposed to show this letter to someone at Baronet Marchman's place."

"*Baroness* Marchman's," the woman corrected her and gestured at the tastefully small brass plaque mounted on the door. "Baroness Marchman's School for Young Ladies," she read. In reply, Kathryn only curtsied and lowered her eyes. Suddenly, she felt the envelope slip through her fingers. The woman had taken the letter and started to close the door, but Kathryn put out her booted foot and stopped the heavy wooden panel from swinging to.

"Owee-me! Owee . . . oweeeee!"

"Are you hurt?" the woman said in alarm.

Kathryn hopped on one foot and clutched the other. " 'Twas only my toe. I shall be all right by the time I see Lady Marchman."

The woman shook her head. "Lady Marchman will not give you a gratuity. Neither will she allow me to. I am sorry. Good day!"

"Please, ma'am . . . you don't understand. Open the letter. If you send me away, I've nowhere else to go." Kathryn let go her foot and tried to ignore its intense throbbing as the woman broke the seal and quickly scanned the letter.

Looking startled, she stepped back and practically yanked

Kathryn into the warm house. "I am Miss Mary Gant," she said, "head schoolmistress. Well . . . actually, I am the only teacher here besides Lady Marchman herself. We employ masters when needed for painting, dancing, pianoforte and the like." She chatted animatedly about the weather as she divested Kathryn of her small valise and cloak, and she placed a chair close to the crackling fire in the largish ante-room. Positively insisting Kathryn sit and warm herself, she began to back out of the room, still clucking like an excited hen who'd just scratched a fat, juicy grub from the earth. "Wait right here, please, miss. I shall tell Lady Marchman you are here. I expect she will be out to meet you soon. I'll ring for tea. Or would you prefer chocolate? Milk, perhaps. Yes, milk would be best, I believe . . . under the circumstances," she said and was gone in a flurry of skirts, leaving behind the pungent aroma of starch.

"Thank you," Kathryn murmured, bemused and astounded at the lady's reaction to her faked letter of admittance. Kathryn knew the entire content of the letter, for she had decided what should be written herself, once she had convinced Ophelia her plan really was the only logical course of action left to them. There was nothing in the missive to provoke such a reaction.

Or was there?

In her haste to recover the diary, Kathryn hadn't had a chance to see the actual instrument. It was supposed to be a simple request for admittance, backed by the promise of a horrendously large banknote to be sent as soon as Kathryn was accepted and settled. But Kathryn had only decided upon *what* would be written; she hadn't decided upon *how* it would be stated, and she hadn't been there when Auntie's butler penned the thing. It was Ophelia who had composed the letter. Plucking the folded paper from the waxed surface of the side table where Miss Gant had left it, Kathryn hesitated before opening it.

The teacher had disappeared behind a closed door on one side of the room. A staircase separated it from an arched, open doorway on the other side of the room. Through the arch, Kathryn glimpsed a long hall that opened onto several rooms on either side. One of those would be the salon where Auntie had left her diary. Now was the perfect time to find it. She would locate the diary within minutes of her arrival and slip out the door, leaving behind only a mystery for the servants to contemplate. That, and a banknote for Lady Marchman to pocket, which Kathryn had hidden in her valise—a note large enough to discourage Lady Marchman from spreading the tale. After all, she wouldn't exactly have earned the money, since her new "pupil" wouldn't have stayed long enough to have afternoon tea. If Kathryn were lucky, she'd unearth the diary and make her escape before she even had to meet Lady Marchman.

But what if she were not lucky?

She'd have to face Lady Marchman, that's what. And judging by Mary Gant's reaction to that letter, not knowing its exact contents might be Kathryn's undoing. She'd just have to read it before she went in search of the diary. Lord! Her plan had seemed simple enough before she'd arrived.

Quickly, Kathryn scanned the foolscap. It was covered with the flowing script of Bendleson's hand. Kathryn smiled at the memory of the butler's poorly hidden delight at having a role in their subterfuge, as she read

My Dear Lady Marchman,

   The young woman I have sent to you is a distant relation of mine recently removed from the West Indies.

   She is emerging from a very traumatic period of her life, during which she lost the six members of her immediate family to the Yellow Jack. We are the only two members of our once-great lineage left alive.

Nothing amiss there. Kathryn read on:

I wish you to admit her to your fine school. I hope to unite the distant branches of the family in marriage AS SOON AS POSSIBLE.

I realize it is an almost unthinkable breach of custom, but please do not insist the gel wear proper mourning clothes. She cannot be married in black, and it is IMPERATIVE the ceremony not be delayed any longer than it must be.

Kathryn's eyes goggled. Marriage? She'd said nothing about including marriage to Lord Arborough in the faradiddle. It must have been Ophelia's idea; Bendleson would never have included such a detail on his own—though Kathryn did note the emphasis Bendleson had used on certain words. Such drama was unnecessary. Yet, she could not be surprised. One could not associate oneself with so strong a personality as Ophelia Palin's for very long without taking on some of her mannerisms. Evidently, Bendleson had succumbed. She read on:

The girl's fortune is quite vast and must yet be settled upon her legally, but there is also the matter of an ancient title entailed in a rather unique manner. There is some talk of her possible inheritance since she is the last of her line. Surely you see that IN HER DELICATE STATE—

Kathryn's eyes widened. Delicate? *That* was an unfortunate choice of words, indeed. Combined with the emphasis Bendleson had used, it might easily be misinterpreted— with disastrous result.

—she is in no position to fend off the inevitable onslaught of legal and social attacks her exceptional situation will bring. You shall understand that I cannot

*divulge further details of this INCREASINGLY compli-
cated matter.*

Increasing? No. It could not be . . .

> *I place my most precious possession in your care.
> It is absolutely imperative that you speak of this matter
> to no one until the legalities are settled. Neither must
> you attempt to make any contact with me whatsoever.
> You will notice she is in disguise. If the girl's present
> position or FAMILIAL LINKS to me became well
> known, there is no telling what might happen to her.*

Kathryn groaned.

> *The girl needs rest and quiet. She is a biddable
> child, but she is rather willful just now, which is not
> surprising, considering HER CONDITION (the trag-
> edy she has just been through, of course), and she
> requires a bit of mollycoddling. Having lost her dear
> mother at such a tender age, she is as yet uninformed
> about certain matters, and I am certain she does not
> understand what is happening to her.*
> *I say again: make no attempt to contact me. I shall
> contact you when it is safe to do so.*
> *Please indulge her whims—and mine—and I shall
> prove myself*
>
> > *Eternally grateful,*
> > *Arborough*

"In my condition?!" Kathryn ground out through
clenched teeth. Good Lord! No wonder Miss Mary insisted
Kathryn warm herself. No wonder she offered milk instead
of tea. Oh, dear! Kathryn couldn't possibly face Lady
Marchman now. The embarrassment would be too great.
She couldn't bear it.

She stomped off to find the diary, no longer worried about

being caught searching. What did she care? It couldn't be any more embarrassing to be discovered with one's hand wedged beneath the cushions than it was to suddenly find oneself *with child*. If Kathryn scowled any harder, her face would stick that way, she was sure, but she didn't care.

Poor Auntie . . . she'd never know her diary was in safe hands. No. Kathryn was going to strangle her first.

Lady Agnes Marchman's teacup clattered to a rest on its fragile saucer. "Lord Arborough? Are you quite sure the note said 'Arborough'?" she asked incredulously. "That seems most unlikely. Arborough is nearly ninety years old. He spends his days in a wheelchair and cannot rise!"

"Apparently," her head schoolmistress said dryly, "he spends his *nights* elsewhere, and at least one part of him *can* rise."

"Mary!" Agnes admonished her but couldn't hide a grin. She cleared her throat. "What on earth are we going to do with the child?"

Mary shook her head. "We cannot turn the poor thing out. She said she has no place to go."

"Under the circumstances, we cannot send her back to Lord Arborough," Agnes said with a nervous flutter of her parchment hand. "It would be most improper."

"Yes," Mary agreed, "we shall have to keep her."

"But how can we keep her? We've no room." Agnes bit her knuckle and stared pensively out the window.

"That does not signify, Aggie. We *must* keep her. You should look on her, the poor mite. To think of that vile old man forcing himself on such an innocent! It is unthinkable. It . . . it is criminal, that's what."

"Criminal or not, we cannot bring the case to the magistrate, Mary. Arborough would claim the babe she carries is not his, and her shame would become common knowledge. She could be left homeless and penniless with no protector."

"Penniless? But she is an heiress."

Lady Marchman's eyebrow rose. "You said she looked fourteen or so."

"Yes . . . oh, I see. With no other surviving relations, the court will appoint Lord Arborough as her guardian—"

"And he will have complete control of her fortune," Lady Marchman finished. "I am just as aggrieved as you are, Mary, but the more she fights this injustice, the more injury she shall sustain. She really has no choice but to marry the wretch."

"God rest his soul," Mary said, and when Agnes slanted her a disapproving look, Mary dimpled and added, "With all possible speed, that is."

"Amen."

The two lapsed into silence as the fire popped and hissed. "Aggie," Mary finally said, "since we cannot turn her out, we shall just have to put her in my old room with Lady Jane Tregally."

"But that room is the smallest in the house. And Lady Jane's guardian will be most displeased when he finds out the private room he paid for is no longer private."

Lady Jane had come to them only the previous morning. Her arrival had disconcerted Lady Marchman because it was long past the beginning of the school term, and because every bedchamber in the large house already housed at least three students. But what was most unsettling of all was that Lady Jane's guardian was a member of the peerage—a lofty member of the peerage at that. They'd made room for her, of course. Mary, who had always enjoyed a room to herself, was now sharing Agnes's bedchamber.

"We simply have no other choice, Aggie."

"But what will happen if Lady Jane discovers the girl's delicate condition? If she should inform her guardian—"

"Arborough's note implies the girl does not realize her own delicate condition—"

"Yes, and we must not enlighten her."

"—and therefore she shall have nothing to tell." Mary made a satisfied gesture. And while Lady Jane is clever, to be sure, I doubt she is worldly enough to discern the girl's condition. It will be many weeks before the girl's figure changes, and she will be gone and wed by then.''

Agnes nodded her agreement. ''Besides, even if Lord Blackshire does find out, he is a good man—''

''Even if he is rather odd for placing his ward in a boarding school.''

''—and I doubt he would spread such gossip.''

''Why in the world did Blackshire place Lady Jane in a boarding school, do you suppose?''

''I do not know, Mary. But we have no time to talk of that now. Our new student awaits.''

Somewhere in the house, a bell rang. Kathryn's sweeping hand stilled under the plump brocade cushion of the divan. This was taking too long. She should have found the diary by now and been out the door. Her hand made its third futile pass beneath the mountain of gaudy pillows. The diary was not there. A mantel clock loudly ticked the seconds off as Kathryn frantically searched the room.

Kathryn opened a glass-fronted cupboard and looked forlornly in the last possible place: an enormous silver vase. No diary. That did it. The diary just wasn't here. Had it been found already? Was it even now in Lady Marchman's possession? Or had Kathryn been searching in the wrong room?

It did not matter, for she had no time to search another.

She could not be found prowling about the house, her hand in a cupboard, reaching for a silver vase! Lady Agnes might doubt the veracity of the forged letter and suspect Kathryn was a robber. She might send word to Lord Arborough to confirm Kathryn's identity!

And then it occurred to her that she really was a robber. Blast! Her careful plan was failing. She was running out of time. In just seconds, she would have to end her search.

But she had to find Auntie's diary.

Kathryn could hear footsteps coming down the hall. The

image of the brave little sparrow flitted into her mind. It must have been terrifying for that little bird to fly through the window of Palin House and steal from the sideboard. But he'd faced his fears and blast it all, so would Kathryn!

Not for the first time, Kathryn made an impulsive decision. She'd do what was necessary to protect her aunt. And if that meant becoming one of "Lady Marchman's young ladies" for an afternoon, she would. In fact, she vowed, she'd stay at the school for as long as it took to recover Auntie's diary or die—probably of acute embarrassment—in the process.

Turning, she ran wildly back to the anteroom where Mary Gant had left her, skidded across the floor, and came to a stop in front of the fire, nearly toppling the chair. She sat down and smoothed her skirt just as the door opened, admitting Mary Gant, who bore a large silver tea tray. Seconds later, a plump, happy-looking woman with gray hair, wearing a tastefully cut green baize dress with a lace collar emerged from the hall. She looked kind and motherly, and Kathryn wondered why Lady Agnes had not come to greet her herself. Probably too stiff-rumped to deign to speak to a girl "in her condition," she decided.

The gray-haired woman extended her hand. "I am Lady Agnes Marchman, Miss . . . ?"

"*You* are Lady Marchman?" Kathryn asked incredulously before she could stop herself. Ophelia's tales had led her to expect Agnes Marchman to wear horns, cloven hooves, and a long, forked tail. She had not at all expected the kind and motherly looking woman before her.

Lady Marchman lifted a shoulder and smiled. "I am she. Does my countenance displease you, Miss—ah . . . ?"

"No ma'am." Kathryn tried to remember if the letter Bendleson had penned had said what her name was supposed to be. She didn't think it had. "Please pardon my manners; I was expecting someone much . . . older-looking. And my name is Davidson, my lady. I am Kitty Davidson." The lie brought a blush of guilty color to her cheeks. She didn't like to lie, but under the circumstances, it couldn't be helped.

"I am pleased to make your acquaintance, Miss Davidson." Lady Marchman sat next to her, took her hand, and patted it. She smiled over Kathryn's shoulder and said, "I see you have already met Lady Jane."

In confusion, Kathryn swiveled in her chair to look into a pair of sparkling, mischievous dark eyes set in a stunningly beautiful face belonging to a girl of about fifteen years. Her elegant features were framed by long, straight, dark hair.

Lady Jane stood in a shadowed corner beneath the staircase, in front of a rich green tapestry. Dressed in green velvet, she was neatly camouflaged, and she knew it. Kathryn's heart pounded rapidly. How much of her search had Lady Jane observed? All of it, by the look on her face. What would she tell Lady Marchman?

The girl stepped forward and held Kathryn's gaze as she said, "Yes, Lady Marchman, we have met, and I must say Miss Davidson is a very interesting new companion. I have had an amusing time getting to know her, and I look forward to furthering our acquaintance."

Clearly, Lady Jane had been spying from her vantage point under the stairs. With one lifted brow, the girl smiled at Kathryn, an expression that gave her to know she needn't worry. She detected no trace of malice in Lady Jane's laughing eyes. In fact, Kathryn found herself flashing Lady Jane a conspiratorial smile in return. She liked the girl instantly, and she rather thought the sentiment was mutual.

"Ah," Lady Marchman said, "how fortunate you find each other agreeable, as you are to share a bedchamber."

Lady Jane looked at Kathryn and winked. "Oh, how delightful, Lady Marchman. I am sure we shall suit very well. We have already found we have much in common."

Indeed, Kathryn thought, with as much amusement as relief, *we both skulk around invading others' privacy.*

Chapter Six

Thank the Lord she was "increasing!"

By the time she was shown her room, given lunch and then tea, taken for a tour of the school, and fussed over by Lady Marchman, it was quite late, and the evening meal was at hand. Owing to her "condition," Kathryn was certain, Lady Marchman had mumbled some excuse about not wishing to subject her to the draftiness of the large dining hall after the rigors of her day's journey and insisted she dine alone in the small dining room—which suited Kathryn perfectly well! She very much wished to avoid having her face become familiar to any of the students at Lady Marchman's School.

Though it was highly unlikely she'd meet any of the daughters of merchants or lesser gentry in one of London's ballrooms, it was not out of the realm of possibility. She decided it was but a trifling consideration.

Besides, she had other things to worry about.

Kathryn tore off a bit of bread and chewed it thoughtfully. Lady Jane was another matter. It would be a couple of years before Jane took her own bow to Society, but when that time came they would meet, and Kathryn was certain clever Jane would recognize her.

She wondered why the girl was here. She supposed it was because her guardian was a single man. Jane's attendance at the school was probably only a temporary measure to protect her reputation while a suitable companion was found to lend them propriety. Jane was certainly not without a fortune, for she was dressed exquisitely. But even without a large dowry, her title and dark beauty alone would be enough secure the regard of some baronet or knight. Oh, yes. Kathryn would certainly be seeing Lady Jane again. But it did not worry her over much. After all, Jane had not exposed Kathryn to Lady Marchman this afternoon, had she?

When the time came, Kathryn would tell Jane the whole story, and Jane would vow to keep the secret of Kathryn's scandalous performance at Lady Marchman's school between them. She would regard such knowledge a delicious lark, just as she had today. Perhaps Kathryn should out with the truth now, confide in Jane and beg her assistance in the search for the diary.

No. Kathryn shook her head firmly. As much as her instincts told her Jane could be trusted, Kathryn knew she could not be certain, and a misplaced confidence would place Auntie's happiness at risk.

The matter settled in her mind, Kathryn put down her fork and slipped from the room, clutching a message she had written earlier. She made her way to the stable, where, from the tall windows of the small dining room, she'd glimpsed a young stable boy going about his chores.

Five minutes later, she was once more sitting primly at table, and the boy was on his way to Grosvenor Square with the message. Along with apprising Ophelia and John of her lack of progress and her decision to stay on awhile longer, Kathryn had also added a plea for a truce between the aged combatants—not that she expected them to declare one. Auntie and John—who'd had a fit over her plan—would be worried by now. She frowned, imagining that the two of them were making each other quite miserable by now.

Always, when the two of them had been thrown into each other's presence, there had been some member of the family to intervene in their spats. But the two of them were alone this time, under strained circumstances, and for many more hours than planned.

Was it possible they would come to blows?

Nonsense, Kathryn chided herself. John would never strike a lady. But of course, Ophelia had no such restriction. And John would no doubt argue that Ophelia was no lady! Oh, dear.

Kathryn wished she could get home sooner, but she knew she would not be home until morning. She was unlikely to be left alone long enough to find the diary. She'd have to search for it after everyone was abed tonight and then she would have to wait until daybreak to return home. London was not Heathford, and it would not be safe to travel alone at night.

Darkness had fallen and the shadowy hallways echoed with the muted giggling of the forty-six girls installed at the school. Kathryn and Lady Jane's bedchamber door was barely closed behind them when the tall, striking girl clapped her hands and exclaimed, "Now, do tell me what you were searching for belowstairs. You *were* searching for something?" It was a statement, not a question.

Kathryn lay her valise on the four-poster. "Searching?" she mumbled with an even calmness she did not feel.

"Oh!" Lady Jane bounced to a rest on the bed, directly in front of Kathryn. "I hope you will not be so tiresome! You may confess your sins to *me* with complete assurance of impunity. Why, when I saw you going through Lady Marchman's salon so minutely, I was overjoyed. The other inmates of this prison are dull indeed, all aspirants to the model of all that is perfect in gentle English Womanhood. But *you*," she declared, "are not."

"How flattering," Kathryn stated dryly, taking off her gloves.

Jane laughed. "I only meant that you are unlike the rest of the girls here. Empty-headed ninnies, the lot of them, unthinking, unknowing, and unseeing. Whereas you, I'll wager, miss nothing, and I'd gladly give a groat or two to know what thoughts *your* brain conjures. You must have been thinking something very interesting when your arm was up to your elbow in that grotesque silver vase, for instance."

Kathryn resisted the urge to roll her eyes. "Lady Jane, I—"

"La, Kitty! You must call me Jane, of course."

Kathryn blinked in surprise at the girl's familiarity. Auntie's lectures had led her to expect nothing but a strict and rather harsh formality among the *ton,* and she found herself drawn to her roommate's straightforward approach in spite of her resolve to resist it. "Very well. *Jane,*" she said, "my mother has—uh . . . that is, she *had* a vase like that one. It is a very unusual design, and its hallmark was located on the bottom of the inside. I was merely checking to see if the two were struck by the same smith."

"Ah." Jane nodded but clearly disbelieved the explanation. "I lost my parents this year. Are both of yours still alive?"

"No," Kathryn answered shortly, hoping her curt manner would pull Jane up short. "They are both dead."

But Jane went on, "How old were you?"

"Ten," Kathryn said, making up a number.

Kathryn went to the washstand and patted her face down with cool water and dried herself, feeling the girl's dark brown eyes boring into her back. She carried a key to her valise on a string about her neck. Her fingers pulled it from beneath her faded blue dress and she set about extracting her night rail from the ratty valise. The sooner she got ready for bed the sooner she could end Lady Jane's inquisition.

Kathryn's nerves were strung up tight as a smuggler's rigging.

Ultimately, Jane was thwarted, since Kathryn never uttered another syllable before blowing out the candle and settling into the feather bed. Kathryn was never more happy to snuff a candle. Jane sighed dramatically and punched her pillow beside her. Kathryn blew a relieved puff of air up through her curly bangs and pretended to fall asleep.

Thank goodness she wouldn't have to face Jane in the morning! The clever girl had given up her questioning with too little resistance, and Kathryn was certain Jane's next siege would begin at first light. Fortunately, Kathryn would not be available! She must have searched the wrong salon upon her arrival. The night would afford her several hours to search under cushions unobserved. And how many cushions could one school have? She'd be gone before the moon rose. She would wait in the stable until morning and send the boy for a hackney coach as soon as it was safe to travel.

All she had to do was wait while everyone around her drifted into slumber. It would be simple. Easy. Straightforward.

It was impossible. Hours later, a frustrated Kathryn still lay listening to the school sighing and settling about her. Oh, to be sure, *Lady Marchman* had fallen asleep with alacrity, but judging by the tossing and groaning Kathryn heard around her, few others were so fortunate.

Lady Marchman snored.

Loudly.

Kathryn herself hadn't slept at all, of course. She'd lain in wait as the hours passed, wondering if the opportunity to arise and search for the diary would *ever* come. Good Lord! The racket coming from Lady Marchman's chamber had been enough to wake the beefeaters slumbering behind the thick walls of the Tower of London. It had gone on for half the night! How anyone ever got enough sleep at Baroness Marchman's School for Young Ladies was beyond Kathryn.

Now, it was half past three in the morning, and the place was finally as still as a dove in the rain. Slipping soundlessly from her shared bed, she mouthed a silent good-bye to Jane, picked up her valise, and crept from the room, closing the door behind her.

As Kathryn descended the back stairs in almost total darkness, a tread creaked loudly underfoot, and she was sure the sudden pounding of her heart rivaled the former clamor of Lady Marchman's grinding snores. Forging ahead, she reached the first floor and looked for the first banked fire she saw, letting its softly glowing coals guide her through an open door and across a room. Drawing from her valise a fresh candle, she held its wick to the embers until it caught and she set about finding the diary.

An hour later, she had almost lost her composure. She'd swept her hand under every cushion in the common rooms. There were classrooms and studies, a kitchen, several small parlors and receiving rooms, two dining rooms, an accounts room, several storage rooms, a drawing room, a morning room, a ballroom and music room, and a studio. She'd found five shillings, a hairpin, a lady's gazette, a broken charcoal crayon, three harp keys (Kathryn assumed the girls did not like music lessons much), and a sticky lump of peppermint, but no diary. The little book just wasn't there.

"What now, Auntie?" she muttered.

It was now half past four, and the kitchen staff would soon be bustling about preparing breakfast. What was she going to do? Kathryn felt panic rising and stuffed it back down. She had to be logical. Where else could the diary be? Someone must have found it and taken it . . . to the library. Of course!

But just as she placed her hand on the library door, she heard a muffled *thump* and the echo of voices from downstairs as the morning cacophony of the kitchen began. Blast! She couldn't risk being caught ransacking the library. She could always say she couldn't sleep and had come looking for a book to read, but how was she to explain the presence

of her valise? And what would happen if she were caught
with the diary on her person?

She was stymied. Foiled. Done for.

There was no other recourse but to end her search right
now. But slinking back to Auntie's house with her tail tucked
and thence fleeing for the country went against Kathryn's
very nature. She had never been a quitter, and she wasn't
about to start now! She would just have to continue on as
one of "Lady Marchman's young ladies" for another day.

She climbed the stairs once more and slipped stealthily
back into bed beside Jane. The mantel clock ticked away
the minutes, and soon she fell asleep. And there he was,
waiting for her.

They were in a garden with darkness close around and a
thick mist swirling about their feet. He whispered all sorts
of endearments, his warm sweet breath skittering across her
neck and ear. And then he kissed her. It was the same kiss
he'd given her in Auntie's garden. Every little movement,
every thudding heartbeat of that kiss she lived once more
in her dream.

She awakened suddenly, perspiring, with a sense of longing. As though she were missing something. It was a foolish
dream.

Foolish. Senseless. Silly.

But, heaven help her, a part of her wanted nothing more
than to go back to sleep so she could return to Blackshire's
arms. Horrified, she willed herself to stay awake. She was
bone-tired and groggy by the time Lady Marchman knocked
softly on the door at dawn and entered the room, carrying
an impossibly brilliant lamp that cast hard-edged shadows
across the room. Both young women groaned, and Jane
pulled the covers over her head. Normally, Kathryn was a
cheerful riser, but Jane, it seemed, was not.

Lady Marchman smiled. "Arise and greet the day, my
girls. There is much to learn before the sun goes down."

Jane groaned again. "Madam, the sun is not *up* yet!"

"Nonsense! The cock has been crowing since a quarter

to five, and if he can drag himself from his roost, then so can—oh my!'' Lady Marchman caught her first glimpse of Kathryn. "Oh my!'' she said again, putting her hand to her cheek. "Are you feeling well?'' She bent closer and squinted. "Oh. But of course you are not.'' She slid a look at Jane and clamped her lips tight, then straightened.

Jane was soon ushered from the room, and Kathryn was ordered to spend the day at rest—which she begged to pass in the library. Lady Marchman consented.

Perfect. Kathryn gave a satisfied sigh as soon as Lady Marchman quit the room. Logic told her that some maid had picked up the diary and returned it to the library. It would probably be sitting on a table waiting to be reshelved, which would make it easy to find. Kathryn would be back home with Aunt Ophelia and John by noon!

Kathryn scrambled out of bed as soon as the door clicked shut behind Lady Marchman, and she hurried to dress herself between bites of toast. She was starving.

She couldn't believe her good fortune. She hadn't had to withstand even one of Jane's questions! The diary was as good as in Auntie's hands. As Kathryn buttoned her shabby blue frock, she relaxed into a dream of ball gowns, waltzes, and strolling in the park on the arm of a handsome gentleman—fancies which would soon become reality. Ah! What fun it would be! Would Auntie restrict Kathryn to pale muslin, or could she be persuaded to let her wear blue satin? Would there be any more masquerades? Would any of the handsome gentlemen she strolled with attempt to steal a kiss? Ah . . . She sighed softly, and her hands stilled on the row of buttons. Kathryn smiled dreamily and stared into nothingness, enjoying the fantasy she'd concocted—until she realized the handsome face hovering so breathlessly close to hers had borne the striking, chiseled features of the Marquis of Blackshire! Kathryn gasped. That demon! Wasn't it enough that he'd invaded her night dreams? Must she admit him to her waking dreams as well? Would she never be free of the memory of his scent, the feel of his hair slipping through her fingers, the warmth of his lips as they moved over hers?

Setting him firmly from her mind, she fastened the last button and brushed her hair until it shone. If her strokes were a little more agitated than they normally were, then that was understandable. She had a right to be a little agitated. She was a burglar, after all. It had absolutely nothing to do with Blackshire. No, nothing at all.

The school hummed with activity but soon settled down as the girls sat down to their morning lessons and Kathryn made her way to the library, the coins for her fare home clinking reassuringly in her pocket. The library was empty save for her. Closing the doors behind her, she leaned against them for a moment. Then she got a good look around her.

She straightened, swallowed, and stared.

Lady Marchman was clearly a bibliophile. The high-ceilinged room was enormous and lined with full shelves. But that wasn't what she was goggling at. The room was in complete disarray. Books lay in stacks on top of and beneath several mismatched tables that had been crammed into the room. The floor was nearly unnavigable for all the jumbled piles choking the floor space. Each tall shelf was neatly marked according to subject: geography, botany, history, languages, and so on—but it appeared that any effort to keep the books in order had gone by the wayside long, long ago. The collection on each shelf was not homogenous by any means.

Kathryn examined the stacks of books on the floor and tables next.

Complete mayhem. Not a shred of order. There were tens of stacks here, probably over a thousand books that were never going to be shelved! And there were several thousand more *on* the shelves themselves.

She blinked. If the diary were here, it would not be easy to spot.

How had Auntie described the thing? Plain, slim volume with an old reddish brown leather binding. Kathryn looked about herself in dismay. That described almost any of the books here. The diary could be anywhere: on a shelf, in a stack, under a table—if it was not already in Lady Marchman's possession. Kathryn's expectation of sharing a merry, triumphant luncheon in Grosvenor Square vanished.

It might take days to search the library.

Then again, the diary might be the first volume she picked up. A flash of Kathryn's customary optimism overtook her, and she dug into the pile of books on the round table. But she hadn't got far when the doors opened, admitting Miss Mary and a small group of girls who engaged in a quiet discussion of literature. Kathryn was forced to abandon her search and flee to a window seat where she hid behind a curtain and pretended to read a book about the Roman gods and goddesses. Mythology was one of her favorite subjects, but in her impatience to get on with her search, she could not drum up any enthusiasm for it today.

The rest of the day was wasted just so, in frustration. One interruption after another kept Kathryn from her search: Miss Mary's class, meals, tea, servants, and at least ten visits from Lady Marchman, who wished to be certain Kathryn was not taxing herself. Kathryn retired early, genuinely tired for all of her nervous vexation, and she was already abed when Jane came in.

The night passed as yesterday's had, with Kathryn—and everyone else—waiting for Lady Marchman's thunderous snoring to subside. As soon as all was quiet and Jane's breathing grew shallow and even, Kathryn once more crept from the room.

But she did not head immediately for the library. Instead, Kathryn went to the kitchen and plundered the larder, emerging with the pocket of her night rail stuffed full of food. Dousing her candle, Kathryn tiptoed outside. The crescent moon had risen, and she was able to walk with some assurance by its pale light. She headed for the small stable situated just beyond a largish kitchen garden and a small, well-kept apple orchard.

And then she felt her skin prickle.

An eerie feeling that she was being watched came over her. Quickly, she edged into the heavy shadows beneath one of the large old apple trees and looked behind her. Nothing moved. The air was cold and surprisingly still after the tumult of the storm earlier in the day. The wet leaves on the ground muffled her footsteps.

They would muffle *anyone's* footsteps, a little voice told her. Nonsense. She was telling herself a tale. She was the only one skulking about the yard. She continued on her way.

She found Thomas, the little stable boy, curled up on a pile of sweet-smelling hay and wrapped snugly in a soft, thick blanket. The poor dear was an orphan, left on Lady Marchman's doorstep when just a baby. Earlier she had guessed he was about ten years old, but in sleep his tense little features had relaxed, allowing their care-worn appearance to ease away, and she could see he was a little younger. Eight, she decided. The boy's blond head was half hidden beneath the blanket, and he snored softly. Kathryn hated to wake him. She touched his shoulder lightly.

His eyes swam with sleepiness. "Yes, miss?"

"You delivered my message?"

"Yes, miss, I done it just like you said."

"And no one knows where you went?"

"No, miss."

"And did you ask the name of the man who answered the door?

"Yes, miss. 'E said it was Ben Dullson."

Ben Dullson? Bendleson!

Thomas stuffed his little hand into one of his empty boots and pulled forth a small envelope. "Here. 'E gave me this. For you."

"Good boy, Thomas. Thank you. You have done well. Now here is your reward." One item at a time Kathryn took the food she'd stolen from the kitchen out of her pocket and laid it in front of Thomas: a huge, cold chicken leg, a large slab of bread, and three tea cakes, the same delicious sort she'd been served upon arriving that afternoon. Then, she pulled from her other pocket a shilling and placed it in Thomas's hand. His eyes goggled. It was clearly more than he'd expected.

Thomas's eyes glowed with unmitigated rapture at the sight of the shilling and the food, and he cast such a worshipful expression up at Kathryn that she thought she might cry. It was clear that Thomas's loyalty—along with anything else he had—was hers.

With the possible exception of the tea cakes.

Kathryn smiled and patted the boy on the head, then hurried back toward the house. She stepped out from beneath the leafy cover of the orchard and skirted the kitchen garden. As she was about to ease open the back door, she glanced cautiously up once again at the darkened window of the school, and her hand froze on the doorknob. She thought she'd seen a movement there. She blinked. Could it have been the moonlight glinting off the mullioned glass? There it was again!

Kathryn deliberately swayed back and forth, watching the moonbeams scatter on the uneven surface of the window glass. That was what had caught her eye, only the reflection of the moon! She sighed in relief, but she stood still for a full minute, staring at the windows just to be sure. She saw no other phantom movements. Kathryn chided herself. No one but Thomas knew she was out here, and Jane was sound asleep.

It was a good thing the moon was not new. Had it been any darker than it was, Kathryn's untrustworthy imagination might have invented a wraith or hobgoblin. She slipped inside and latched the door behind her.

As soon as the door was closed, a shape emerged like a graveyard wraith from the shadows at the far side of the lawn. The tall man swiftly crossed to the back door and, finding it locked, swore softly. He'd gone to some trouble to convince the downstairs maid to leave the door unlatched.

He had almost been inside when the door opened and *she* had slipped from the house into the garden and nearly discovered him. Ducking behind a tree, he took note of her furtive movements, and then, like a fool, he'd followed her and watched to see what she was doing. By the time he realized she was only delivering food to the stable boy, it was too late to make it back inside without being seen. He cursed himself and withdrew from the yard. His business here would have to wait for another night.

Kathryn crept through the house in total darkness. The moonbeams had her spooked, and she was loath to light a candle. She wanted nothing more than to dart into her room and burrow into the safe comfort of her bed. Kathryn forgave herself her silly fit of cowardice. She supposed being a burglar entitled her to a little paranoia.

She really had nothing to be scared of. She still believed it likely she would find the diary tonight. Then, after a short detour to fill Thomas's pockets, she would be gone.

The library, with its heavy velvet curtains, seemed even darker, and the gloom finally forced her to light a taper. The weak light wasn't much to search by, and she went from shelf to table to stack, opening book after book, hoping to see pages filled with Auntie's familiar scrawl, but her hopes were dashed. Her back ached and her eyes stung from squinting by the time the cock began to crow and the familiar humming in the kitchen told her it was time to give up her search once more.

She hurried upstairs and opened her chamber door soundlessly, only then realizing she had not yet read the note Thomas had given her. There was nothing to do but wait until morning light. Unlocking her valise, she tucked the note inside and locked it closed once more. Replacing the key's chain around her neck, she went over to the washstand and washed her hands rather loudly. If Jane suddenly demanded to know where she had been, Kathryn would say she could not find the chamber pot and went outside to use the privy. Hence the hand washing.

Moments later, she slipped into her bed. Her still-badly bruised foot was throbbing painfully, but she was so tired she could feel the soothing numbness of sleep creeping over her in moments.

Sleep came surprisingly fast—to one of the occupants of that chamber. Lady Jane lay awake long after Miss Kitty Davidson's breathing had evened out and Lady Jane was sure her bedmate was fast asleep. Kitty had been in this room all evening, alone. She'd been excused from what was evidently the nightly routine of sewing lessons and Scripture reading. Lady Jane wondered why. One thing was certain: it was *not* because Kitty needed to rest from her journey. That was just an excuse for Lady Marchman to keep Kitty isolated, Jane was sure. After all, stitching and listening to Scriptures were not at all strenuous. No, there was another reason Kitty Davidson was being allowed to hibernate away from the rest of the students, and Jane had been eagerly awaiting the opportunity to ask Kitty all evening.

Of course, there was still Kitty's intriguing search of the parlor to be inquired about. And Jane certainly did intend to inquire. Especially after what she'd just witnessed from the window. What was that girl looking for, anyway? When asked the first time, Kitty had stubbornly pretended not to know what Jane was speaking of. Oh, yes, Kitty Davidson was harboring secrets. Fortunately, Jane was more determined and stubborn than any other girl could ever hope to be.

At least that's what darling Nigel always told her.

She listened carefully to Kitty's breathing, assuring herself her bedmate was indeed asleep. Then, moving from the bed, she checked the pockets of Kitty's wrapper. Nothing but a few crumbs. Some kind of cake. Tea cakes, such as she and Nigel were offered upon their arrival yesterday morning, by the sweet smell of them. And what was that smell? Roast chicken? Why was Kitty toting food about the grounds in the middle of the night?

Jane made a mental note to watch what her roommate did with her food at each of tomorrow's meals and then crawled carefully back into the bed. Should she question Kitty? She wasn't sure, but it didn't matter now anyway. Any questions would have to wait until tomorrow.

Besides, Jane would need the light of day to pick the lock on the lamb's valise.

Chapter Seven

"Devil take it, Blackshire!" Sir Winston pounded on his desk and shoved at his blotter. "If I cannot trust the Blue Devil to keep a fifteen-year-old girl safe, how can I trust him with the safety of King and country?"

Nigel smiled insolently at his superior. "The same way you have always trusted me, sir."

"Indeed—reluctantly!" The gray-haired man pounded the desk again.

As architect and master of the English Army's covert operations, Sir Winston was one of the most respected—and feared—men in Europe. But he had formed an almost paternal bond with Nigel, who had begun his service to Sir Winston at a relatively tender age. The old man always professed to have no confidence in Nigel. It was his way of reminding him not to become overconfident, and whatever abuse he heaped on Nigel always came in proportion to the danger or importance of Nigel's current mission.

"Lady Jane is in no danger. If I do uncover any evidence that Lady Marchman is involved in espionage, I shall pull my ward from the school immediately."

One of Nigel's counterparts, another covert operative, had heard Lady Marchman spewing some startling intelligence at a morning call: a string of English code words uttered as the lady recited a snippet of an odd French poem she'd learned "from an acquaintance." And then, at a milliner's shop a week later, another poem, this time embedded with two known French military passwords and the place-names of important English objectives on the Peninsula. But Nigel didn't see how it could have been anything but coincidence.

"Sir, I have come to know many spies in the course of my service, and I am certain Lady Marchman is not one of them."

In fact, Nigel wondered why his particular talents were being wasted on a case such as this one. He was accustomed to a more . . . vigorous sort of mission, and spending his time idling about a girls' school chafed his impatience.

"I am aware of your doubts, Blackshire. I know you think your assignment to this case is absurd. That is precisely why I summoned you here today."

Nigel looked past Sir Winston through the third-story window. Beyond, the Thames sparkled in the slanting afternoon sun, gilding Westminster Bridge and the barges passing beneath the span. Nigel extracted his pocket watch from his close-fitting azure coat. It was almost time to take Jane to Hyde Park as he'd promised, but Sir Winston, his mouth pressed in a tight line, only continued to pace behind his ironically unimposing desk. Perhaps his rheumatism was plaguing him today, Nigel thought, for the old man knew as well as Nigel that the Marchman surveillance was not worth his current level of agitation. Nigel cleared his throat to jar Sir Winston from his agitated stupor. He hoped to end this interview quickly, for Jane would be vexed if he missed their drive altogether. A vexed Jane was a most unpleasant prospect—and Nigel was already in a foul mood as it was.

Why his cousin had chosen him to be the girl's guardian was beyond Nigel's understanding. Nigel was not exactly known for his good humor. Just the opposite, in fact. And he had little tolerance and even less patience.

Unfortunately, Jane delighted in taxing both. Nigel was constantly threatening to lock her up in the dungeon of his Northumberland estate. Half the time he was serious. He waited patiently for his chief's next insult to his cunning, his intuitiveness, but it never came. Instead, Sir Winston stopped pacing, sat down tiredly, and ran his fingers through his white hair.

"Nigel, I wish you would have got my approval before you involved your ward in this."

At the chief's uncharacteristic use of his first name, Nigel lifted his brow. "The next time, I will ask you before I proceed."

"You are lying." Sir Winston narrowed one eye. "I hope."

Nigel inclined his head a fraction of an inch, but his easy smile vanished. "This mission is more vital than you told me, isn't it?" It was a statement, not a question.

"It is more serious than any of us knew," Sir Winston said and carefully steepled his fingers. "The English Army is poised to strike in France. Of that matter I cannot say more, even to you," he said almost apologetically.

Nigel nodded, and his superior went on.

"It has taken many months of preparation to bring us to this point. We have moved slowly, so as not to forewarn our enemy. Because of our careful preparations, England's position is now very strong. Victory is nearly in our grasp. But a great part of our strength lies in Napoleon's ignorance. We have deliberately given him the impression that England is a lamb. A lamb that has strayed into the wolves' den. The coming offensive should be the pivotal moment that brings us our realization of triumph. But if Bonaparte learns the truth before we strike, if we falter now . . ." He let his words trail off and rubbed his fingers beneath his hard-set lower jaw. His eyes grew steely and his voice took on a hard edge to match.

"Intelligence has informed us that plans for the English offensive are in the hands of the enemy as we speak."

"How did this happen?"

Sir Winston held up his hand. "A weak link in our chain of security." His expression grew grim. "It has been culled. That is not our concern." Intelligence believes the plans have not yet crossed the Channel. Every operative I have at my disposal is on alert and in place. If we do not intercept them before they reach the Continent, we may well find ourselves fighting our battles on English soil before year's end. We expect our enemies to pass the plans in the course of the next two weeks. They must be stopped."

Nigel raised an ironical eyebrow. "And you suspect dotty old Lady Marchman to be capable of engendering Bonaparte's trust in such an important mission? Surely the French have other, more reliable lines of communication."

"Of course they do. But we cannot leave any of the known conduits unwatched. And do not dismiss Agnes Marchman so blithely. She is cunning and quick."

Nigel wisely reserved his opinion on that point. *"Known* conduits? I thought I was assigned to this case to investigate the *possibility* that Lady Marchman is a French sympathizer."

"You were. But," he said, tossing a thick sheaf of papers onto Nigel's lap, "Hargraves just finished his investigation of Lady Marchman this morning and sent this up to me."

Nigel opened the file. It contained the standard background check, which he'd already seen. Nigel flipped through to the end. A few new sheets had been added. Financial records. Nigel studied them. "Payments," he said at last. "Regular, large payments from an unknown person or persons." He looked up.

"Made in English banknotes, usually from a different bank each time. The origin of the payments were obviously meant to remain a secret, but we were able to trace at least three to France . . . and check the date of the first."

Nigel did and then closed his eyes. Lady Marchman had

received the first payment over forty years ago. He hated to imagine the damage those forty years of undetected activity had done. Cunning and quick? She'd be cunning and dead, if Nigel proved she was a spy. Old woman or no, he would see her swinging from the gallows. He was passionate about his beloved country, and he had no sympathy for those who would betray England.

"Blackshire, normally I do not care how the Blue Devil gets things done, as long as they *are* done," Sir Winston said acerbically. "I have at times thought you take unnecessary risks, and, while it would be a great shame to lose you, England would survive. There are others who would take your place. You are expendable," he said, "but Lady Jane is not."

Nigel nodded. "No, sir, she is not. And had I known about this"—he rapped the papers in frustration against the edge of the desk—"I would have found another method of infiltration." He tapped the ocean blue sapphire nestled in his cravat. "If I am able, I shall insinuate myself into a position of trust there and remove Jane to the country with a sudden case of the ague or some such. There is a young schoolmistress, and if I can get inside her—" He was about to say "defenses," but his chief interrupted him, holding up his hand.

"I don't care to know whom you will be getting inside of, Blackshire," he said humorlessly. "Just do what you must and get your ward out of there." He stilled suddenly. "No. There is no time for that now. The plans could pass at any time. Today. Tonight. If they *are* passed, she shall be in much more danger than she is now. War on one's home soil is not kind. I am afraid that Lady Jane must remain at the school until the mission's conclusion." He stood and resumed his pacing, sparing no glance in Nigel's direction. "Shouldn't you be taking tea with Lady Marchman rather than wasting time here in my office?"

The meeting was over. Nigel left. Today, Lady Marchman was leading her students on an educational expedition through the Egyptian exhibits at the British Museum, "the clutches of boredom," as Jane had called it. He decided to liberate her before the end of the field trip and take her driving in Hyde Park early. If the plans were to pass through Lady Marchman's fingers, she would not choose so public a place as the museum to move them forward along the chain, so Nigel and Jane would still go for their drive. Besides, there was no other place for Nigel to debrief his unwitting accomplice. He was counting on the detailed reports his loquacious ward was certain to give him.

He turned his phaeton toward St. James's. A bonnet in a shop window had caught Jane's fancy last week—a bonnet he'd refused to buy for her, pointing out that she owned thrice as many bonnets as any sensible girl needed. But Sir Winston's words echoed in his mind. War was not kind. The old man hadn't had to remind Nigel of that. He'd fought on the Continent when he was not much older than Jane. As he'd trooped across Spain, he'd seen firsthand what war had done. The bloody image of one young girl haunted him now.

Jane could never have too many bonnets.

"Oh look, Nigel," Lady Jane said, sitting next to him on the soft brown leather seat of his crane-neck phaeton. "There is Lord Bankham. He is an acquaintance of yours, is he not? Do let us stop. I desire an introduction."

Nigel eyed his ward. She was harder to keep in check than an untried pair in a king's parade. He put out his hand and imprisoned her fingers, just in time to stop her from wiggling them at that rakehell, Bankham.

"Nigel, you are hurting me."

"If you stop trying to twist free, my grasp will not hurt."

"Oh, you beast! Do not let this opportunity pass. I am wearing Lord Bankham's favorite color. I promise to be cordial."

Nigel shot a frown down at his ward. "That, my dear, is what I am worried about." Jane was becomingly dressed in a bottle green gown. "And how do you know Bankham's favorite color?"

Jane glared right back at him, but Nigel could see a ghost of a smile floating in her deep brown eyes. Her hand stilled in his, and he allowed her to withdraw her white-gloved, slender fingers.

"I think I shall lock you in my dungeon after all."

"Either that, or introduce me to Bankham." She dimpled and looked wistfully over her shoulder at Bankham's smart high-perch phaeton as it rolled past on an adjacent pathway some twenty yards to their left. "Why do you not drive a high-perch? It is more stylish. It is the Prince Regent's favorite, you know."

"A flash high-perch phaeton such as Bankham's is lighter and more prone to tipping than this carriage, and it is therefore better—"

"—for keeping me safe," Jane finished for him in a singsong voice. "I'd rather be fashionable. And, speaking of fashionable, Nigel, it would serve you well to pay more attention in that regard. The color blue certainly looks well on you, but you wear it every day." She pulled at the fine camlet cloth of his coat. "Too much of a good thing. People might think you eccentric."

Nigel knew what people thought, and he bloody well did not care. Wearing the color blue had nothing to do with fashion. Neither did it have anything to do with his code name, Blue Devil. In fact, he'd got his code name *because* he wore blue, and not the other way around. He always wore something blue. He had never explained his reasons to anyone, and he never would, so he pretended to ignore Jane's remark about his hallmark color.

"My crane-neck phaeton will turn more tightly than a high-perch will."

"To better avoid handsome young bachelors and deprive me of any hope of wedded bliss, I suppose." Jane ran her slippered toe over the polished silver moldings which edged the low, curving doors. "And something else I do not know is why we never drive that path.'' She nudged Nigel. ''That is the one Bankham prefers.''

''Precisely.''

''Ah. This ride has been very educational, Nigel. Much more so than that musty old mausoleum.''

''Museum,'' Nigel corrected.

''Humph!''

Nigel smiled. He had discovered many things to admire in Jane since his cousin died and left her in Nigel's care. She was a beautiful, spirited, intelligent girl, and she was going to make someone a wonderful wife. She was also going to lead whomever she lured into the parson's mousetrap a merry chase for the rest of his days. He rather thought she'd even be able to keep that rakehell, Bankham, in line. If truth be told, it was Bankham who needed protection from Jane and not the other way around.

''Why are you smiling?''

''Must I have a reason to smile at you?''

''Yes,'' she countered, suspicion coloring the tenor of her words.

''So . . .'' He ignored her. ''How do you find the accommodations at Lady Marchman's?''

''They are adequate. Quite comfortable, actually, if a bit . . . small.''

''Are you given enough food?'' Nigel asked, remembering his days at Eton, where, as at every other exclusive boys' boarding school in England, the food was so unappealing that the meager portions rarely caused a complaint from the boys. ''If you find yourself hungry, send a message right away to—''

''Oh, no,'' Jane said. ''The food is abundant and delicious. Cook is French and as plump as they come. She cannot resist her own creations.''

Cook was French. Nigel filed the information away.

''Except for today's tour of the mausoleum, I am actually enjoying the school very much—though I must still question your judgment at placing me there—especially during the Season.''

''I told you: I am often away from home while in London, and it is not appropriate for a young lady to stay in a house alone.''

''Nigel, why is it that I am too old to stay alone without becoming scandalbroth, but I am too young to have a come-out?

''If you would prefer, you could go to stay in Northumberland. I shall be traveling there in late autumn, and—''

''No! Uh ... no,'' Jane moderated her voice, ''Lady Marchman's School is good for me. I need exposure to all sorts of people. You said so yourself.''

''So I did.'' Nigel shook his head. In spite of her initial, vehement protestations, Jane was obviously unwilling to leave Lady Marchman's. The thought gave him pause.

He knew the last year had been hard on Jane, living with him as guardian. Jane was always being banished to one or another of his country estates at a moment's notice whenever Sir Winston called Nigel to service. She had no friends her age, and since Nigel had no family and little time to entertain, he worried she was lonely. Though she was canny and wild, she was also a girl about to become a woman, and Nigel believed Jane needed female companionship.

Inevitably, the thought of marriage needled Nigel again. His marriage could provide Jane with a steadying influence. His marchioness might even make it possible for Nigel to make his way from one side of a ballroom to the other without having to assist some delicate young lady who happened to swoon in his path. And in spite of what he told Jeremy, he did feel a certain responsibility to the title. Finding True Love seemed more and more improbable as the years passed. He would soon be thirty—his bloody birthday was once more creeping up on him like a great black spider.

Maybe he should just give up and choose one of the current crop of Diamonds. He couldn't think of one unmarried female who wouldn't walk willingly, even eagerly, into a loveless marriage with the Marquis of Blackshire.

Or could he?

The fairy queen had popped into his mind. She certainly hadn't been eager to further their acquaintance. He wondered, remembering that one, hot kiss they'd shared, if he might be able to convince her otherwise. But the point was moot, for Titania's true identity was still unknown to him.

Nigel sighed and rubbed the knotted muscles at the back of his neck. He grew tired of waiting for his bride to walk into his life. Perhaps he should marry now and start a family. He could find a woman he could admire, even if he could not find someone to love, and he was certain to love their children. Would it not be better to marry now and put an end to his uncertainty? What was he waiting for, a leprechaun to appear and lead him to the lady at the end of the rainbow? A fairy to wave her magic wand and—

A fairy, a wand.

His mind kept returning to the fairy queen.

He dwelled upon her gallant and clever rescue of Lydia and her violent indignation—however undeserved—over Nigel's role in the matter. He pondered her kindness to the pirate and her cunning escape from Nigel in the garden. He savored the memory of their embrace. Of how her hesitancy had given way to full participation. Of how she had melted into his arms. She stirred something inside Nigel, something which left Nigel bemused and . . . and wanting.

When this mission was over, he'd find her. And then he'd . . . he'd . . .

He'd do nothing at all. He couldn't. He could not persuade her that he had done nothing wrong without dishonoring Lydia, and that was something he would not do.

Impossible. Devil take it! On just one mission in service to his country, he'd broken out of a French dungeon, single-handedly ambushed four military couriers, and ridden half-way across France, stopping only to seduce a general's wife in order to gain access to vital information—all with broken ribs and one eye swollen shut.

And that mission was proving to be far easier than solving his personal problems.

"Of what were we speaking?" he asked Jane.

"The people at Baroness Marchman's School."

"Meet anyone interesting?"

"Oh . . . yes. Yes, I have. Most of the girls seem rather vapid, actually. But there is one who is . . . very interesting. She is my roommate."

"Your *roommate?* Were you not shown to a private room yesterday afternoon?"

"I was, but a new student arrived an hour or so after you'd gone and I was settled. She and I are alike, I fancy."

Nigel watched as Jane's gaze became unfocused again and, staring off into the sky, her mouth molded into a slow, lopsided grin. Obviously, what Jane had found was another girl with the heart of a trickster. Were Lady Marchman exonerated, as Nigel fervently hoped she would be, though the facts thus far were damning enough, Nigel would feel sorry for her and send her roses in apology.

"Jane, do behave at Lady Marchman's. You must not give her cause to dismiss you. If you do, I promise I *shall* banish you to Northumberland."

"Bankham hates Northumberland."

Good. Nigel sighed. Then Jane would certainly stay out of trouble, and he knew it would take considerable force of will for her to do so. She was a trouble magnet, just as an unguarded meat pasty was a street-urchin magnet; she was pulled to it naturally.

A clap of thunder boomed and echoed in the distance, and Nigel pulled the carriage in a tight circle. The clouds had been scudding in from the south since he'd left the buildings of the Home Office. The distinct, biting promise of a cold rain had crept into the air, and Hyde Park, normally filling at this fashionable hour with fine carriages, was emptying rapidly. He whipped the horses up into a brisk trot and headed for Lady Marchman's. "Would you care to return to the park tomorrow?"

"Oh . . . no thank you, Nigel. That is unnecessary; the ride was just long enough. Besides that, Bankham only drives here twice a week, Tuesdays and Sundays."

Perhaps I should introduce Jane to my superior, he thought testily. She was obviously a better spy than he was. He was amazed that she hadn't yet discovered his service to the Home Office.

Nigel blinked.

By the devil! Jane *would* make a very good operative at that. She was clever, loyal, brave. Too impulsive, perhaps, but she knew how to temper her natural impulsivity when the need arose. Nigel realized, too, that Jane would be safer if she were aware of his mission at the school and the danger they could both fall into if he took a wrong step. If he suddenly were forced to tell her to flee, he did not want her to plant her hands on her hips and demand to know why.

That decided the matter. He set his jaw. Sir Winston would definitely not approve of what he was about to do, but it would not be the first time. Jane was already a covert operative, whether she knew it or not.

It was time Nigel told her some things.

Chapter Eight

She'd read the note from Grosvenor Square as soon as Jane had left the room that morning. As Kathryn had suspected, the message was not of any real importance. It was full of Ophelia's dire predictions for the outcome of this "outlandish misadventure" as well as multiple venomous assaults on the character and disposition of John, who had scrawled across the bottom of the missive a warning that using Thomas to carry messages put her at risk of exposure. He urged her not to send Thomas again unless it was absolutely necessary.

Poor John. Kathryn doubted he was enjoying his stay in London very much at all.

Lost in thought as she searched through the stacks of books in the library, Kathryn didn't notice anyone's arrival until voices echoed down the hall. She quickly retreated to her window seat with a book and glanced at the mantel clock. Seconds before four o'clock, and Lady Marchman and Miss Gant were not expected back with the students for another hour. Kathryn hoped the voices signaled a simple delivery or the arrival of a calling card.

As the clock began to strike the hour, Kathryn noticed a small, ornately framed looking glass on a stand next to the domed mahogany clock on the mantel. Smiling, she tiptoed over to the mantel and angled the mirror so that, from her perch at the window, she could look into it and see the small anteroom at the front door. She was not disappointed. As the clock finished announcing the hour, Cook, a fat, floury woman with a red face, bustled down the hall from the kitchen, passing the library without glancing inside. She opened the front door and two figures entered, one tall, broad-shouldered, and commandingly upright, the other slight and lithe. It was impossible to see more, for the day had turned gloomy with rain, and the single lamp near the door to the library provided little illumination in the entryway.

Cook grumbled something unintelligible, but decidedly French, and turned on her heel.

"Enchanté," the man intoned when Cook had passed out of their hearing. He bowed gracefully and then helped his female companion off with her pelisse. Kathryn's pulse quickened.

The lady giggled. "Do try to be understanding about Cook's tart nature."

Kathryn knew that voice, too! It was Lady Jane's!

"From what I gather," the girl told the man, "she has a husband who is always leaving her in London to roam the countryside, where, it is rumored, he visits a light-skirt who wears red—"

"Jane!" the man cried. "You will quit such talk. At once!"

Kathryn's blood froze. Yes, she was absolutely certain she had heard the gentleman's voice before; it was so familiar. She wished she could place it. Who was he? They were alone together, which meant he could only be Jane's guardian. Jane hadn't mentioned his name. Was he a friend of her parents? Or worse, someone she'd met briefly at Ophelia's ball?

"I am glad I placed you at Baroness Marchman's School," he said quietly, confirming Kathryn's guess. "It was indeed a good move."

"You had no choice," Jane answered him. "You had to bring me into this. It was the only way you could—"

"Jane!" He shushed her. He lowered his voice even further, and Kathryn strained to hear his next words. "Be careful of what you say."

"Oh! Yes . . . yes, I shall! I shall be observant, too—as you instructed. And careful."

"Good. Remember, you must be careful not only of what you say, but of what you do, pet. You are not to take an active role in this. You are only here to keep watch. You are to report anything unusual to me."

Kathryn wrinkled her brow. Jane's guardian had instructed her to be observant? To report "unusual happenings"? What could it possibly mean?

"Come along!" he said. "We shall adjourn to the salon and ring for tea and amuse ourselves observing Cook's bad temper until Lady Marchman returns."

Kathryn's heart beat wildly in her chest. She huddled deeper into her window alcove. Oh Lord, what was she going to do? She'd certainly meet Jane's guardian as she moved in Society, and if she let him see her face now, he would recognize her later. Recognize her and know that she'd carried out this outrageous masquerade. He'd certainly ask her about it. And he might tell others what he'd seen. What was she going to do? There wasn't even time to hide!

Jane's guardian's voice boomed down the hallway. "The main salon is this way, I believe. Yesterday, I saw a card table there." Kathryn said a quick prayer that they would move away from the library.

But God, it seemed, was in a perverse mood that day.

Instead of walking into the nearest salon, the pair came down the hall toward the library. The only way to conceal her face was to toss her skirts over her head—which was unthinkable—or to run for the stairs and hope he did not see her clearly.

"Ohh!" Kathryn moaned her panic, splayed her fingers over her face, and bolted for the stairs.

"Feel like losing your pin money again?" he boomed. "How about a game of—umph!"

Kathryn had misjudged their proximity. As she rounded the wide, open doorway of the library, she slammed into the tall, surprisingly solid and robust person of Jane's guardian.

On top of everything else, she'd just been caught eavesdropping.

His strong arms were curled lightly around Kathryn's back to keep her from falling. She was embarrassingly close to him, but she did not wish to step away. She peeked through splayed fingers at Jane, whose amused expression was enough to make Kathryn truly nauseated.

It was imperative that she secure this man's goodwill. How else could she persuade him to keep her masquerade at the school a secret? Being exposed as an eavesdropper was *not* an auspicious way to be introduced to him.

Kathryn dreaded seeing censure in the eyes of Jane's guardian.

Yet even if her success at finding the diary had not hinged upon his good opinion of her, Kathryn would still have been embarrassed. Eavesdropping was impolite, to say the least, and she was mortified at having been caught. She felt her cheeks burn as color rose to fire them.

The last time she had eavesdropped was in that awful closet when she'd had to endure listening to that devil Blackshire savage an innocent maid, Lydia, the poor darling. The image of the black-eyed marquis danced in her mind, and Kathryn was sure she felt the color in her face rise even higher, if such a thing were possible. She fixed her gaze firmly on the floor and regained her balance.

Jane's guardian stepped back when Kathryn was at last standing without his support, and Jane spoke.

"Nigel, allow me to introduce Miss Kitty Davidson."

Nigel?! A toll of warning clanged in her head. That name ... that voice ... no, it could not be!

Kathryn looked up, and her mouth dropped open.

The devil was staring back at her.

A mixture of surprise, amusement, and suspicion marched across the sharp planes of his handsome face as he towered over her. As she watched, his grin turned from amused to sardonic. The wispy seeds of recognition swept over his features. Kathryn felt herself blanch. If he identified her as Titania, poor Aunt Ophelia truly would be ruined. Blackshire would expose Kathryn to Lady Marchman without delay, and Ophelia's diary would never be rescued from her clutches. Then, if whatever secret it contained did not entirely ruin Aunt Ophelia, the story of Kathryn's shocking masquerade as one of Lady Marchman's students would—for Kathryn had no doubt Blackshire would delight in maliciously telling the tale, were he to discover that it had been she who had witnessed his attack upon Lydia.

That it had been she dressed as a fairy at the masquerade.

That it had been she who had swatted his rump with her wand.

That it had been she who had delivered him that insolent, malicious, and very public cut direct.

That it had been she who had melted into his arms and kissed him like a strumpet at twilight and then escaped him without even letting him see her face. And, Kathryn realized, her heart sinking, even if Blackshire did not recognize her as Titania, and even if she were able to recover the diary, she would still be at his mercy. For, if she were ever to enter London Society, he would see her sooner or later and know she had posed as one of "Baroness Marchman's young ladies." She would have to rely on his honor as a gentleman not to give her secret away. And Kathryn already knew how little honor Nigel Moorhaven, the Marquis of Blackshire, possessed, the demon.

Not a shred. Not an ounce. None.

Yet how much pleasure could one such as he extract from besmirching the reputation of a plain miss from the country?

Yes. She would be beneath his interest, she reasoned wildly. She could still have her Season. She would avoid him, attending only the less fashionable balls, perhaps. She would scan rooms as she entered and keep careful watch for him, leaving immediately if he made an appearance. She would avoid the park, Vauxhall, and St. James's. The opera, Astley's, and Almack's. With any luck, she would find her true love and be safely and happily married by the time Blackshire recognized her as the waif from Baroness Marchman's School for Young Ladies.

But—oh!—what if her luck did not hold?

What if she careened headlong into him, as she just had today, in some other, horrifyingly public venue? And what if he chose that horrifyingly public moment to expose her—and poor Aunt Ophelia—to all?

The only saving grace was that Blackshire had seen nothing of her face at Auntie's masquerade ball but her eyes. Thank goodness he had not had time to pull off her mask! It was bad enough that he'd seen her eyes. They were a distinctive ice blue, but she doubted he could guess her identity from that alone. Though their color was rare, it was not unique. She and Aunt Ophelia would be safe from his venom until Kathryn took her bow to Society.

Jane moved to touch Kathryn's elbow. Once again, Kathryn St. David—with an assumed identity—found herself being formally introduced to the despoiler of innocents as Jane said, "Kitty Davidson, may I present my guardian, Nigel Moorhaven, the M—"

Jane did not finish announcing Blackshire's title, for Kathryn startled her by doing the only sensible thing under the circumstances. She closed her distinctly colored eyes tightly shut, pretended to swoon, and fell at Blackshire's feet.

Chapter Nine

Nigel looked down at the girl and sighed.

Jane's bow mouth made a little O, and then she laughed. "I see the rumors are true. The young ladies really do swoon at the Marquis of Blackshire's feet!"

"Rubbish." Nigel snarled. "This one isn't old enough to spell 'marquis,' much less swoon at the mention of one. And what rumors? Who have you been listening to this time? No," he said irritably, holding up his palm, "on second thought, I don't wish to know."

He sighed again. He really was in a foul mood. It had been gathering like a storm cloud all week, and the closer it got to his birthday, the darker his mood became. He wished he could simply do away with the entire day, the entire week. Hell and blast, the entire month! He longed to ensconce himself in his library with a case of brandy while the occasion passed with him insensate, as he had each year before Jane had come to live in his care. But he wouldn't have had that luxury this year, even if she'd not been his responsibility. Not with this damnable investigation.

He knelt and scooped the child from the floor. She was

light as thistledown floating on a breeze. Nigel cradled her still form in his arms and looked down to examine her. When she had fallen, she had luckily managed to avoid both a thump on the head from the sharp-edged armchair and a graceless slump over the ridiculously overstuffed ottoman in front of the chair. Satisfying himself that the girl was unharmed, he cast his gaze over her face. Smooth skin curved flawlessly over high cheekbones and a rounded face. Short, dark eyelashes dusted her ivory complexion. A large, faded blue satin ribbon, tied in a bow, nestled in her tight blond curls. Her feet, peeking from under a blue skirt edged in faded yellow lace, were bare; her carelessly tossed slippers lay in a jumble near the couch. He looked at her face once more. There was something of the familiar there . . . did he know her? Was he acquainted with her parents, perhaps?

She was not from a well-to-do family, judging by the condition of her clothing. But Nigel counted as friends people from many stations of life. He paid little attention to class distinction.

"How old is your Miss Davidson, Jane?"

"I'm not certain. Lady Marchman said we are almost of an age—which I took to mean either fourteen or sixteen."

"Sixteen?" He thought she looked younger. "Fourteen is more likely." He looked again at the little-girlish cut of her ill-fitting dress and a wave of sympathy washed over him. The fabric, though clean, was worn and shabby, and it was plain to see the garments were old. How long had this young lady been without new clothes? He did a quick mental calculation. How could her parents afford to send her to school if they could not afford a new gown more than once every three or four years?

Poor girl.

He looked down at her lovely face and imagined what she would look like properly gowned. She was a comely lass, even at fourteen. Given a few years, she'd be able to charm the feathers from a chicken.

Or a marriage proposal from a bishop.

She probably had the lads of whatever village she came from coming to blows for the privilege of carrying her over the threshold. Perhaps that was why her parents had sent her off to school. Perhaps they hoped that with an education to accompany her beauty, she might marry well. She'd need both, with no dowry to offer. And these horrendous clothes! Nigel hoped her parents would be able to do something about that problem.

He stood gazing down at her cherubic moppet face. Her eyelids were twitching, and for a moment he wondered if she were shamming after all. No. She had no reason for a false swoon, for she hadn't heard his full name and title. She was just coming to, that was all.

He noticed a deep, mended rip at the shoulder of her dress. "This garment ought to be ripped off and tossed," he muttered, pinching the thin fabric of her sleeve and giving a little tug.

The cherub's eyes jarred open, and she began to squirm and wriggle to get down. Nigel's eyes grew wide as he suddenly discovered parts of her were surprisingly rounded in a most uncherubic way! Perhaps she *was* sixteen!

"Unhand me at once!" she demanded. "You shan't have a stitch of my clothing, and if you rip the fabric, I shall tell the *Times* or the Bow Street Runners or . . . or both! She scowled at him.

Nigel closed his eyes and then shook them open. "What? What makes you think I want to—" Oh. Hadn't he just grumbled something about getting rid of her clothing? He laughed. "No, I assure you that is not what I—"

"How dare you laugh! Put me down. Now, I say!"

But instead of setting her on her feet, Nigel just held on to her and smiled. He was a master of smiles. He bestowed them to disarm, tame, charm, or seduce. They were always calculated, created purposefully and executed without any accompanying mirth of heart to cloud his judgment. But not this one. It had come about on its own. It had no purpose, no reason for existing, but Nigel could no more have stopped its coming than he could have stopped breathing.

His expression seemed to infuriate her, for she frowned and struggled even harder to be free of him.

Nigel's grin widened. And he knew exactly why. In all of his days, even before inheriting, no lady, young or old, had ever struggled to be free of his touch. Yet Miss Davidson was struggling. Struggling and growling, the little hellcat. He couldn't help chuckling.

"Put me down!" she sputtered.

"But you are recovering from a swoon," Nigel told her.

"I am not!" She sounded outraged at the very idea.

"Oh. I do beg your pardon. But it certainly *looks* as though you are recovering," Nigel said, pointedly eyeing her pinching fingers and stabbing knees.

Instantly, she stilled and tossed her head, eyes flashing. "Put me down *please.*"

Nigel obeyed a sudden impulse to provoke her, and he added, "You are weak. In fact, I think I should not allow you to recuperate from your swoon here in the library."

"Allow? Allow!" she sputtered. *"You* will not allow?"

"Where is your chamber? I will take you to your bed."

"The devil you will!" she cried. Quick as a ferret down a rabbit hole, the cherub-turned-hellcat reached up and yanked a lock of Nigel's hair. Since she was evidently quite recovered—and since he was standing conveniently over the plump window seat cushion—Nigel dropped her.

She landed on her bottom, glared at him, and swung her feet to the floor, then raised a triumphant blond eyebrow. "Ah, it seems you are correct," she said while primly arranging her skirts. "I must be weak after all"—she slid him a sly look—"for I could not pull as hard as I wanted to."

Nigel should have been furious. Instead he found himself . . . exhilarated. Challenged. He realized she had swooned before Jane had announced his title. Nigel was glad. He wondered how she'd react when she heard the word "marquis." Would her delightful indignation metamorphose into the predatory speculation and corresponding speculative greed he was all too used to seeing in young ladies' eyes? He hoped not. He was enjoying her enmity too much!

"Miss Davidson," he said, grinning once more, "you do not seem the type who makes a habit of swooning. I am concerned. So, like it or not, I intend to carry you upstairs to your chamber—with Jane accompanying us, of course. If you move to harm me again, I shall bind your hands and feet for the journey."

"And will you gag me as well?"

"No. Your spiteful tongue amuses me."

Miss Davidson stubbornly crossed her arms and, clamping her jaws tight, looked away.

"That amuses me, too," he told her and was rewarded with a flash of irritation in her eyes. "Jane," he directed his ward, "go have hot water sent up to your chamber. Also go upstairs and see that Miss Davidson's night rail is ready and her bed turned down. Then come back here." He looked around. Jane was standing, stock-still, staring at the two of them, a bemused expression on her face. He coughed and tossed his head in the direction of the hall, and for once she followed his orders without question, turned, and left. Nigel sat on a delicate Chippendale chair and, leaning back, tried to make it clear that he was going to stay long enough to see his orders carried out. Though Miss Davidson refused to look his way, he saw her red lips thin into a line at the sides.

She was enraged.

He was delighted.

In spite of the perverse satisfaction he was getting from rubbing the hellcat's fur the wrong way, his cause was actually noble. It was not wise to ignore a genuine swoon, and Nigel knew it had to have been genuine, for Miss Davidson had certainly not been attempting to impress him with the delicacy of her feminine sensibilities. On the contrary, he had the distinct impression she would cheerfully do him an injury if she could. Miss Davidson looked to be in fine fettle now, but a sudden faint could be a sign of all sorts of maladies, and the girl should have the attention of a doctor. Lady Marchman was due back in less than one hour. He would guard the stubborn Miss Davidson to make sure she stayed in bed, and then he would inform Lady Marchman of the incident. Chances were, he was wrong about her. Chances were Miss Davidson was simply a swooner, the sort who could be sent into a genuine cold fall at the mere glimpse of a garden frog or rearing horse. There were many like her in London, Nigel thought. She was not unique. He'd wager her anger would disappear magically at the mention of his title, too. She'd be fawning over him in seconds, just like all the rest. Irritation stabbed him, and Nigel looked away from her.

"Where is Jane?" he muttered. She was probably off poking into some dark recess of Lady Marchman's boudoir, going against his express orders. She was always doing exactly the opposite of what she was told. "Devil take her, the rotten wench, she—" Nigel stopped abruptly, for Miss Davidson was staring at him openly. He shut his mouth and smiled at her. Her gaze snapped back to the window, and he returned to his brooding, though his ire was no longer directed toward Jane but inward, toward himself. What was the matter with him? Such an outburst was inexcusable.

He knew exactly what the matter was.

His birthday. It was almost upon him. In a few days, it would engulf him like a flood tide, drowning him in horrible memory, and nothing could stop it.

It stole his concentration, something he could not afford right now, not with the Marchman case breathing down his neck. He had a right to be on edge, he told himself.

He shook his head at the delicate silhouette of Kitty Davidson. But for her presence, he could have put this unexpected boon of time in the empty school to use. Maybe the stolen war plans were here in the house, waiting for Lady Marchman's accomplice to arrive and take them on to

France. This would have been a good opportunity to search for them.

Blast! He wasn't going to let a bad-tempered country chit get in the way of his duty. He'd lock her in her chamber if he had to, with Jane to guard her.

And where was Jane, anyway?

Nigel sat, trying to think about his mission, about where— and for what—he would look first, but he was very distracted by Miss Davidson, who was fidgeting with the golden fringe on the couch, twirling her delicate fingers around and around. Pulling, tapping, brushing delicately under the tips of the fringe. Her fingers were long and surprisingly mature. He wondered if she liked the pianoforte or if she hated it and neglected her lessons. That would be a pity, for her passionate nature would give her music a depth of feeling so often lacking in the efforts of the other London chits. The strains of a Mozart concerto thrummed though his imagination, and Nigel sat, momentarily entranced by the movements of her hands. So precise . . . yet feather-soft, like those of a dancer. Suddenly, Nigel looked away. Jane was taking an awfully long time.

Miss Davidson was peering between the heavy velvet drapery, which nearly blocked the weak light that shone through the tall, narrow, library window. Most of the windows in the house, Nigel noted, were similarly shrouded. The better to obscure the truth. He wondered if it were Lady Marchman's guilty conscience or a fear of the gallows which drove her to keep the house dark. Perhaps the room would soon be light again. Lady Marchman had mentioned a school outing to view the magnificent glass window at St. Margaret's Church and the architecture at St. Dunstan's in-the-West, to be held two days hence. Perhaps he should wait until then to search the house. Lady Marchman would be back soon. Nigel's thoughts drew him on an intense study of the room. He scanned it, looking for possible hiding places for the war plans.

"Do pictures and bud vases displease you particularly?

Or do you always scowl?'' Miss Davidson asked after a time, in tones that were not of the drawing-room variety.

"I do not scowl."

"You are scowling at me right now."

Was he? He had not been aware of it. "I do apologize. Young ladies as beautiful as yourself deserve nothing but smiles." He expected her face to soften for his compliment, but he was disappointed.

Her eyes sparked with ire once more, and she crossed her arms and looked away. "You waste your smiles on me, then."

"Not at all, for you are beautiful. A fair blossom, just beginning to open." One with thorns, Nigel thought.

"You insist I am a flower? Then I am a briar rose," she said smugly, echoing his thoughts.

"Exactly," Nigel said, without hesitation.

For a fleeting moment, Miss Davidson's eyes danced, and the corners of her well-shaped mouth twitched upward. The almost-smile transformed her face, and in that moment Nigel thought he glimpsed what the briar rose would look like in full bloom. Her hard frown quickly returned, but Nigel let the beauty of her smile's image pool and eddy in his mind along with the other memory he carried of her smooth, sleeping face.

"You don't frown often," he said.

"I frown all of the time. Do not think you are getting special treatment just because I frown at you this—why are you laughing?"

"Because, cherub, your face has no frown lines. In fact, what you have is a set of laugh lines. You must be a happy girl by nature, so what have I done to set your rudder so hard against me?"

"Cherub?" she asked archly. High color suffused her cheeks. He watched it spread in fascination. He'd pricked her ego. Her diminutive size must be a sore spot with her.

Nigel hid a grin. He stood and bowed low. "Forgive me, Miss Davidson. I did not mean to say 'cherub.' "

"That's better!"

"What I meant to say was 'imp.' "

"Imp!" Her expression clouded over and Nigel could have sworn he heard thunder.

"Yes," Nigel affirmed with satisfaction. "A mischievous little spirit-being. A sprite. A fairy."

"F—fairy?" she repeated.

"Yes. You know, Queen Mab . . . Titania . . ." Nigel watched as her face blanched suddenly and she swooned again, her curl-festooned head and shoulders slumping to a rest on a pink silk pillow.

From the doorway, Jane giggled. "Ha-ho! Twice in one day. Nigel, you must turn down your wick. Your charm lamp is burning out of control."

Nigel rolled his eyes. There wasn't a frog or rearing horse in sight. It had to be him. What had he said? Cherub, imp, sprite, fairy. All harmless. Certainly, he'd said nothing so noxious as to cause a swoon. A thrill of fear ran up his spine. Perhaps Miss Davidson was truly ill. Nigel stood and cleared his throat to mask his alarm.

"You are correct, Jane; you and Miss Davidson do indeed have something in common. You are both shameless eavesdroppers."

Jane wrinkled her nose. "Well . . . Kitty is an eavesdropper, to be sure, but I do not believe she is shameless—though she is a quick learner, I'm certain. I don't know . . . do you think I can teach her to be shameless?"

"You could teach Oedipus to be shameless. Is the water ready upstairs?"

"The basin is being filled now. You may carry her up in a minute or two—as long as she hasn't clawed your eyes out, in which case she will probably be more than willing to lead you upstairs and then, I suspect, to nurse you back to health herself." She laughed wickedly.

What the deuce did she mean by that? "Are you implying Miss Davidson has formed some instant *tendre* for me?"

Jane nodded, already ascending the stairs.

"Rubbish!" Nigel muttered. Miss Davidson did feel strongly about him, that much was certain, but what she felt was obviously not affection. As he carried her upstairs, she roused enough to glare at him, which satisfied him that nothing serious was amiss, though he'd report her fainting spells to Lady Marchman anyway. He left her in the care of one of the maids—and Jane, who expressed a desire to help see Miss Davidson settled.

Waiting in the front parlor below, he concentrated upon the case, until a sudden cacophony of muted, high-pitched voices gave him notice that Lady Marchman and the students were back, and Nigel rounded the corner just in time to see Lady Marchman pass out of sight through a doorway down the long hall. He also caught the sweep of Miss Davidson's gown as she ducked into the library. She had not followed his orders to stay in bed. Nigel's eyes swiveled upward. If Kitty was downstairs, then where the deuce was Jane?

Jane, quite naturally, was bent over, squinting through a keyhole and listening to a most interesting conversation. Lady Marchman and Miss Gant were speaking alone. Unfortunately, she was forced to avoid discovery by a passing servant before she got all of the details. But she left well satisfied anyway. It seemed one of the girls at the school was expecting a visit from the fairies. It was not something she would tell Nigel, both because Jane could see no relevance to his case and because she was sure Nigel would be scandalized by the knowledge that Jane had any inkling of—or interest in—where babies came from. And she certainly wouldn't tell anyone else, either. No, the knowledge would be her secret. Hers and Lady Marchman's and Miss Gant's, Jane amended.

Chapter Ten

With Jane gone, Kathryn was free to return to the library. She had to find that blasted diary. She had no time to lose. Jane said her guardian—her "dear sweet Nigel," as she'd called him—took a great interest in her education and planned to visit the school often, which meant chances were good Kathryn would be thrown into his company again, a circumstance she must avoid. For the longer Kathryn was in his company, the greater the chance that he would recognize her as Titania from Ophelia Palin's ball.

If he connected her to Ophelia, it would not be long before he found out who she was, which would be disastrous for poor Ophelia.

And the longer she was able to pull the wool over his eyes and masquerade as a schoolgirl in front of his nose, the angrier he would be if he discovered her true identity. Kathryn cringed, thinking how such a wicked man might react to having been so easily deceived.

He would be enraged.

Not that Kathryn intended to let him discover her ruse. She wasn't going to let him find out. She would avoid him, and as soon as she had Auntie's diary in hand, she wouldn't just hire a coach back to Grosvenor Square, but she'd hire one to take her all the way back to Heathford.

She knew she could never have her Season now. Never take a place in Society. Blackshire would recognize her. He would know about her masquerade at the school. From there it would be easy for him to discover her connection to Ophelia. And it would not take a great mental leap to realize that Kathryn was Titania. The one who'd slapped him with her wand, given him the cut direct, and kissed him alone in the garden.

Oh yes! He would certainly have enough tales to tell!

He wouldn't even have to embroider them. He'd ruin her reputation, her Auntie's, even her parents'. And what about poor Lady Marchman, whom Kathryn had begun to suspect was not as vile as Aunt Ophelia liked to think she was? Would Blackshire's black-hearted venom ruin her as well?

Kathryn had no choice but to retire to Heathford forever, once she'd found the diary.

Drat Blackshire!

It galled her to accept defeat at his hands. He was cheating her of her Season, of her chance at finding a loving husband. He was disappointing Auntie and her parents, who would not be happy to see Kathryn's youth fade into childless spinsterhood. And of course, she would have to give up her friendship with Jane as well.

After placing a line of pillows under the covers to make it look as though she were still in bed, she crept downstairs. The girls were at tea, and the school was relatively quiet, but the buzz of a muted conversation emanated from the library. Drat! She listened at the doors, recognizing Lady Marchman's voice and a man's voice—Blackshire's perhaps?

A sharp rap of the knocker sounded on the heavy wooden front door of the school, and a servant hurried past to answer it. Kathryn crouched behind a large chair, concealing herself as a lady swept inside and toward the library with a soft rustle of silk. She trilled a greeting to Lady Marchman in the musical syllables of a French accent, and Kathryn smelled the sweet tang of lilac perfume carried on the draft from the open front door.

There was no chance of searching the library now, and Kathryn didn't wish to spend any more time cooped up in her chamber. She dashed for the front door, taking her cloak from its peg as she passed.

The rain had slowed to a drizzle, and she strolled the grounds over shaded paths winding among large tree trunks and manicured hedges. The air was chill and an almost unnatural stillness gripped the world, as though all of London, both men and beasts, had sought shelter from the elements. She looked down the street, toward where it disappeared into the mist.

Was her own true love here in London at that moment? What did he look like? What was he doing? Was he even now thinking of her? Or wondering when they would meet?

"I am sorry," she whispered into the air. It was unlikely they would ever meet. Heathford was out-of-the-way, and her parents did not seek friendships outside the country circle. Kathryn and her true love would never meet now. No matter how much she desired a Season in London, she would not take the risk. Blackshire was too much of a menace.

A shiver of loneliness crept miserably up her spine.

Kathryn allowed herself a moment to wallow in self-pity. Though she had always denied any real interest in the fashions and frippery so popular with the ladies, secretly she had wondered what she might look like dressed in a beautiful gown with her curls drawn up on the sides and pinned like a crown high on her head. She had dreamed of dancing until dawn and being regaled by the sweet poetry, songs, and flowers of a stream of ardent suitors. It was not to be.

Lady Marchman's beautiful French visitor glided through Kathryn's consciousness, and Kathryn could not help comparing herself to the elegant lady. Kathryn's skirt did not swish with silken luxury around her ankles. Her hair, which had gone unwashed since the night before her departure from Heathford, did not smell of lilacs. Mild jealousy stabbed her. She hadn't even seen the lilac lady. Hiding behind the chair, she'd had to rely on her other senses. She'd heard the silk and smelled the perfume. Now she wondered what the lady who wore silk and perfume must look like. Kathryn would wager that the lady would never be able to masquerade as a girl of fifteen! She would never be dismissed as a child by handsome strangers. She would be beautiful and sophisticated, a sought-after young beauty. A woman who would catch the eye of every eligible young man—including the Marquis of Blackshire.

Kathryn looked up at the house. The library jutted out into the garden. He was in there, still. And so was the lilac woman. Unbidden, Kathryn's feet took her off toward the tall, narrow library windows. Camouflaged beneath the cover of a large, purple rhododendron bush, she peeked into the marble-framed window and froze.

Blackshire's polished black Hessians were only inches away from her nose! If the window had been open, she could have reached out and touched him. Her heart pounded madly enough to shake the house off its foundation.

Resisting the urge to shrink toward the water-soaked, leaf-strewn ground, Kathryn willed her heart to still. She was close enough to see warp and weft of the fine material of his deep blue coattails. His legs were closely encased in buff-colored breeches, and Kathryn could see his sinewy strength clearly outlined—as well as a good deal of everything else the man possessed. Heaven help her, she could not look away. Blackshire was not the pudding-bodied dandy her parents had led her to expect all privileged London males to be. One's legs did not acquire that kind of muscle with lazy disuse. No, Blackshire was an active man, like her father.

If only he were like her father in other respects! If he

were, he would be gentleman enough to keep her secrets, but Kathryn doubted Blackshire would forgo the sinful pleasure of plunging her and poor Aunt Ophelia into disgrace without some greater reward than keeping his own sense of honor intact. No, Blackshire would need some stronger consideration than that.

Wait ... perhaps Blackshire could have it both ways. Perhaps she could strike some sort of bargain with him to keep her secrets for but a Season. Then, even if Kathryn did not find a husband, she could still go home with Ophelia well satisfied and none the wiser. But what had she to offer him? Kathryn had nothing of value to offer in exchange for his silence. Nothing save her feminine honor, and giving *that* to him was unthinkable.

Her mother had explained that husbands and wives undressed to ... to be together. He would have access to more than her lips. It would mean having his hands on her skin, his eyes taking in every contour of her naked form. Dear Lord, it would mean the marquis would take off his clothing as well, and she would see his long arms, his long legs, and his long—

Dear Lord! Where were her thoughts taking her?

In the wrong direction, that was certain. If they ... were together, Blackshire would not be her husband, she told herself sternly. He would not take his clothes off at all. He would unbutton his pantaloons and toss her skirts clumsily over her head. They would meet in a closet somewhere, or in a pantry, or if she were really lucky, in a stable ... with sweet-smelling hay, and a soft woolen blanket to lie on, and a soft rain pattering on the roof close overhead. ...

Her senses went a-begging as images of what she and Nigel Moorhaven might do together sifted languorously through her mind, and Kathryn realized suddenly that she had forgotten where she was and what she was doing. She was standing there quite still, staring with unfocused vision into the leaves of the rhododendron. Perhaps it was her mental distress at the thought of poor Auntie's suffering, or perhaps it was a sudden, cold wind that wafted around the outside corner of the library, but Kathryn felt a swath of gooseflesh form up her spine.

Or perhaps she was just a little fascinated with the images she had conjured, fueled as they were by the memory of his strong arms curled about her shoulders, his hands curved possessively around her waist, his sweet breath sending chills skittering up and down her spine, his warm lips coaxing, demanding, taking.

She shook herself.

The man was like a great, black spider, and she had been caught in his web, just like all of the other, innocent, unwise chits. But she was not innocent—or not entirely, she told herself—and she would free herself.

She *had* freed herself.

She stamped her foot upon the cold earth as though to prove the point and looked around her. Blackshire had moved closer to the lilac lady. Kathryn assessed him coolly. No, he was really nothing at all like her father. Her father had acquired his strong body through honest toil, working along-side his own men, his hands in his own clean earth. Kathryn doubted Blackshire had ever worked a day in his spoiled, miserable life. Perhaps he got those muscles riding to the hounds or swimming in the sea at his estate in Brighton. Perhaps he sparred regularly with Gentleman Jackson.

Or maybe his legs had grown strong chasing after fleet young girls and eluding the devil.

Kathryn tore her gaze away and looked for the visitor, but a glimpse of Lady Marchman's gray serge skirt and Blackshire's legs were all the vista afforded. She moved over to the next window. This time, she had a view of Blackshire's profile and a full view of the visitor's face. Kathryn frowned. The lady's delicate features were made even more fragile-looking by long, straight blond hair that shone in spite of the poor light. The pink silk walking gown she wore, with its matching, fur-trimmed pelisse, was of the first stare of fashion. Her skin was flawless and her posture regal. Kathryn doubted if her expensively shod feet had ever touched the bare earth, and she would certainly never be caught stooping under dripping wet rhododendron bushes spying on her betters.

If she had any betters. She looked like a princess.

Kathryn glanced at Blackshire to gauge his reaction to the lady and was stunned. His face was transformed. He smiled at the lilac lady with even, white teeth, his sculpted lips turned up in a disarming, boyish manner. By the light of day, he did not look at all like a devil. In fact, he looked more like an angel. But as she looked at him listening to the lady speak, Kathryn tingled with an intimate awareness, and she was certain his smile did not go deeper than his features. Despite his merry, carefree expression, Nigel Moorhaven was wary, unsettled.

But not half as unsettled as Kathryn was. She was jealous! Jealous of the attention Blackshire was paying the lilac lady. She pushed away the emotion with violent denial. It was unwanted.

Unwarranted . . . unbelievable . . .

And undeniable.

The marquis had been smiling at Kathryn just that same way barely an hour ago. And he'd smiled at her in a very different—but no less compelling—way when he'd kissed her in Auntie's garden. But Kathryn was sure that when he'd smiled at her then, the smile had come all the way from his heart.

His black heart, she reminded herself.

His smile now was a façade. But by the sound of Lady Marchman's muted laughter and the lilac lady's gay expression, Kathryn was the only one who was aware of Blackshire's current discomfiture. She stood, silently fixed on the tableau before her, until a movement at the far window opposite hers caught her eye.

A red felt hat bobbed up and down, peeking over the sill. Suddenly, the hat rose a little higher and a pair of gray eyes popped into view for a split second, meeting squarely with

Kathryn's, before bobbing out of sight once more. It must be the gardener. Kathryn hurried away, escaping a possible lecture on spying.

Too bad she could not as easily escape the green-eyed monster that followed her with teeth bared.

Jealous? Yes, she admitted to herself. She was jealous of the French lady, but must the reason be Blackshire?

She had reason to envy the lilac lady, who was no doubt free to search the world over to find her one true love. Kathryn was envious of the lady's opportunities. Of the attention of men in general and not of Blackshire's in particular. Jealous of the attention the lady was receiving from Blackshire? Faugh! It was nonsense. She had no reason to be jealous over anything Blackshire did. She did not desire his attentions, after all!

Drat that miserable diary! Where was it? She wanted nothing more than to get away from Blackshire, from the school, from London altogether. She wanted to lose herself in the solitude of the hills.

Kathryn stamped her foot again and strode away from the library defiantly. For someone who desired solitude, she suddenly found what little of it she had was making her feel much too . . . alone.

Nigel watched as the fashionably dressed young woman laughed gaily, and he listened as she and Lady Marchman shared the latest *on-dits*. "Ah, Agnees, my dear friend!" Madame Briand exclaimed after a particularly spicy bit of gossip, "I so look forward to calling on you."

Lady Marchman beamed. "Ah, Yvette! Not half as much as I. How very glad I am you were able to call again so soon this time." She turned to Nigel. "Yvette and I have often remarked that we seem more like sisters to each other than friends. From the day a friend of Yvette's introduced us, a week has never gone by when Yvette has not called here."

"A friend of yours, Madame?" Nigel said, trying to make

it seem as though he were feigning polite interest, when in fact he was alert to every syllable.

"*Oui*, my lord."

"A lady of my acquaintance," Lady Marchman supplied. "Celestine Jenoit. She has since moved back to France." A note of sadness trembled in her voice. "We were quite close—quite like Yvette and I, but now I never hear from her." She launched into a verbal cataloging of all the disasters that may have befallen her "friend," Madame Celestine Jenoit.

Nigel stayed long enough to be sure no recognition sparked in Madame Briand's coal black eyes as she addressed him before excusing himself and finally taking his leave.

Nigel was sure he had seen Madame Briand before. Except that she had been a mademoiselle—and her name had not been Yvette. That name was false, just as, he suspected, was the name "Celestine Jenoit."

After Kathryn left her vantage point outside the library, she had wandered toward the small kitchen garden, where the fragrance of the rain-battered herbs rose to greet her. A church bell rang in the distance, and she had looked up in time to catch sight of Blackshire as he boarded his phaeton and departed.

She got a perverse satisfaction from the knowledge that the lilac lady's charms had not had the power to hold Blackshire for long, though she recognized the notion for what it was, another stab of jealous asperity. She reached down and picked a sheaf mint and crinkled it to bring out its fresh fragrance and inhaled deeply.

"Lud!" she muttered to herself. "If my wits can be scrambled just by a silly kiss or by a glimpse of a manly smile and a bit of sinew, perhaps Mama and Papa were right to keep me penned in the country."

But she knew there was more to her sudden feeling than mere reaction to a virile, jaunty smile or a handsomely turned leg. After all, she'd seen John Bothwell naked once, though he'd been up to his waist in river water, and Robert Brice had the most beautiful smile, and both young men had stolen kisses from her once or twice.

A little voice asserted that neither of their kisses had affected her the way Blackshire's had. But that was pure nonsense! His kiss was no different. It was just a short pressing of the lips and a closing of the eyes. It was nothing.

It was everything.

She closed her eyes. Neither of her country suitors had ever caused her to be so all about in the head. She hadn't lain awake at night thinking of their kisses, only to go to sleep and dream it all again. Blackshire seemed possessed of an almost magical power over her.

"Perhaps he truly *is* a demon," she grumbled and wandered toward a fluffy carpet of yellow sunshine, a patch of newly budded daffodils.

After she rambled outside for a few minutes, heavy sweet-smelling raindrops began to fall again, clattering upon the new green leaves and down upon her head. She jogged lightly to the front door and ducked inside. All was quiet. The students must have been at their French lesson—which, unfortunately was conducted in the library, for Lady Marchman had an extensive collection of French literature. Good, Kathryn thought, moodily. She had no desire to pore over a mountain of dusty, musty old books today, anyway. She would much rather go outside and smell the rain-washed air and pretend she was back in Heathford. She'd just sneak back upstairs and borrow Jane's umbrella.

She placed her bonnet and cloak upon her peg and started for the stairs, but she paused when she heard voices emanating from a parlor. The voices were soft and difficult to ascertain, but the word "book" clearly sailed to Kathryn's ears.

What book?

Could whoever it was be talking about the diary? Had it

been discovered? She crept soundlessly to the closed door and put her ear to it.

"La," she heard Lady Marchman exclaim, "the thing was full of such daring exploits. Why, I do believe it was the naughtiest thing I've ever read."

Kathryn's mouth went dry, and her body shook with apprehension.

Lady Lilac's voice trilled in laughter. "You weel not share it with the pupils, will you, Agnees?"

"Oh, heavens no!"

"Then eet is where they cannot find eet?"

"Most assuredly."

"Someplace very safe?"

"Oh, yes. Quite safe. It is not out in the open."

"Eees eet in your chamber?" the lady persisted.

"Yvette! Why do you plague me so? If you must know," Lady Marchman began and tittered nervously, "I have misplaced the book. But do not worry for the innocence of any of my girls. The book is so miserably well hidden that even I cannot find the thing."

"Oh, my ladee! Do not say so! We must find it. Immediately."

"My dear Yvette, I am certain it is just wedged under some of Mary's belongings upstairs in our chamber. I would not be so careless as to lose something you had given me. *Childe Harold's Pilgrimage* is not gone forever."

Childe Harold?! Kathryn nearly collapsed with relief. They were speaking of a book by Lord Byron and not one penned by Ophelia Palin!

Mopping at her perspiring brow, Kathryn retrieved Jane's gray parasol. Downstairs, she had to put the cumbersome thing down in order to don her cloak again. But before she could slip out the front door, in stepped the dancing master.

Having been excused from the daily dancing lesson, Kathryn knew Monsieur Revelet only by the hilarious description given her by Jane that morning. He was a pinched man, short yet gangling, and not at all what one would expect from the typical suave dancing instructor. In a plain, olive green short coat and mustard-colored breeches, he was dressed unfashionably; Kathryn could see that even with her unpracticed eyes.

He was not even particularly graceful. But he *was* fashionably French—which is what must have persuaded Lady Agnes to hire him.

Kathryn thought of the lilac lady and her trilling accent. Evidently, Lady Agnes had a fascination for the French, as did most of the *ton,* and she cultivated their acquaintance.

Upon seeing her, Monsieur Revelet fixed Kathryn with a look of distaste and waggled his finger.

"Ees good your school geeves lessons in deportment, no? For I think zee young lady's manners need—how do you say?—refinement." Kathryn stared at him incredulously, and he continued. "Listening to others in secret ees very bad, I think." With that, he walked with an air of calm superiority into the library, Kathryn staring after him.

How did he know she'd been eavesdropping?

As he passed into the salon, the lilac lady greeted him with a slight nod of recognition. And then, in a breathless, panicked tone, he cried, "Lady Marchman, Lady Marchman! I think there is a fire outside! Come into the library. Hurry!"

Kathryn's eyes narrowed and she wrinkled her brow. Monsieur Revelet's manner had changed from calm smugness to alert fright much too quickly! The high-pitched, startled-rabbit tone of voice he was using now did not match the manner of the man who had chided her for eavesdropping only seconds before.

Something was amiss.

Kathryn decided to investigate this fire for herself. Dashing outside, she looked for flames but saw none. Finally, she spotted a thin wisp of smoke curling up into the still, moist air just beyond the tall hedgerow bordering the lawn. It did not look very serious, and she was certain Monsieur should not be so agitated.

She darted under the rhododendrons and peered into the

library as she had before. Lady Marchman and Monsieur Revelet were still standing at the far window, and the lilac lady—Where *was* the lilac lady?

Craning her neck, Kathryn caught sight of the woman. Standing on one of the topmost rungs of the tall library ladder, her pink silk skirt waving in a most shocking manner, the lady slipped her slender fingers into the top of her silken bodice and plucked from her generous *décolletage* what appeared to be a small sheaf of papers. Quickly, she tucked the papers into a slim, brown leather-bound book on the highest shelf, grasped an impossibly low rung of the ladder, and swung down, accomplishing a maneuver that would have made a monkey at the menagerie envious. Smoothing her skirt, she then pasted a concerned look on her face and addressed the two at the window, who turned around. Kathryn cursed the drizzle and the closed windows, for she couldn't hear what was said, but it wouldn't have mattered if the day were fine and the windows open. Her heart was beating so hard, she would have had difficulty hearing herself speak.

Had she just seen what she thought she had? Had Monsieur Revelet actually created a diversion so that the lilac lady could hide her papers in the library unobserved?

There was one way to find out.

Kathryn quit the rhododendron bush and struck out for the hedgerow. She hurried down the length of the gnarly old yew hedge, her booted heels crunching the wet gravel of the drive. At the end, she discovered a sleeping nag hitched to an unattended gig pulled to the side of the drive, a gig that must belong to the dancing master, she was certain, for there lay some soggy sheet music on the wooden seat.

On the other side of the hedge, a small pile of wet, green branches had been set afire. Upon closer examination, Kathryn found a block of paraffin at the base of the pile, which had been needed to ensure the fire would continue long enough for Lady Marchman to see the plume of smoke. For Kathryn held no doubt that that was exactly what had occurred. Someone had deliberately set the fire, and Kathryn was fairly certain she knew who had done it. She strode purposely back around the hedge to search for some evidence in the shabby, two-wheeled cart she'd passed.

It wasn't difficult to spot.

Kathryn spoke soothingly to the horse, who had awakened and was rolling her eyes nervously, sniffing the smoke in the air. Quickly, Kathryn examined the gig, discovering why the man had left the laboriously copied sheet music out in this weather. Lifting it aside, she discovered beneath the sodden music a block of paraffin and a jackknife.

She also found a red felt hat. Red felt, such as she might have assumed would be worn by a gardener! He'd been spying on the people in the library. Kathryn was outraged. Her first impulse was to inform Lady Marchman of what she'd seen without delay.

But she couldn't. After all, he'd seen her spying, too. Were she to inform Lady Marchman of her discoveries, then Monsieur Revelet would not only deny her story, but he would probably tell Lady Marchman he'd caught Kathryn spying.

Which, of course, was the truth.

Either way, Lady Marchman might never trust her enough to leave her alone again, and then Kathryn would never find Great-Aunt Ophelia's diary.

It began raining in earnest, and, since the library was occupied, Kathryn huffed in frustration and retreated to her bedchamber. She was very tired. She had not had a whole night's sleep since before she'd left Heathford. Perhaps she would just close her eyes and take a nap. She climbed into the bed and stared at the gray plaster ceiling.

She remembered Blackshire telling Jane to be observant, to be careful of what she said aloud. And now people were spying and starting fake fires and hiding papers?

What did it all mean?

It would have been much less surprising if she'd seen the lilac lady steal an object from the room, perhaps one of

Lady Marchman's valuable first editions or a small, silver picture frame. But to go to such lengths to hide a sheaf of papers? Who was she hiding them from? It certainly wasn't the dancing master. He was the one who had created the diversion that had allowed the woman to place the papers on the shelf in the first place. He had to have known what she was doing. But that still didn't answer why she had done it. Kathryn knitted her brows together and twisted the edge of the bedsheet. Perhaps the cache of papers was meant for him.

Perhaps it was a love letter.

Lady Marchman, high-stickler that she was, would never leave her two French acquaintances alone. They would have no opportunity to speak privately or to pass their love note unobserved. Yes, Kathryn reasoned, that explained everything to a nicety.

Everything but Blackshire's remarks to Jane. Hadn't he told her to be observant? To report to him?

And then there was that enigmatic look of recognition that had passed from the lilac lady to Monsieur Revelet. It was not one of love, or even of the sort of anger born of a lovers' quarrel. It was ... passionless, which didn't make any sense at all, and blew Kathryn's theory to shreds. But if the papers were not a love letter, what were they?

And what was their connection to Blackshire and Jane?

And one more little detail nagged at her. The book the papers were hidden in was a slim, brown leather volume. Could it be Auntie's diary?

The gray afternoon light seemed more like twilight, and Kathryn, accustomed to country hours, grew drowsy. She yawned and drifted into a deep sleep, hoping she would be able to hold a lighted candle and climb the narrow library ladder at the same time without tumbling down.

Owing to the school schedule, she doubted Monsieur would have an opportunity to retrieve the book this afternoon or evening.

But Kathryn would.

* * *

Nigel drove from Baroness Marchman's School for Young Ladies to his town house in Berkeley Square and, waving off the assistance of his butler, shrugged out of his blue coat on his way to the library. He had some thinking to do. He helped himself to some brandy and sat down in one of his brown leather chairs before the fire. Before those last few moments in Lady Marchman's parlor, he had been able to cling to the belief that Lady Marchman was completely innocent, that this whole investigation was based on some horrible misunderstanding.

But the appearance of ''Madame Briand'' had shattered those comforting thoughts. On his fingers, Nigel ticked off what he knew about *her* so far: Briand was French; she was masquerading under an assumed identity; and she apparently paid regular and frequent visits to Lady Marchman.

Nigel abandoned his hope that Lady Marchman was not entangled in some evil business. He rubbed his eyes, remembering how the old woman's lined face had filled with concern at the mention of Miss Davidson's plight, how she had confided to him that the girl was in some trouble or other and might need a friend in high places—meaning Nigel, of course. He remembered the conflict he'd seen in her eyes when she'd obviously wanted to tell him something more about Kitty, but felt she could not, for some reason. And he recalled how her eyes sparkled at a jest he had made, how she had dimpled like a young girl when he bowed over her hand upon taking his leave.

And how very much he wished he were not the one who would be responsible for sending her to the gallows.

Nigel had captured all manner of people during his years in service to his country. But always, he'd known his quarry was sinister. He could feel it in his bones. This time, however, he couldn't feel it. He felt only the warmth of Lady Marchman's glowingly girlish smile. The touch of her papery hand lingered in his heart. It was not the icy grasp of a villain.

He swore. He was getting soft. Perhaps it was time to tell Sir Winston it was over. He could give some excuse or other—time to marry and get a son. It was half true. It was time to get married and—was he going mad? He was only nine-and-twenty. The Earl of Reeve had waited to wed until he was nearly forty and still had found a sweet, biddable, and intelligent young wife. Nigel knew he had time to wait.

Trouble was, he didn't want to wait.

Suddenly, Miss Davidson's lovely face popped into his mind, and the feeling her image provoked was definitely not one of fatherly—or even of brotherly—protectiveness.

Maybe he *was* going mad. Miss Davidson was but sixteen. And *he* was bloody well nine-and-twenty! He'd never considered courting one so young before, and he bloody well wasn't considering it now. Sixteen! She wasn't even old enough to *look* at. She was, however, old enough to get someone into deep trouble. Well ... that someone would not be Nigel.

It did not matter that the Earl of Reeve had been nine-and-thirty upon his wedding day and had taken to wife a girl of only sixteen. It did not matter what was acceptable to Society; wedding a child was *not* acceptable to Nigel. Nigel tossed down the rest of his brandy and poured himself another. He was not going to court a dashed sixteen-year-old and that was that. He banished the image of Miss Davidson from his mind and conjured up Madame Briand's instead.

Where had he seen that woman before?

He was certain they'd met, probably on one of his missions on the Continent. Perhaps she had been wearing a disguise when he'd seen her before. A different hair color? Or different clothing? No clothing at all, perhaps?

Nigel tried to remember the faces of the ladies he had taken to his bed—or to their beds. But it was not one of their womanly images that came to mind. It was the image of another woman, one he had never taken to his bed, a woman he could have if only he was willing to wait for her to grow up. A mature Kitty Davidson, fully blossomed, sharp-tongued, and full of fire. Her lithe, naked body stretched out on his bed. Her eyes half closed in passion as he lowered himself over her and . . . and . . . .

He growled. Where the devil were his thoughts taking him? Kitty was not yet a woman grown. It didn't matter if he was imagining what she might be like several years hence. Today she was but a child, and he had no deuced business thinking of her in such a manner!

Nigel took another draft of brandy and tried to concentrate on the satisfying burn down the back of his throat. Perhaps that was his trouble. Perhaps he'd had too much brandy. Nigel put the half-filled glass aside.

Staring into the fire, he allowed himself a smile. He half hoped he was still unmarried a year or two from now, just so he could see her face when they met at a ball or at the opera. He would gauchely remind her of how she had treated him today. He chuckled, wondering if she'd blush and lower her eyes or whether she would scratch his eyeballs out for his impertinence. Nigel liked his eyes right where they were, but then again, he rather hoped she wouldn't blush, either. He'd hate seeing her with all her magnificent fire gone.

His smile fell. He wasn't likely ever to find out. After the story Lady Marchman told him today, he knew Kitty would never make her bow to Society. Lady Marchman told him she'd arrived with nothing but the clothes on her back and a night rail stuffed into a pitiful satchel. Her family had died, and she'd had nowhere else to go. Girls of her station, with no relations and no fortune, did not have a come-out.

He would never waltz with her across the shiny marble floors of a ballroom.

Nigel thought about Lady Marchman's strange assertion that the girl needed someone influential to befriend her. Was Kitty in some sort of trouble, or did she simply need what could be had for the price of a few guineas, a new gown or two?

One thing was certain: Lady Marchman knew more than

she was willing to tell. When pressed, she had clamped her lips tightly together and stubbornly refused to say more.

Nigel strode to his desk and scratched off a missive to one Madame Vensois's, a clever, pleasant woman with whom he'd become well acquainted during the year he'd kept his first mistress. She made the most beautiful gowns, and she could be depended upon to be discreet. A second note was directed to Jeremy Scott.

In light of "Madame Briand's" appearance, Nigel knew he needed another man on the scene. Jeremy had been one of Sir Winston's operatives almost as long as Nigel. He was a good man, a keen investigator, and a loyal friend.

Jeremy would keep watch when Nigel could not.

Impulsively, Nigel added a scrawl to the bottom of his letter to Jeremy, a request for a favor. Would Jeremy carry out a discreet investigation on one Miss Kitty Davidson?

Summoning a footman, Nigel sent the letters immediately. That done, Nigel thrust Kitty Davidson firmly from his mind, barked an order to his valet, and stalked to the stables. Perhaps a good, hard ride would clear his head.

Chapter Eleven

Nigel wiped at his brow with a sky blue handkerchief and reined in his stallion. The horse's black, velvety mouth was flecked with foam, and Nigel's rib cage was sore from the exertion, but the good, hard ride had done nothing to drive the image of a grown-up Miss Davidson from his mind. It was still there, taunting him with a sense of familiarity. But that wasn't the worst. His body taunted him, too, with a blatant physical response whenever he remembered the feel of her in his arms. She certainly hadn't felt like a child.

He swore.

He planned to spend the early afternoon productively at his club, trying to ferret out any information he could on Lady Marchman and her late husband. Though her current station in life precluded her acceptance into the highest of social strata, Lady Marchman was still a titled member of the *ton*. Her husband, Nigel had found out, had been a high-stakes gambler who had lost virtually everything on his wedding day. If there was anything more interesting than that to know about him, someone at the club would probably be the one to share it with Nigel.

But he knew he would be unable to concentrate on the case.

He dismounted and walked his horse parallel to the Serpentine until the animal was cool enough to take a draft of the water there. Nigel wished it were that easy to cool himself.

Was he a degenerate? Was he mad? Would he be forced to hand himself over to the Bedlamites? He was lusting after a mere slip of a girl. She was a child. And he bloody well was not! Instead of the image of a grown-up Miss Davidson, he deliberately focused instead on one of Kitty bedecked with those ridiculous, bouncy satin bows atop her head.

That did it.

His libido screeched to a halt, and Nigel blew out a deep breath, relieved to know his gentlemanly honor was intact, to know he wasn't interested in Kitty Davidson, the sixteen-year-old. And all he had to do to banish the much-too-alluring image of a grown-up version of the chit was to imagine those enormous bows nestling in that shiny halo of blond curls of hers.

Nigel blinked.

Shiny blond curls . . . blue eyes . . .

Of course! Nigel slapped his thigh, spooking his horse. He suddenly realized why Miss Davidson, with her glorious curls and wrathful blue eyes, her slight build, and her spiteful tongue seemed so familiar to him. He'd had the feeling he'd met her before, and now he realized why.

She bore a strong resemblance to the fairy queen from Ophelia Palin's ball!

He laughed out loud, garnering curious looks from passersby. It wasn't the impossibly young Miss Davidson who'd sent his senses a-begging at all, but the fair Titania. Thank God. He wasn't the true devil he had begun to suspect he was.

He marveled at the resemblance, but it was easy to see why he had not recognized it at once. He'd never seen the fairy's whole face, after all, just her lovely blue eyes, her mouth, and her hair. If he saw the two side by side with no masks, he was sure, the two would look nothing alike. Besides, the fairy was slightly taller than Miss Davidson, wasn't she?

He wasted no more time in trying to discern the reason it had taken him so long to understand his wayward libido. Miss Davidson was gone from his mind, and he had work to do, he told himself. Enough of this nonsense. More urgent matters awaited his attention. Even now he could be at his club, interrogating the old boys at the whist tables. He wondered how much it would take in lost wagers and fine brandy to loosen the right tongues. Nigel sighed and headed for home. His clothes would need to be changed and his horse stabled for the night.

But an hour later instead of being ensconced in a comfortable chair at the club, cheerfully losing at whist, Nigel found himself paying a social call on Ophelia Palin.

The club would still be there after his visit to Palin House, and the high-stakes gamblers generally showed up at the club much later than the rest of the crowd. A lost hour was a small price to pay for his sanity.

He had to exorcise the sudden madness that had overtaken him when he had first beheld the fairy queen, the flare of attraction that had swept over him like a wild thing, claiming his reason and driving him to take her into his arms and taste her lips. He'd been unable to concentrate on anything since that night. His desire for the fairy had even driven him to an unreasoned and unacceptable lust for the Davidson chit.

But no more.

He would find out who the fairy was, escort her to a ball or to the opera, find her as superficial and frivolous as the rest of the crowd of fainting dainties, and be done with it.

Sure. And the Prince Regent was a monk.

Something inside warned him it might not be that easy to regain his balance.

He handed his horse's reins off to the blue-and-scarlet

liveried groom who waited in front of the immense house on Grosvenor Square. As he waited in the vast grand entry hall of Palin House for the butler to return from announcing his arrival, Nigel remembered his reaction to the fairy on the night of the ball. The mere sight of her had stirred him, mentally and physically. Beauty abounded in London, and Nigel could have his choice. But it was not the fairy's beauty alone that had claimed his reason. He didn't even know what most of her face looked like. No, it was the way her eyes cast uncertainly about the room, the way they flashed their sapphire fire when he first spoke to her, the way they danced as she publicly insulted him! It was her clever and gallant rescue of Lydia, someone she didn't even know. It was the way she had yielded to his kiss, sighing into their embrace as though sating a hunger long denied.

Nigel couldn't help noting the absence of a wedding ring on her hand.

Ophelia Palin knew who she was. The butler returned and showed him into a small, garishly decorated salon done in shades of orange, Ophelia's favored color. Here and there among the visual chaos were splashes of purple: a vase, a pillow, a painting. As he entered the room, Nigel's eyes rested on these as a drowning man might rest on a piece of floating flotsam.

"Why, Lord Blackshire! What a pleasure it is to see you again so soon, my boy!" the couch appeared to say before Nigel realized Ophelia reclined there, neatly camouflaged in a flaming orange gown among a pile of flaming orange pillows. "To what do I owe the pleasure of your company?"

"Yes, my lord," a man said, stepping from a window alcove, "To what do we owe the pleasure of your company?" Though clean and tidy, he was dressed in the clothes of a workingman.

Nigel's eyebrows lifted and he looked to Ophelia for the necessary introduction, but his hostess was too busy looking daggers at the man to perform it. Evidently, Nigel had walked in on some sort of dispute.

''Have I come at a bad time?'' he asked. He'd had this experience before. People were almost always ''at home'' when the Marquis of Blackshire called, whether they were ready to receive him or not.

''Yes.'' ''No!'' They spoke at the same time.

Ophelia glared at the man again, while the man smiled at Ophelia saucily before walking forward with his hand extended toward Nigel.

''Pleased to meet you, my lord. I'm John Robertson, a friend of the family.''

Family? Nigel thought. He was unaware that Ophelia had any family, but he kept the thought to himself. Mr. Robertson's heavy accent spoke of his low birth, even if his clothing did not. Nigel took the rough, callused hand the older man offered him and, smiling, shook it firmly. ''Do I detect a trace of a Scottish brogue, Mr. Robertson?''

''Aye, that you do, laddie. My dear mother, rest 'er soul, was a Scot,'' Mr. Robertson said, allowing his mother's influence to creep into his words even more heavily.

Ophelia, still glowering at Mr. Robertson, held out her hand to Nigel. He crossed to her and bowed over her fingers before sitting down next to Mr. Robertson on a couch opposite the one Ophelia sat upon. Not looking at Mr. Robertson directly, Ophelia said, ''John, please see that tea is served immediately.''

''Yes *ma'am!*'' John said, springing crisply to his feet, snapping his heels smartly together, and tugging his forelock.

Nigel was momentarily confused. So . . . John was a servant? Had he not just introduced himself as a friend of the family? Nigel's eyes followed the man across the room, but instead of quitting the room to fetch the tea, John moved to the braided red silk bellpull and yanked it, then returned to his place on the couch, grinning smugly at Ophelia.

What was going on here? Nigel wondered. Whatever it was, it was certainly no place for a guest, yet Nigel hated to leave before he learned the identity of the fairy queen.

He had best be out with the reason for his visit as soon as possible.

"My dear Miss Palin," he addressed Ophelia, "I am afraid my reasons for coming to see you are duplicitous. It is not the mere pleasure of your company I seek, but a formal introduction to a certain young lady who attended your masquerade ball."

"Oh?" Ophelia said, a mask of unknowing innocence falling over her.

Nigel wasn't fooled. Ophelia knew exactly of whom he spoke, but he decided to play the game her way.

"You must know the one. She smiled at everyone," he said. "Everyone except for me. She danced with every man fortunate enough to ask her . . . but me. And she was gracious with everyone . . . but me, whom she insulted. You must know who she was. She returned to your side after each dance. I even saw her kiss you."

"Many young ladies kiss their hostess's cheek, my boy."

"Ah . . . she is so young then? Is this her first Season?"

Ophelia chuckled. "Good shot, my boy, but you'll have to do better than that to get me to reveal who she is or anything else about her."

"Then you do know the identity of the lady I seek."

Ophelia laughed. "Of course I know who she is. She was the great treasure I was revealing at the ball. Did you not figure that little puzzle out, young man? You and every other unmarried gentlemen in Town, it seems, wish to know who she is. Half of them were here this morning. She pointed to the pile of calling cards on the heavily carved, red chinoiserie table beside her. Of course I know who my treasure was!" She cackled. "I'm just not going to tell you. Not yet, anyway. You shall just have to be content with 'the mere pleasure of my company.' " She motioned a maid to place the gleaming, burnished gold tea service on the table.

Ophelia poured for Nigel and was about to replace the pot when John Robertson cleared his throat loudly and pushed his own cup practically under her nose. Ophelia poured for him as well, but she overfilled the teacup and the near-to-boiling liquid sloshed over the rim of the delicate, gold-rimmed saucer and onto John's hand. Ophelia made no move to apologize, and it was John's turn to glare. Nigel glanced at the ornate, silver mantel clock. He did not intend to stay a moment longer than the polite obligatory fifteen minutes. He wasn't going to learn the fairy's true name today, and these two were obviously not getting along. He wondered again about Ophelia's mysterious family and about John Robertson's connection to it as he sipped his tea and answered a barrage of questions from John, most of them embarrassingly personal.

He was grateful when he could make his escape at last.

Ophelia rose and hurried to the window as soon as Blackshire was gone.

"All right, what's wrong wi' 'im?" John asked behind her. "He a little too cosy wi' the bottle? Too shallow in the pockets? A womanizer?"

"What are you jabbering about?" Ophelia shot over her shoulder. "The marquis is wealthier than I, and he is a respected and powerful member of the House of Lords. A champion of the poor, and a sought-after guest at all of the most important social gatherings. A perfect gentleman."

"Then you're daft, woman!" John thundered. "Why did you not tell 'im it was Kathryn he's lookin' for?"

Ophelia was peeking around the heavy, fire-colored velvet drapery, watching for Blackshire to mount his horse, but she spared a second to roll her eyes at John. "You ignorant farmhand. You know nothing of Town life."

"Drop the airs, you old windbag. I ken when a man is smitten. That look in 'is eyes . . . 'tis the same anywhere, country bloke or no. Seems to me if a well-titled, well-turned, well-heeled gentleman wants to get to know our darlin' better—"

"Excuse me, madam," Bendleson interrupted them, "but this letter has just arrived, and—"

"I'll take it," John said, snatching the plain white envelope from the butler and hustling him out the door. "We're involved in some very important business. See that we aren't bothered." He closed the door in Bendleson's impassive face and turned back to Ophelia. "I was saying that if a gent like the marquis wants to lovey-dovey up to our darlin' girl, then we should be doin' everything we can to help 'im." He waved the letter at Ophelia for emphasis.

"Men!" Ophelia huffed, forgetting for a moment that Blackshire, like John, was one of that cadre of exasperating male creatures. She seized the letter and tossed it carelessly onto the couch. "Even you cannot be so ignorant, Mr. Robertson." She refused to call him by his first name. "The marquis is indeed smitten, as you say, but that is precisely why we must not tell him who she is."

John sputtered indignantly. "A—are you sayin' that . . . that my Kathryn isn't good enough for the likes o' 'im?"

"Of course not! *My* Kathryn is good enough for the Prince Regent."

"That's not sayin' much, from what I 'ear."

Ophelia looked around wildly and whisked herself over to hiss in John's ear, "Do not, for heaven's sake, be heard publicly maligning the prince ever again."

John looked around. "There's no one 'ere but us two," he said.

Ophelia rolled her eyes again. "The servants are everywhere, whether you see them or not," she whispered.

"But—"

Ophelia covered his mouth with her hand. "There is no time to explain the intricacies of servant-master relationships to you now, Mr. Robertson. And as for not revealing Kathryn's identity, suffice it to say that a woman's mysteries will only make a man's attraction for her grow. A woman comprehends these things," she said, "and for once, I trust, you will not insist that you know as well as I."

"Well, I'm not a woman."

"Heh," Ophelia commented.

Ophelia sat, drinking her tea and thinking, refusing to discuss the matter until the repast was over and deliberately prolonging her silence. She genuinely needed the time to consider.

On the night of the masquerade, if she had thought Kathryn had any real chance of attracting Blackshire's sincere attention, she would have bound and gagged the stubborn girl with Blackshire's own blue satin cravat to keep her from insulting him as she had. What had got into her grand-niece? Why had Kathryn taken such a sudden dislike to the marquis?

And what was that business with that Grantham chit? Now there was a piece of work! If the two of them had been feeding some mongrel kitchen scraps, then Ophelia was a giraffe.

And she would have sworn on a stack of diaries that Blackshire had been in on that outrageous Banbury tale about feeding the mongrel, too. How she wished she'd been able to pry some answers from Kathryn at breakfast the very next morning!

She sighed with frustration. Any fool could see the two of them were meant for each other. But Kathryn would not be convinced, of that Ophelia was certain.

It was a pity, too, for even if Agnes Marchman found Ophelia's diary, she would not expose her secrets if Ophelia were connected to Blackshire. Blackshire's influence was too great. Agnes would not risk disgracing *him*.

Which meant Ophelia had to orchestrate a betrothal, or at least some public understanding between Blackshire and Kathryn straightaway. She simply had to bring the two of them together somehow, and without delay. But how? Ophelia bit her lip and thought hard.

After a while, a smile spread across her face and she clapped her hands together, startling John, who was staring into his empty teacup.

"Wipe the crumbs from your lip, and answer me a question, old man. The moon was but only approaching full last night, correct?"

"Aye, an' what's the matter wi' that? Not bright enough to bay at yet?"

For once, Ophelia did not take umbrage. She flashed a rare smile at John and tapped him on the hand. "I'm going to see that marquis is brought up to scratch!" Ophelia suddenly felt as giddy as a tot on Christmas eve. Her insides were bubbling like a glass of sweet champagne. She gave a fruity chuckle. "With any luck, my dear, we shall both have to curtsy to Kathryn by the first snowfall of winter."

His eyes widened. "You're serious, ain't ye? What do ye 'ave in mind?"

She laughed again. "You don't want to know."

John gave her a pinched, sideways look and regarded her a moment with narrowed eyes. Finally, he nodded his head. "Ye're right. I don't."

Ophelia was a little disappointed. Not about being unable to confide her plan to John. He was a man, after all, and he just would not understand. But she still found the urge to tell someone irresistible—and she would need an accomplice to carry it all off. But who?

The answer came to her suddenly.

Literally.

A footman entered the room to announce Miss Lydia Grantham, who was urgently desirous of an audience with Miss Ophelia Palin.

Ophelia nodded her consent, and the footman went to fetch the visitor. As Ophelia waited, she slid a look over at John. "I was overset with excitement a moment ago. Do not think that because I called you 'dear' that I look on you with any charity at all."

"I know that, woman! Think me stupid, do ye?"

"Yes."

"Liar." John snarled.

"Humph!"

John waved off her rude disdain with an equally rude gesture. "Crikey, woman, let's stop arguin' for once. We're wastin' time. I don't know what you got planned, but if it gives Kathryn a clear shot at that fine gentleman, then I don't care.''

"For once, John, we are in complete agreement." Too late, Ophelia realized she had used John's given name. But he appeared not to have noticed her blunder, so she rose to retrieve her writing materials.

Behind her, John said smoothly. "Kinda feels nice for once, agreein' about somethin'. Don't it . . . Ophelia?''

"Humph!" Ophelia plopped down on an Egyptian-styled chair as Miss Grantham entered the room. The girl dropped a nervous curtsy, and John, gauchly declaring himself uncomfortable with "woman talk," excused himself.

Then Ophelia fixed her gaze on Miss Grantham, and for the next half hour, her eyes never left the gel. She'd come asking what everyone else had been asking Ophelia since the night of her masqued ball: the identity of the fairy queen. Ophelia pinned her with her most intimidating stare and asked Miss Grantham the very questions she should have asked Kathryn on the morning after the ball. She was merciless. Direct, blunt, abrupt, and unyielding. Miss Grantham was surprisingly resistent, quite adept at verbal deflection and even outright lying, but at last she crumbled under Ophelia's assault, and her story tumbled out. Ophelia discovered Miss Grantham had a good heart. She'd come to thank the fairy, she said. She'd made a terrible blunder that night. She'd known the marquis did not want her, and really she did not wish to wed him, either, though she respected and admired him. She'd tried to compromise herself only because she feared her uncle would soon force her to wed someone she cared for not at all, just to be rid of her. She ended her tale, saying she was grateful to the marquis and the fairy, and she wished she could make it up to them somehow.

A slow smile spread across Ophelia's face. She'd found her accomplice.

"Lydia, my dear," she said slowly, "you were not successful at trapping the marquis the first time, but perhaps, with my help, you shall be on the second.''

"Oh, but I have no desire to marry him," Lydia protested.

Ophelia almost laughed aloud. "Then you will not object," she asked quietly, though she knew the answer, "if the fairy queen is compromised instead of yourself?"

Lydia's eyes widened. "Go on," she said.

Ophelia rang for more tea and settled in to explain everything to Lydia: the fairy's identity, the cut she had dealt to Blackshire, Blackshire's interest in her—and finally her own plan to bring the two together. Lydia was more than happy to help and went on her way with a promise to return early the next evening.

Ophelia sipped her tea with satisfaction. How she would enjoy the look on Agnes Marchman's face when she realized the Marquis of Blackshire was to be Ophelia's nephew!

Settling back onto her flaming orange couch and sighing with anticipated relish, Ophelia was disturbed by something crinkling under her. It was the letter Bendleson had delivered earlier. Somewhat absently, she pulled it free and broke the seal. She quickly scanned the letter and her hand fell, the letter fluttering to the floor, forgotten. "Oh dear!" she said.

"What's it?" John demanded, sauntering back into the room unannounced and uninvited.

But Ophelia was too stunned to complain. The letter was from Kathryn's loving parents, who had not fully approved of their daughter's visit to London in the first place. Kathryn's cautious parents, who thought London was a bad influence. Kathryn's distrustful parents, who thought Ophelia could not be relied on to maintain a proper atmosphere for their daughter's first Season.

Kathryn's dratted parents, who were en route to London even then.

Chapter Twelve

"Are you quite certain?" Mary Gant asked incredulously, looking at the papers Agnes had just handed her. "Why would Madame Briand do such a thing?"

"I do not know, Mary, but do it she did. I saw her reflection myself, in the glass of the library window. She was behind us you see, and . . . well, you are holding the evidence in your hands."

"I cannot make any sense of it. This appears to be a map—" She traced the lines with her fingertip.

"Of France. Yes I know. And there are snippets of words and phrases in French, though few of them rhyme."

"Why should they rhyme?"

"Yvette is quite fond of composing poetry and fonder still of reciting it for me. At first I did not think she was a very accomplished poet, but I have heard her poems so often that they have grown on me. I confess I have even repeated a few of them to my friends. French poetry is so *en vogue*, you know."

"That explains what the papers are, then," Mary said, refolding the sheets of foolscap and laying them aside, "they must be her poetry composition notes. But why did Yvette hide them in the library?''

"I am sure I do not know." Agnes turned out the light and punched a comfortable nest into her feather pillow. "I would like to ask her, but I am not sure it was entirely polite to remove them—even if they were hidden in my own library without my permission. Do you think I should put them back?''

"Let us sleep on it, Aggie.''

Light stabbed into Kathryn's eyes and a tremulous, soprano voice sang out, "It is a fine morning, Kitty. Rise and greet the world.'' Lady Marchman threw open the windows to admit not only the blinding light of late morning, but also a fresh spring breeze.

"Morning?'' Kathryn asked groggily.

Lady Marchman laughed. "Yes. Well, it is almost afternoon, really. Lady Jane informed us you had gone for a walk yesterday. It must have tired you, for she found you asleep here just before dinner last evening.''

Morning! Kathryn suppressed a groan. A wasted chance to search the library unobserved. She was disappointed in herself. She wasn't turning out to be much of a burglar. Poor Auntie!

Lady Marchman tied the heavy green woolen curtains back and turned around. "When I saw you sleeping so peacefully, I was torn between your need for sleep and your need for nourishment. But since sleep won and you missed supper, I expect you are rather peckish this morning. Nicolette will be up with a fully laden breakfast tray presently.''

"Nicolette?''

"One of the upstairs maids, dear. Oh my, your clothes are in a state.''

Kathryn looked down at her borrowed blue dress. It was wrinkled beyond belief from having been slept in and on, and she had drooled as she slept, so a large, dark spot spread embarrassingly across her bodice. Her hand flew to her hair, which was a tangled mass of blue satin and flattened, knotted curls. "Not exactly fit to appear at Carlton House, am I?"

"Or any house," Lady Marchman said and chuckled.

"How about a gaol house?"

"They would refuse to keep you."

"A dog house?"

"He would bury you." They both laughed, and Kathryn wondered not for the first time at what Great-Aunt Ophelia could possibly have found to dislike in Lady Marchman. The kind woman treated Kathryn more as a beloved niece than she did a mere boarding student. She had a warm and gentle way about her.

"It is no matter," she said, gesturing toward Kathryn's dishevelment, "for a package has just arrived for you, and unless I miss my guess, you will be pleasantly surprised at the contents." She smiled enigmatically and tugged on the bell pull. Almost instantly a maid appeared, carrying a large, white box. She placed it on the bed.

Kathryn looked up at Lady Marchman questioningly.

"It came this morning. I'm not sure whom it is from. Go on, child. Open it," she said. And Kathryn did.

In the box lay a lovely walking dress of white muslin sprigged with blue delphiniums. A matching shawl, dainty lace gloves, and a small bonnet trimmed with a spray of the blue flowers nestled on top. There was no card. Ophelia must be responsible, but of course Lady Marchman would assume the dress came from Lord Arborough.

Lady Marchman smiled kindly and left.

The maid Nicolette supervised the filling of the hip bath and remained to help Kathryn dress. Kathryn encouraged the lively young woman to chat, and soon she was telling Kathryn of her latest beau—the dancing master, she confessed to Kathryn—who often visited her after hours, when they strolled together outside. They'd even talked of marriage. Nicolette was in raptures.

Kathryn was more confused than ever.

Breakfast, bathing, and dressing in her new ensemble took

a surprising amount of time, and as she had been allowed to be such a slug-abed, she passed into the library well after twelve o' the clock. Her heart beat a furious staccato rhythm as all afternoon she waited for an opportunity to climb the tall library ladder and see if the papers were still there. But students and teachers came and went, downstairs maids passed the open double doors, and a gardener worked trimming the rhododendrons outside the windows, which Kathryn had thrown open to receive the cool breezes and the dancing sunlight. She contented herself with surreptitiously searching the library for the diary by casually wandering among the shelves and untidy stacks, feigning interest in first one volume and then another. By teatime, when a maid came bustling in with a tray, Kathryn was almost certain the diary was not on any of the lower shelves. Neither was it in one of the stacks of books piled on top of or underneath the tables.

The maid closed the window. "Drafts are bad for you, miss. So says me mum. She allus has me wrapped up tight when I'm sick-like. You're lookin' better, but if you don't mind my sayin', you'd best keep that window closed till you're sure you're over your spells. And her ladyship said you're to eat every speck, miss." The maid indicated the laden tea tray, smiled, and left. Kathryn's stomach rumbled its obeisance, and yet she did not sit down to tea just yet.

Everyone else was at tea, too. The library was empty. Now was her chance to get at those papers! She could see the book from where she stood.

Soon she was teetering on the topmost rung, reaching for the book she thought was the correct one. Her fingertips had just brushed the aged leather cover when she sensed, rather than saw, a movement behind her.

Chapter Thirteen

Kathryn moved her fingers purposefully on to another book, and she climbed carefully down. Without turning around, she opened the book and shuffled slowly to a window seat, pretending to be engrossed.

"That would be very convincing—to someone unaccustomed to chicanery," Jane said, behind her, "but, unfortunately for you, I know a fellow sneak when I see one."

Kathryn suddenly noticed that the words in the book were upside down. She looked up at Jane questioningly. "Whatever do you mean?"

"Oh! You know very well what I mean. What is upon that high shelf?"

Kathryn looked up where Jane pointed, directly at the spot where the papers were hidden. "Books, it appears to me," she said blandly. "Did you escape lessons?"

"No. I escaped tea. I was much more interested in what you were doing off by yourself than I was in a cup of tea. And you," Jane said, coming to sit beside Kathryn, "were interested in ... something other than tea as well." She shrugged her shoulder in the direction of Kathryn's almost untouched tea tray. "Care to enlighten me?"

"About what?"

Jane sighed. "Very well. If you will not tell me what you were doing perched on that high shelf, I cannot force the knowledge from you. But I certainly can ask how you came about that lovely dress you are wearing. I know you had no such finery when you arrived at the school."

"Oh? And how did you determine that?"

"I picked the lock on your valise, of course."

A thrill of panic seized Kathryn. "You what?" If Jane had found the note Thomas had delivered to her from Ophelia . . . bells in heaven! She could only hope Jane hadn't found the concealed compartment at the bottom of her valise.

"I picked the lock. But, as you know, I found nothing of interest."

Kathryn relaxed a little and gave Jane an indignant sniff. "Since you have told me you invaded my satchel, why did you not just ask me for the key?"

"Because you would not have given it to me. And because I did not know what sort of person you were. My instincts told me to trust you, but after seeing you searching the parlor, I thought you might be a robber." Jane laughed. "I had to find out if you were good or bad."

Kathryn's face burned with crimson fire. "I see. And has pawing through my meager private possessions helped you to reach a conclusion?"

"No. Your visit to the stables did that."

"You were watching! I knew I saw a movement at a window. But it was not the window in our chamber and so I thought—"

"I had sneaked into Martha and Anne's room. They have the best view of the orchard and garden."

Kathryn narrowed her eyes at Jane.

The girl held up her palm. "Do not look at me that way. I approve of your visit to young Thomas."

"What makes you think I visited Thomas? You canno'
see the stables from that window. The orchard blocks the
view."

"I overheard Cook the next morning complaining abou'
a missing chicken leg and some biscuits. She keeps track
of every crumb, I vow. And the pocket of your wrapper was
full of crumbs."

"You leave no stone unturned," Kathryn remarked.

"And no book," Jane said, reaching out to turn Kathryn's
right side up. "I pride myself on being thorough." Jane
wrinkled her nose. "Little Thomas, however, is not such
an easy pebble to be overturned. He stubbornly refused to
acknowledge your midnight visit, though he still had grease
marks on his mouth and sleeve the next morning."

"Thomas is a good boy," Kathryn said quietly. "He has
no parents. He deserves better from life."

Jane nodded. "As do you. You are not an evildoer. Now,
tell me. What are you searching for?" Kathryn only glared
at Jane, who laughed and tossed her head. "In spite of
whatever nefarious activities you are indulging in—no, do
not bore me with a denial! In spite of the fact that you hold
secrets, I believe you are a good person at heart." She tipped
her head to one side. "How long have your parents been
dead?"

Kathryn blinked back shock at Jane's forwardness. She
had only encountered such bold behavior in her own parents
and in Ophelia, and she had never had to fend off such a
direct question from others. It took her by surprise. "Oh . . .
it, ah . . . seems like forever."

"I know what you mean," Jane mused, then asked suddenly, "How many years?"

"Eight!" Kathryn blurted out, her nerves all aflutter at
having been caught atop the ladder. God's green goose!
Kathryn's heart pounded in her ears. She'd already told Jane
that she'd lost her parents when she was ten! If "Kitty
Davidson" had been an orphan for eight years, then that

made her eighteen years old! And if Lady Jane did some arithmetic, she would catch Kathryn in a lie.

But Jane appeared not to have noticed the discrepancy. Instead, she frowned her sympathy. "Eight years is a long time. Do you miss them?"

"Oh, yes. Dreadfully," Kathryn said. That statement, at least, was truthful, for at that moment Kathryn would have happily traded her parents' companionship for Jane's. The girl was staring out the window, pensively twisting a lock of her raven hair. Sudden guilt assailed Kathryn for she realized Jane was an orphan. "You ... must miss your parents as well."

"Yes. I do. But Nigel is a darling. He is such a dear, and we get along famously, though really we are from different worlds."

Yes, thought Kathryn, Jane belonged on Earth, and Blackshire belonged ... somewhere decidedly balmier.

"He does suffer from an occasional moodiness," she went on, "but everyone succumbs to the blue-devils now and then. Other than that, he's utterly perfect. And yet you were determined to dislike him from the moment you laid eyes upon him. I cannot understand why. You seem such a reasonable person, Kitty." Jane's eyes widened and she smiled. "Saying your name reminds me of Kettle."

"Kettle?"

Jane smiled. "My cat."

"What an odd name for a cat!"

"Kettle is odd—oddly marked, rather. White on top and black as a kettle on the bottom. Two of her kittens have the same coloration, but her other four are striped. Would you like one? Perhaps I can find homes for all of them here at the school. Nigel would like nothing better. Kettle and her brood were strays, and he complains bitterly about them."

"That does not surprise me. He does not strike me as a man with an abundance of compassion."

Jane laughed. "La, it was Nigel who rescued Kettle and her kittens and brought them home to me. Found them under

a thorny hedgerow. Muddied his trousers and tore his shirt
getting them out, too. And if that isn't enough proof of his
compassionate nature, when our housekeeper scooped Kettle
and her brood up to take them out to the stable, it was Nigel
who insisted the lot of them be installed in the house. He
said it was just too cold outside. Now,'' Jane said, placing
her hands on her hips, ''does that sound like the behavior
of an ogre to you?''

''Hmm!'' Kathryn said, and lifted her shoulders.

The response seemed to satisfy Jane for a moment, for
she went to a window and used the weak reflection there to
fuss with her hair.

Kathryn stood behind her, quivering.

Blackshire had rescued the cat from outside Aunt Ophelia's!

Could it be, as Jane insisted, that the evil marquis was
not as evil as Kathryn thought? Ophelia, it seemed, had
badly misjudged Agnes Marchman's character. Perhaps
Kathryn was mistaken about Blackshire's as well. Perhaps
what she'd seen upstairs at Palin House had been some
hideous misunderstanding, as Blackshire had tried to persuade her.

She remembered the tender way he had held her in the
salon, his laughter and his smile—a smile, it seemed to
Kathryn, which had reached his eyes—and his concern that
she should be seen by a doctor. She remembered the way
Auntie had dimpled and smiled at him, the way the sensible
Lady Marchman had so easily confided in him. And she
thought of Jane's effusive praise of her ''darling Nigel.''

She shook herself. No. His influence over them and her
own questioning of his character now only underscored the
dangerous power he wielded, the power to fascinate the
unwary. Jane and Lady Marchman and even Ophelia had
fallen under his spell. Kathryn would not. If he chose to
take the cats home with him or to keep them in the house,
then it must have served his purpose to do so. Maybe his
house simply had mice. Whatever the reason, she was certain

it had nothing to do with compassion. She took a deep breath, girding herself to defend against the onslaught of his false charm.

But a small part of her couldn't help cherishing a hope that she was somehow mistaken about the scoundrel. She closed her eyes, trying to shut out the memory of his touch, his silken voice, his lips tasting hers. Dear God, why had she allowed it? But she knew the answer. Not only had she allowed it, she had wanted it. She'd been done in by his show of tender concern for that poor baby bird. She'd been all too willing to forget about what she had seen and heard upstairs and give in to the intense attraction she'd felt from the moment she'd seen him.

She'd been a silly little country mouse without an ounce of sense.

"What morose thoughts have shaped your expression?" Jane asked. "Do not wallow in them, for today, I vow, I cannot afford you any sympathy. My heart is filled only with gladness, for Nigel has promised to take me for a drive in the park on the morrow," she said brightly. "They say the park is where many love-matches are formed. I am hoping to finally be noticed."

"By whom?"

"La, only by the most excellent and beautiful of men. Quinn, Lord Bankham. He always drives in the park on Tuesday." Jane hugged herself and shrugged, transported for a moment, Kathryn was sure, into the imaginary arms of her "most excellent and beautiful of men." How lucky Jane was, Kathryn reflected, watching the girl's shining face. Her life lay before her, like a thick, red carpet strewn with white rose petals. She would have a come-out, and she would have her choice of clever, handsome, wealthy suitors. Perhaps she would even marry the man about whom she was now daydreaming.

Kathryn looked down at her hands. "It sounds lovely," she whispered, knowing she would never enjoy any of those wonders. Not now. Blackshire's knowledge of her masquerade here at the school would prevent that.

"Would you care to join us?" Jane asked. "I am sure Nigel will have no objection to your accompanying us, and—"

The marquis strolled into the room and interrupted her. "You are certain Nigel will have nothing to say about it?"

Jane glared at Nigel, who did not return her gaze for his eyes seemed fixed upon Kathryn. He was resplendent in an embroidered waistcoat of royal blue and a coat the same shade as his dark hair. He wore close-fitting, buff-colored breeches and tall, brown boots that made him seem even taller than before.

Kathryn hated the way her heart beat so much harder in her chest at the sight of him. Hated the way her eyes were drawn to his lips. He was attractively imposing. Dangerously handsome. Disturbingly masculine.

And he knew it.

She looked away, swallowed, and when she looked up, he was watching her. She defiantly returned his gaze, but he greeted Kathryn's studied belligerence not with an answering enmity, but with a knowing, slightly amused expression. Kathryn looked away once more and instantly regretted it, for out of the corner of her eye, she saw him smirk, the popinjay.

"Jane is correct, Miss Davidson. I will have nothing to say about whether you accompany us or not, as my ward is obviously in charge of everything. She is a controlling, manipulative little witch." His words were carefully chosen to insult, but his expression plainly showed his intent was not malicious.

Jane swatted her guardian playfully and then stilled. Kathryn couldn't be sure, but it seemed as though a silent communication passed between the two. Though Jane's face was turned away from her, Kathryn could see Blackshire's features clearly. He was once more wearing the carefully bland expression she had come to think was studied, constructed, and maintained for the world's benefit. His eyes were fixed firmly on his ward's face, and though Jane's face was not visible, Kathryn still had the distinct impression that the girl silently mouthed a word or two to Blackshire.

It must be her imagination.

But no—there! Her eyes widened. Jane was definitely making some sort of hand gesture to him. It wasn't her imagination after all. Immediately, Jane turned on her heel and passed on her silent way out of the room, leaving the massive doors open for propriety, and leaving Kathryn alone in the deserted library with the Marquis of Blackshire.

Nigel watched Jane go, his heart thumping a little harder in his chest. Had he understood Jane correctly? She'd held up all ten of her fingers, made two fists, then held up eight fingers. Then she'd mouthed the words, "She's eighteen," waggled her eyebrows, and withdrawn.

Was that possible? Was tiny Kitty Davidson really eighteen years old? What the devil was she doing at a girls' school then? She should be at home, possibly married, maybe even caring for her first child. He supposed her parents simply hadn't been able to come up with the blunt to send her to school until now. The thought crossed his mind that she may be the spy he was looking for, but he dismissed the idea as soon as it occurred to him. Miss Davidson was no spy. Of that he was certain. She had neither the guile nor the heart for such work. She displayed her feelings openly, and Nigel guessed that she'd suffocate under the weight of them if she tried to conceal them.

His inattentive attention wandered back to the remarkable idea of Kitty's being old enough to have a child. He imagined her standing with a child clinging to her skirts. The image disturbed him somehow. Perhaps it was because she looked little more than a child herself, though the soft curves he'd discovered hidden under that awful rag she'd been wearing when he'd picked her up had certainly been enough of a clue to the contrary. The gown he'd sent and which she now

wore was a vast improvement. The sprigged muslin clung
to her body, and though her curves were not voluptuous, on
her slight frame what curves she did possess suited her quite
nicely indeed. She was really a comely little thing, and the
blue-flowered dress perfectly set off her blue eyes and crown
of shiny yellow curls. Madame Vensois was a miracle
worker. When the chit returned home, she would be well
attired, well educated, and able to catch herself a suitable
husband. Perhaps a shopkeeper or a clerk. Maybe even a
vicar or a farmer with a large holding.

And, Nigel realized, her wedding day wouldn't be very
long in coming, for, by Jove, Kitty was eighteen. Her parents
would be unwise to wait much longer, and hadn't they
already proved their shrewdness by sending her off to school
in the first place?

"You look lovely today." His tone of voice, more growl
than purr, surprised him. He chalked his sour temper up to
the impending arrival of his birthday and resolved to moder-
ate his tone of voice. "That shade of blue just suits you."
His eyes roved critically over the sprigged muslin gown
he'd sent. Yes, she was quite attractive. She wouldn't have
any trouble finding a husband. She shifted under his perusal
and blushed becomingly before seating herself behind her
tea tray.

"Lady Jane is more elegantly attired this afternoon than
I, but you did not compliment her, my lord."

"My ward is already secure in my regard. Too secure.
She believes she can behave however she pleases with impunity. Yet I assure you I gave her no offense. She is too
concerned with how I feel about you to be concerned with
my lack of manners toward herself." He took one of the
small biscuits from her plate. "She fancies you have formed
some sort of instantaneous *tendre,* you see."

Kathryn gave an unladylike snort. "For you?"

He nodded, smiling, for the very idea was amusing. Looking into Kitty Davidson's eyes was like looking down into
the mouth of a volcano.

"Yes. She says we are perfect for each other."

"Sure," she muttered, "and I am a hedgehog."

"A hedgehog?" Blackshire shook his head. "Well . . . I will own you are small and adorable—"

Kitty sniffed loudly.

"—but you are much more prickly."

She scowled at him, and Nigel suddenly wished he had not provoked her. He found that he very much wanted to see her smile at him instead of frowning.

"You must excuse Jane's fancies. Like every other female her age, she is too much consumed with thoughts of marriage," he said, "and her preoccupation has her imagining romantic feelings where none exist. Particularly where she herself is concerned, but in others as well. I suppose I should not be impatient with her. She is fifteen, after all."

"You are not being fair, my lord. Not all fifteen-year-olds are consumed with thoughts of romance. Some of them are quite self-possessed and know their own minds and feelings very well. Take me, for instance."

"You?"

"Yes," she said, looking down at her skirt and plucking at some imaginary imperfection. "I myself am near fifteen, and you cannot claim that my thoughts are dominated by romantical nonsense, now can you?"

Nigel chuckled. "You are not an accomplished liar."

"P—pardon me?" she stammered.

"Your cheeks are flaming, you are fidgeting, your breathing is a little too rapid, and your pulse is beating a visible staccato at your throat." He crossed his arms across his chest and grinned. "Besides, Jane just told me you are eighteen."

Kathryn gulped air. "Oh dear! I—I can explain. There is a perfectly good reason why I—"

Blackshire stuck out his palm. "Please. You do not owe me an explanation. Your reasons are your own. And your secret is safe with me. We shall speak no more of it."

Kathryn was slack-jawed. Bewildered. Flummoxed.

Kindness was the last thing she expected from Blackshire. He walked to the large globe that stood on a cluttered table and spun it absently.

"Your defense of my ward pleases me," he said.

"She is my friend." It was true. She'd only known Jane for a short time, but for whatever reason, the girl had decided to befriend her. She'd seen her up to her elbow in a silver vase, skulking off to the stables past midnight, and stealing food from the kitchen, and hadn't said a word—unless she'd told Blackshire.

"Good," he said. "Since you are such good friends, perhaps you will agree to accompany us on our drive in the park today. Jane is absurdly enamoured of a most unsuitable young man. She imagines he is ready to whisk her off to Gretna Green, though they have never even been introduced. Perhaps you can make her see her own folly. Or, at the very least, distract her and keep her from making a fool of herself."

"Very well, my lord. Perhaps I can."

But Kathryn had no intention of trying to convince Jane that her regard for Quinn, Lord Bankham, was silly. No. Instead, she would contrive to bring about the introduction Jane so fervently desired—and which Blackshire, evidently, did not. A moment before she'd been willing to assign to him the quality of kindness. But keeping Jane from meeting the young man was heinous. He might very well be a wastrel and a cad, but at the very least Jane should be introduced to him and allowed to make that judgment for herself.

"Jane will be delighted that you have agreed to join us."

"No, my lord. Delight is dependent upon an element of surprise, and with Jane, I am certain the notion that people will not ultimately do exactly as she desires never enters her stubborn little mind."

His black eyes sparkled like sunlight glinting on the brook back home. A disarming smile softened the curves of his sharply angled face, and before she could stop herself, Kathryn's own traitorous features mirrored his pleasant expression. She saw his eyes open wider and his lips parted, revealing even, white teeth.

She wanted to kiss him again.

The desire welled up suddenly, taking her completely by surprise.

Kathryn did her best to hammer her own features back into a semblance of poised indifference and forced herself to hold his gaze. Obviously noting her sudden change of demeanor, Blackshire coughed softly, straightened, and pulled a frown, but his eyes could not hide his mirth, and his dimples were deep enough to take shelter in.

And then he winked at her.

The scoundrel was mocking her! If he expected her to dissolve into silly giggles, he was mistaken.

"My lord," Kathryn asked sternly, "why are you so opposed to the idea of your ward marrying Lord Bankham?"

"Ah. You know his name, then. Jane has already confided in you." He appeared not to have noticed her tone of voice. A smile still lurked upon his face as he went on. "Well, as to marrying Jane off, I cannot declare the idea unappealing. It would be a relief to burden some other poor devil with the responsibility of riding herd over Jane. But Bankham is not the right man for her."

"Shouldn't Jane be the one to decide that, my lord?"

"No. Not at her age."

"What do you propose to do, lock her away and introduce her to the man she will marry on her wedding day?"

"Oh." He raised a mocking brow. "Why, I hadn't considered that, but I shall give it some thought. Thank you."

Blast him and all men with his attitude! They refused to recognize innate good sense when it marched forward and planted them a facer. Certainly Jane entertained fantasies—but only because that was all she was allowed to entertain as of yet! Kathryn knew how that felt. She doubted there was a girl alive who did not. If she had been allowed to have her London Season when she should have, she would not be in the mess she was in right now. Drat it. She shoved her teacup onto its saucer with a clatter and found the motion so satisfying that she gave the entire tray a second shove, the tray slid across the slick, shiny waxed table and onto the floor, shattering the delicate teacup and its saucer and sending brown tea flooding into the carpet.

"Botheration!' she cried and knelt to pick up the broken pieces. Blackshire just stood where he was, and Kathryn did her best to ignore him.

"Do you always clean up after yourself like that?" he asked blandly. "The maids are employed for occasions such as this." His tone suggested that he found her fussing with the growing stain distasteful.

"Do you always leave your messes for others to take care of?" she tossed back at him, keeping her head bent to her task.

"Actually . . . no. No, I do not."

She gave him a look that clearly said she didn't believe him. But he smiled and knelt beside Kathryn, helping to move the broken pieces back onto the tray and then blotting the tea-soaked carpet with the napkin.

"I should call for a housemaid," Kathryn said. "That stain should be treated with—"

"Bicarbonate of soda. Yes. I know. Do not forget and let it dry, for if you do, she shall have to work twice as hard to get it out."

Her hands stilled then, and she looked up at him wonderingly. He frowned. "What?"

"I . . . well, I just wouldn't have imagined you would know about such things, or that you would ever give a thought to—ouch!" Kathryn jerked her hand away, and it immediately blossomed red with blood. A shard of the cup had cut her little finger. She hadn't any time to snatch a napkin from the tea tray before a drop of her blood ran down her finger. Quickly, she drew her injured hand over her lap, where the blood dripped with a crimson splash onto the snowy muslin. "Ohhh . . . the stain will be impossible to get out. I've ruined this lovely dress."

"I think not," Blackshire said. Taking up the napkin, he moved closer and pulled her hand into his lap. Quickly, efficiently, he examined the injury before wrapping the injured finger in the square of linen and pressing her hand with his own. His skin was warm and dry and felt silky against hers.

"Wha—what are you doing?" she stammered.

"I am stanching the flow of blood."

"The cut is not large."

"No, but it is deep. What did you think I was doing with your hand in mine?"

Kathryn stared at his fingers where they made contact with hers, for it did not feel like any normal human touch. Where she should have felt flesh, she felt only fire. More proof that he was a demon, she thought.

But even demons, she supposed, could deliver medical assistance.

He shifted his hand to apply firmer pressure to the wound with his middle finger, a move freeing his thumb, which began to trace tiny, slow circles in the sensitive skin on the back of her hand. She snapped her eyes up to his face, but he was staring hard at the floor and did not seem to notice what his own hand was doing. Or if he did, he obviously did not think it extraordinary. Kathryn tried to relax and ignore it, too, but she found it impossible. The circles widened to span the breadth of her hand, and his brushing touch grew lighter, until, instead of trying to ignore it, she was almost straining to discern it. Outside, the birds stopped singing, the wind stopped blowing, the rain stopped falling, the world stopped turning.

And Kathryn stopped breathing.

"Iodine," he intoned. Their eyes met and he shrugged. "A little secret I learned from our old housekeeper when I was a boy. She put me to work whenever my parents were away."

"You? Cleaning stains and polishing furniture?"

"Lemon juice and fuller's earth. Works wonders on

wax." He threw her a wry smile. "I am not the blackguard you seem to think I am."

"So Jane tells me. She dotes on you. Tell me, my lord, do you return her regard at all? Or do you scorn her privately as well as publicly?"

"You do me an injustice. Young ladies such as Jane," he said quietly, "can be tiresome at times. But they can also be very charming, even . . . beguiling. I suppose that is why I am willing to drive in the park with them."

Kathryn knew she should jerk her hand away. He spoke softly then, his voice somehow more of a caress than even his gentle hand. "If Jane were to exhibit good sense . . . as you do . . . I might be willing to"—he squeezed her hand—"to travel much farther."

His meaning was clear. Where she knew her heart should sting with icy disdain, she felt her heart pulse with a warm glow. She stared at his fingers wrapped around hers and whispered, "Don't touch me."

"Don't tempt me," he echoed and leaned toward her.

She snatched her hand from his and clutched the napkin to her own injury. "I . . . you . . . you must leave now, as Lady Jane has left and we are quite alone. I do not think Lady Marchman would approve. And," she said with a toss of her head, "neither do I."

Nigel blinked, and his head cleared suddenly, as though he'd been under a spell. By the devil! She was giving him the shove-off! He stood, bowed stiffly, and quit the room without another word. He stepped outside and moved to his carriage, where his tiger, James, a boy of eleven, appeared to be half asleep. He was sitting with his back to the trunk of an old oak tree, next to another, smaller boy—Lady Marchman's young stable boy Thomas, Nigel clarified as he approached. They both appeared to be nodding off. A ball, improvised from a tight wad of rags, sat motionless between them, and it was obvious the two of them had tired themselves out playing together. James's fingers were much too loose around the reins of Nigel's pair of high-strung blacks. Nigel issued a sharp rebuke and climbed into the seat. He jerked the reins from the startled tiger's hands, and the poor boy barely had time to scramble aboard the back of the carriage before Nigel whipped the horses into a brisk and reckless gallop.

Nigel was incensed, though he didn't know whom he was more furious with, himself or the young groom.

As the carriage rolled along, Nigel's ire cooled, and after a time he was left with only mild irritation.

"Lovely day, James," he remarked. "Easy to be lulled into sleep on a day like today."

"Thank you, my lord."

They both knew Nigel was apologizing, but that wasn't enough for Nigel. He believed people should speak their thoughts plainly. Like Miss Davidson did. Nigel swore a silent oath. She had spoken plainly all right. She'd told him not to bother pursuing her, for she wasn't interested.

Was that what he'd been doing? Pursuing her?

What had come over him? Certainly, a young lady of eighteen was marriageable. There was no question about that. Men took eighteen-year-old brides every day. But not men like Nigel. Nigel had seen battle. He'd killed in the name of his country. And that was not all he had done. In covert service, he had also seduced a number of women. It was a task he rarely relished and never asked for, but it was one for which he was very well suited, apparently, for he was always successful. Yes, he had seen too much, done too much, lived too long, to even think about marrying an innocent girl of eighteen years.

His mother had been only eighteen when she'd married his father. Eighteen, and married to an old man who had no more in common with her than a worn boot had with a rainbow. How could Nigel have forgotten that? How could he have let himself believe, even for a moment, that Kitty could ever be anything more to him than his ward's friend?

He swore again, this time aloud.

"I really am sorry, my lord," James said from behind him, thinking his master's irritation was directed at him.

"No, James, it is I who should apologize," Nigel admitted, attempting to force Kitty Davidson from his mind. "It was wrong to snarl at you back there."

"Not a bit of it, my lord. It was wrong to be snoozin' when I should ha' been takin' care o' yer cattle. It won't happen again."

"Good man."

Nigel frowned. James *was* almost a man. He would not be able to tiger for Nigel much longer. The boy was growing out of his striped livery, and soon he would no longer be able to fit on the narrow tiger's platform installed on the rear of the carriage. Nigel was going to have to find another youngster to take his place. An image of Thomas, the little boy who worked at Lady Marchman's, leaped into Nigel's mind. Jane had reported that Miss Davidson had taken food to the stables for the boy in the dead of night. Nigel wondered at her generosity. She'd risked getting herself into trouble for the lad. He must quite need more food. But if she continued supplying it, she'd get them both into trouble—and Thomas could find himself on the street. Nigel considered the lad's plight for a moment. He'd make a perfect tiger, if Lady Marchman could be persuaded to part with him. He'd speak with her about the matter first thing tomorrow morning.

But Nigel did his best to ignore returning to dwell on the thought of Kitty Davidson's tender self-sacrifice and to steep himself in his own irritation instead.

What had got into him back there at Lady Marchman's?

Nigel flicked the reins too hard, spooking his cattle. Damn if his heart had not skipped a beat when Jane had mouthed to him that Kitty Davidson was eighteen! Kitty Davidson, who looked absolutely charming in that flower-strewn dress. He had thought he was grown beyond being moved by the sight of a beautiful young woman years ago. But he had been wrong.

She looked like she belonged in a garden.

His garden.

And therein lay the trouble.

Nigel was determined to marry a lady closer to his own age. Even without his mother and father's situation to steer him, he certainly would never have wanted to wed a chit fresh from the schoolroom, a shivering, timid waif who would obey his every command. No, Nigel wanted a wife who could match him move for move, one who was not afraid to best him, if she could. And the trouble with that, of course, was that most women his age were married. Lately, he'd begun to suspect he'd done himself out of finding an intellectual match by foolishly insisting on a love match as well. He'd thought he had waited too long.

But then Jane had mouthed the word "eighteen" at him, and his logical, practiced resolutions had spun off their axis. Eighteen was certainly old enough to marry. No one would look askance at his courting her.

Kitty Davidson was a blossoming rose, not a shrinking violet. A thorny rose with a fiery center. She wasn't afraid of him. She had no interest in obeying him. Her tender years were no hindrance to her spirit or her intelligence. And when she had broken that teacup and reached for a napkin instead of the bell pull, Nigel had been stunned. There was no denying the attraction he felt for her. Even now, he was plagued by the memory of her surprisingly rounded body nestled against his chest as he'd carried her upstairs on that first day, the soft contours of her legs and hips against his open palms. His senses went a-begging as he imagined her in his bed.

Nigel's hands gripped the reins too hard. He'd known the pleasure of many women. And he always knew as soon as he touched them how it would be between them. Instead of simpering and lowering her clear blue eyes whenever her opinion differed from his, Kitty Davidson stood straighter, flared, and spat fire. He knew that Kitty Davidson could scorch his bed and burn her mark into his very soul.

As soon as Nigel arrived home, he took up the decanter of brandy and sat in his favorite chair and swore some more.

With her sharp wit and agile tongue, she would be a popular and lively addition to the most fashionable salons in London—if she ever managed to marry well enough to be admitted there. A sudden image of Kitty assailed him: Kitty, standing at the back door of a yeoman farmer's cottage, wearing rags to which several children, clustered about her feet, clung. Kitty, with tired, sunken eyes and sore, red hands. Swearing again, Nigel put down the decanter. He needed to think about his investigation, and he knew the brandy would only channel his thoughts toward Miss Davidson. He rubbed his temples and tried to concentrate.

For all he knew, the war plans had already been passed. There were several expatriate French visiting or working at Baroness Marchman's School, though only one—Madame Briand—seemed likely to be involved. She could well serve as a link in the chain of communication across the Channel. "Yvette" came and went on a regular basis. She was obviously either picking up information on its way out of England, or she was dropping it off. Nigel was overlooking something—or someone. There was another person involved. Someone in the chain was missing, someone who either already was or soon would be right under Nigel's nose. He could not simply apprehend Yvette Briand. Her accomplices would be alerted, and the plans would only find another way across the Channel to Bonaparte. No, Nigel needed to find out who comprised the other links in the chain.

Chapter Fourteen

Kathryn awoke with the sun. The first light of dawn was just painting the edge of the sky a breathtaking blue. Nigel. The name stole into her foggy thoughts like a ray of early light. She had dreamt about him again.

In her dream, they had been walking along together over a country hill. He had pointed to the deep blue morning sky, which matched his coat. Then the sky reached down and scooped him up toward heaven, but he had tumbled down and dissolved upon hitting the ground, only to disappear into the earth.

Did he always wear blue? She'd never seen him without it yet. She had to admit the color suited him. He had looked so handsome yesterday in his bottle blue coat, a diamond pin winking from the folds of his immaculately tied cravat like the morning star in the sky outside her window.

He was very like a star, she mused. Mysterious and inaccessible.

She tore her gaze from the sky. Yesterday, Kathryn had been shaking with anger as that devil Blackshire had all but admitted to her that he was going to do whatever was neces-

sary to keep Lady Jane from meeting her young man, Bankham. Why? Why, if he found Jane so tiresome, so difficult
to keep in check, did he not contrive to get her married as
quickly as possible? Did he derive too much pleasure from
denying others happiness? Or did he gain something else
from his continued guardianship of the girl?

The answer came to her in a flash of understanding. Jane
was an heiress, or so the loquacious maid Nicolette had
informed her importantly. And since Blackshire was Jane's
guardian, he would have control of her inheritance until she
married. Of course! That was why he wouldn't even let Jane
meet Lord Bankham. He wouldn't let her marry until he
had to—and then, since he had complete control over her
finances, it would be easy for him to force her into marrying
a man of his choosing, a man with whom Blackshire would
no doubt make a deal, a very lucrative deal for them both.
But not for Jane.

She supposed she should not be so very upset about it.
Her parents notwithstanding, love matches were uncommon
among the *ton.* Marriage was more often than not a simple
transfer of wealth.

A few feet away, Jane snored softly in their bed. Kathryn
was glad to see the girl sleeping soundly, for she had turned
in early complaining of a megrim and had slept fitfully. Too
fitfully for Kathryn to escape to the library without fear of
waking her, unfortunately, and the topmost shelves of the
library remained regrettably unsearched. Kathryn was as
quiet as she could be while she dressed. Pulling on the
blue-sprigged muslin, she found herself wishing she had
something else to wear. He'd already seen her in this yesterday.

Nonsense! She did not care what he thought of her. He
was not interested in what she wore, anyway. He was more
interested in what was under her clothes, the beast. An image
of Lydia, clutching her torn bodice and careening down the
hall away from Blackshire, flashed into her mind. Savagely,
she pulled on the dress and fastened its openings. She didn't

give a fig about what she wore today, she told herself. The sprigged muslin would be just fine.

Last night Jane had advised Kathryn of the day's plan. Their drive in the park had somehow grown into a morning's outing. Kathryn's insides felt like they were knotted.

A whole morning in the company of Nigel Moorhaven.

A whole morning diverted away from her search for the diary. But there was no help for it. She had already agreed to accompany Jane and Blackshire to the park. Besides, Jane's predicament must be almost as bad as her own. If Blackshire had his way, Jane would marry some ogre of his choosing, or if she chose not to give in to Blackshire, she would end up unmarried. A spinster. An old maid. An ape-leader.

But not if Kathryn could help it.

Her anger with Blackshire had slipped silently away overnight to be replaced with a firm resolve to do whatever she could to help Jane in her quest to meet Quinn, Lord Bankham. Kathryn *had* to think of a way to save her from Blackshire's greed. Jane would be introduced to Bankham today if Kathryn had to throw herself in front of the man's carriage to get him to stop!

She trembled at the thought of Blackshire's reaction to such a ploy. He would explode with anger. He would be incensed. Especially after she had rebuffed his obvious advances yesterday in the library.

She shivered with dread.

At half past seven o' clock, Nicolette knocked softly on the door. She entered carrying a large, white box. She put it where Kathryn directed and left. Inside the box rested a delicate concoction of pale lavender muslin with an airy lace overskirt of the bluest violet. Satin ribbon rosettes trimmed the shoulders and the high waist. A wide-rimmed bonnet trimmed in *faux* violets, another pair of lace gloves— off-white this time—and slippers that looked too large along with an impossibly tiny reticule. Kathryn was delighted.

Kathryn changed into the gown and then went in search

of Thomas. The muslin and lace swirled lightly around her as she walked, and the long tails of the satin sash floated in the breeze. She recognized that it was in the first stare of fashion. It was the finest gown she had ever had, and it made her feel wonderful. Good, dear Aunt Ophelia! Oh, but Ophelia simply had to stop sending clothing. She would have to carry it all away when she left Baroness Marchman's, lest the lady attempt to return the clothes to Lord Arborough's! Two gowns were enough. Her valise was not large, and any more than this and she would have trouble carrying them. She would send a message with little Thomas the stable boy, imploring Auntie to send no more. But ten minutes later Kathryn's pleasure in the lovely dress was forgotten, for Thomas was gone.

He was no longer in Lady Marchman's employ, said the head groom, and none of the servants knew where the lad had gone. But a maid did say she'd seen the little boy walking off with his possessions this morning, just after Lord Blackshire had arrived.

Blackshire! That explained it all. Kathryn's blood began to boil. Yesterday, from the windows of the library, she'd watched that demon take his leave. She'd seen him march away, stiff with anger. She'd heard him take his wrath out on his tiger, the sharp syllables of his rebuke floating to her on the moist air. She'd watched Thomas trudge back to the stables with his pitiful rag ball in his hand. Blackshire must have blamed Thomas for his tiger's lapse in duty. The devil must have come back to the school early this morning specifically to have Thomas dismissed. Such cruelty was unspeakably evil!

Seething, Kathryn hovered just inside the front door, waiting for Blackshire to arrive. Poor little Thomas. He had no parents, no family. He was alone in the world. Where could he go now? And what would he do when he got there? What would he eat? Where would he sleep? Did he even have his blanket with him, or was that school property?

"Ohhh . . . !" Kathryn snatched a pillow from a chair

and hugged it, crying silently until, at a quarter of nine, eyes dry and hot, Kathryn heard the sounds of a heavy carriage pulling into the drive. She dismissed the maid who came to open the door and opened the door herself, leaving it ajar and standing behind it, waiting for him.

The expression on his face changed as he pushed open the door the rest of the way, at first registering pleasure at the sight of Kathryn and then puzzlement and shock as he realized Kathryn was angry.

But Kathryn wanted to be sure he knew exactly how angry she truly was.

"I hate you," she seethed. "You are vile and despicable," she added, not leaving anything to chance.

His eyes narrowed into lazy slits as he regarded her in a bored fashion. He fiddled with his shirt cuffs.

"What," he drawled, "have I done, now?"

"I'll tell you what you've done, you blackguard—as if you did not know! Ha! You've hurt a little boy. Do you think he is like a bit of rubbish you can just cast away? He has a name and feelings. And he did not just cease to exist. Even now he is somewhere out there"—she pointed to the street—"lonely and . . . and c-cold." She almost sobbed the last sentence. She swallowed hard. "You have made an enemy of me this day, my lord," she said, "and do not think that because I am of poor consequence that I cannot be a thorn in your side. Indeed, I will be a stake in your heart unless you find him forthwith. I will—"

"Are you speaking of Thomas?"

"You bothered to learn his name, then? You surprise me, you devil. You demon. You heartless, vile, wretched, cruel, cold, unfeeling—" Kathryn sputtered to a stop, for Blackshire's shoulders were shaking.

The man was laughing!

"How dare you?! How dare you laugh?" Kathryn had had enough. She drew back her arms and began to pummel Blackshire with her fists. Immediately, he caught her wrists, but she did not meekly end her assault. Instead, she hauled back her foot to kick the dastard in the shins. Blackshire, though, anticipating her attack, drew her tightly against him, pinning her arms between them and easily avoiding the blow her feet would have delivered. When she gathered her breath to protest, the warm, clean masculine scent of him robbed her of words. She stilled, suddenly acutely aware of his body wherever it pressed so intimately against hers. His flat, hard belly. His powerful thighs. His long fingers and wide palms, which molded themselves to the small of her back. And, though she fought against the memory, she remembered exactly how it had felt to be kissed by him. It had been intense, exciting, intoxicating. . . .

"Look at my carriage," he said, loosening his hold on her, but not letting completely go. "Go on, look."

"I don't care about your fine carriage." She sneered. "Do you think your wealth impresses me? Your blasted carriage could be fashioned of gold and I—" But she *did* glance at the carriage, and her tirade came to an abrupt halt, for there was Thomas, standing proudly erect at the head of Blackshire's horses.

"Thomas! Oh, Thomas . . ." Blackshire released her fully, and Kathryn ran to the boy and scooped him up joyfully, spooking the horses, who whinnied and shied. Instantly, Thomas spoke to them, clucking nonsense as Kathryn hastily put him down.

"Crikey, miss, the 'orses! Do be careful. I'd 'ate to lose me job before I'd worked me first day through."

For the first time, Kathryn noticed what Thomas was wearing. He was dressed in striped livery and wore new shoes.

"Come to think of it," the boy clarified, "I'd 'ate to lose me job before I'd worked the first 'undred years or so." He turned adoring eyes up at Lord Blackshire, who had approached at a sprint when the horses shied.

He firmly grasped Kathryn's shoulders and thrust her away from the pair, whose eyes were still flashing white.

"Good work, Thomas. You handled the team expertly. I knew you would be perfect as my tiger."

"Your tiger!" Kathryn gasped.

His warm hands lingered on her shoulders, his fingers splayed so that his thumbs rested on the sensitive skin at the base of Kathryn's neck. She shivered, and he lowered his hands.

"I—I was mistaken," she told him. She could not bring herself to utter an apology. The man was still a devil. She must not forget his treatment of Jane and poor Lydia. She turned to Thomas. "You look splendid, Thomas lad."

The boy shoved his shoulders back and his chin rose a notch before he leaned over to her and whispered, "His lordship 'ired me away from her ladyship this morning, before the cocks crowed. Paid for me, he did. Took me to his palace. I got a hefty raise, a new suit of clothes wif shoes, this 'ere uniform, an' a real bed to sleep in. I get to sleep in the 'ouse, miss!" He grinned. "An this morning I ate me breakfast round a *table* wif a bunch o' other lads. They're right uns, they are. All o' em. Includin' 'im!" He hooked his thumb at Blackshire and, leaning toward her, whispered reverently, never taking his gaze from the marquis, "The lads told me 'e goes to Parly-mint and orders the king to help poor folk!" His eyes wide, he flashed her a significant look and then peered back toward Blackshire. "His lordship's a hero, an' no mistake, miss! They all talks about 'im." He beamed at the marquis.

Kathryn blinked, incredulous. Her last ally had defected to the enemy. She followed the boy's gaze up to Blackshire's handsome face. The man wore a smug expression. Kathryn narrowed her eyes at him, but to her disgust the disfavor she was trying so hard to make obvious only succeeded in releasing from him a smirking grin. At that moment another carriage barreled down the street and drew to a halt before them. Its driver hailed Nigel loudly and jumped down. His dark brown hair glinted with a reddish cast in the morning sunlight. He walked with a slight limp but otherwise carried

his large frame gracefully. He insulted Blackshire good-
naturedly and bowed low over Kathryn's hand, flashing
dimples.

She liked him immediately.

Blackshire made a smooth introduction as though nothing
unpleasant had just occurred between Kathryn and himself.
Mr. Jeremy Scott, he said, had served in the army with
Blackshire and had been invited to accompany them on their
outing.

The pleasantries out of the way, Kathryn ruffled Thomas's
silky blond hair. "I am so happy for you, Thomas."

To Blackshire she said, "A word with you, my lord."
He followed her back to the front door. Without looking at
him, she said quietly, "I was wrong, my lord. I made a
hasty assumption and I regret my subsequent accusation and
display of enmity. Yet I promise you that if you ill-treat that
boy in any way, I shall make you regret it." With that,
she drew herself up to her full height, which was woefully
inadequate for the purposes of intimidation, and stalked off
to find Jane. The sooner their excursion was begun, the
sooner it would be done with.

Nigel watched her withdraw into the house, her back
indignantly upright and proud and her chin tilted high in
the air. She was dressed in yet another of Madame Vensois's
creations, a violet and cream muslin concoction that seemed
more suited to a temptress than to a schoolgirl. At least on
her. The light, sheer fabric clung to her swaying hips as she
walked. At his elbow, Jeremy said, "Couldn't hear what
she said from over there, but I didn't have to." He nodded
his head in Kitty's direction, his eyes taking measure of her
stiff, indignant carriage. "Bad-tempered little baggage, is
she not?"

"Yes." Nigel did not look away from her, but followed
her dignified progress back up to the front door of the school
with his eyes.

"Quick as a ferret."

"Yes."

"And twice as mean."

"Yes."

"You like her, don't you?"

Nigel stood mute.

"I thought so." Jeremy smirked. "So that is why you wanted me to investigate her. Here I thought I was helping to probe the Marchman case. Had me up all night. Lost a bloody fortune at White's before sundown, and all you wanted to know was the pedigree of a skirt? Couldn't you just ask her? Who is she? A teacher here?" He gestured toward the school. "A young lady of good family come down in the world?"

"You tell me. You are the one who carried out the investigation."

"Would if I could, old man, but I didn't find out a deuced thing about her. No one has ever seen or heard of your Miss Davidson."

"She did not simply materialize from nowhere, like a ghost."

"No." Jeremy nodded after Kitty. "More like an angel."

"Someone has to know where she came from." Nigel tugged at his sleeves irritably. "And she is not 'my' anything."

"That so?" Jeremy said, rubbing his chin and watching Kitty climb the steps to the front door of the school. "Good."

Nigel felt a sudden urge to plant Jeremy a facer but got hold of himself before the impulse did. "I suppose you were too busy attempting to recoup your losses last night to carry out the investigation as I asked you."

Jeremy's face clouded over at Nigel's sharp tone, then quickly took on a seriousness that was well known to Nigel. "I tried my best. I swear it. Haven't slept at all. You said your need of the information was urgent, and I believed you. There just wasn't any information to be found, Nigel."

Nigel frowned. "No information. Probably means she is one of any number of young ladies of gentle breeding who have been so thoroughly buried in the country all of their lives that no one in Town has heard of them.''

''You *are* smitten with her, aren't you?''

''Nonsense.''

''What else could cause you to overlook the possibility that she may be assisting Lady Marchman with her treachery?''

Nigel was stunned by his friend's question, for there was no denying the fact that Jeremy was right. Nigel had not even considered Kitty as a suspect, not even after he had learned yesterday that she had been lying about her age. His fingers tightened into a fist. ''Kitty Davidson is not a suspect,'' he said firmly.

Jeremy hooted with laughter. ''Well then, if she's not a suspect, then you *are* chasing her, eh? But is she not a little too young for you, Nigel? She can't be a day over fifteen.''

Nigel moved to his near horse and checked a strap he knew hadn't a thing wrong with it. ''Yes. She is too young, as a matter of fact. But maybe not for you. She's eighteen. Though she's pretending to be a good deal younger than that, and if you tell anyone I told you so you'll be in for the thrashing of your life.''

''Is that the reason you wanted me to investigate her? Because you found out she was older than she let on?''

''Yes,'' Nigel lied. ''I know her real reason now, though, and it has nothing to do with Lady Marchman.'' Nigel actually knew nothing of the sort, though he'd guessed accurately enough, he thought; it wasn't hard to deduce her story. Oh, he might be missing one or two details of her story, details he'd hoped Jeremy might uncover with his investigation, but one thing was absolutely certain: Miss Kitty Davidson was not a spy for Napoleon Bonaparte.

''I shall carry out a more thorough investigation when my task here at the school is finished,'' he told Jeremy.

''I say''—Jeremy cut the air with the flat of his hand— ''you don't seem to understand, old man. I did a thorough investigation. There is no information to be had on the young lady. Not anywhere in London, anyway.''

Nigel was unperturbed. The lack of information meant only that Kitty's parents must be more obscure, more lacking in status than he had guessed. The door of the school closed behind Kitty, and Nigel affected a bored stance.

"The ladies should be out in a few moments," he told his friend. "We'll be on our way to the park then."

"The park? Ladies?" He backed away. "Oh, no. Jane and a schoolmistress chaperon." He shook his head. "Not on your life, old man. I came here to make my report to you, not to squire some pinched, dried-up schoolmistress about town."

Nigel pulled the strap tight and tucked it in. Then he looked at Jeremy seriously. "I've turned up something at the school that convinces me I need another pair of eyes here—yours. But you'll be no help unless you have a good excuse to spend time here at the school. So . . . not only are you going to squire a lady about town, my friend, but starting right now, you are unofficially and diligently—yet falsely—courting her."

"Now, Nigel . . ." Jeremy began with a ferocious scowl.

Nigel laughed at his friend and enjoyed watching him sputter and fume until Jane and Miss Davidson emerged from the school. "I say!" Jeremy exclaimed. "Do you mean to cast me as Lady Jane's suitor or as Miss Davidson's?"

Originally, Nigel meant it to be Jane, but after what had happened yesterday afternoon in the library . . .

"Miss Davidson," he said, not quite clear of his own motives.

Jeremy turned a speculative glance in the lady's direction. "Falsely, eh?" he told Nigel sotto voce before advancing and bowing too long over Miss Davidson's hand.

It was Nigel's turn to scowl.

Spring had finally decided to wrest winter's hold on London, and the air had warmed to a comfortable level by the time they drove through the gates of Hyde Park.

The four breakfasted in the shade of a spreading plane

tree. Blackshire produced a basket of delectables and
Thomas spread a large buff-colored quilt over the ground.
The food was delicious and the company merry, had Kathryn
been in any mood to enjoy them, which she was not. Neither
did she enjoy the walk they had after breakfast, the kite
flying, the carriage racing, nor the icy lemonade Mr. Scott
had bought for her from a vendor. She couldn't even enjoy
the flattering attention Blackshire's friend was paying her.
She was too busy being watchful for the arrival of Quinn,
Lord Bankham.

And when that gentleman finally made an appearance and
Kathryn had practically got herself run over in contriving
to make him stop his carriage long enough for Jane to have
the desired formal introduction, Blackshire's attitude was
maddeningly unperturbed. For he seemed more concerned
that Kathryn be unharmed than that Jane and Bankham had
finally had their bow and curtsy.

But all through the morning's diversions, not once did
Blackshire say or do anything objectionable. There wasn't
even one sour glance. Blackshire was a perfect gentleman.

The easy nature of Jeremy Scott, the laughing, teasing
eyes of Jane, and the sight of Thomas and Mr. Scott's tiger
frolicking as little boys should relaxed her to the point where
she began to enjoy herself. It appeared that whatever deviltry
Blackshire was bent upon, he was not determined to embark
upon it today. The weather was fine, the company gay, and
dear little Thomas was so very happy.

The lad's praise for his new employer echoed in her
mind, and she wrinkled her brow. She could understand
Blackshire's being able to pull the wool over Lydia and
Jane's eyes, and even over Auntie's, but if Thomas were to
be believed, Blackshire had all of London's poor deceived
as well. She wandered over to the boys, who were splashing
barefooted in the Serpentine, intending to quiz Thomas for
more details of what he'd heard about Blackshire, but Jane
and Jeremy followed right along behind her. Talking to

Thomas about the marquis was impossible without making it obvious she was fishing for information.

Nigel stayed in the shade and watched the five of them. What was Kitty doing? Suddenly, he chuckled, for she had shed her slippers and joined the boys in a hunt for tadpoles. He'd been very wrong about her. She was not the sort of miss who would shrink back and faint at the sight of a frog. At intervals, Kitty and the boys splashed Jane and Jeremy, who sat together on the bank, setting leaf boats to sail. The group's shouts and pleasant laughter carried on the wind, and Nigel drew a deep breath as a memory came to him.

He was holding on to his mother's skirts as she showed him how to find tadpoles, their shoes on the bank of a pond on his family's ancestral estate, Havensham. It was one of the last days they spent together. How lucky he had been to have her at all!

As he watched Kitty Davidson cavorting in the water with the boys, completely unconcerned by the curious and sometimes disapproving stares of those who passed, he wondered if she longed for children of her own. He watched her bend over and peer into Thomas's cupped hands, an O appearing on her lips. She would be a wonderful mother, as his had been.

It was nearly eleven o'clock. Lady Marchman's field trip to St. Paul's Cathedral was today, and Nigel had been careful to ascertain that there were no visitors, French or otherwise, scheduled to call at the school that day. According to what he'd told Lady Marchman, his outing with Jane and Kitty was supposed to be an all-day affair, but he actually planned to return to the school when the students and their chaperones left early in the afternoon. He would search the house for the war plans.

He'd decided that the spies must be using the house as a drop point to pass the plans. One spy would leave them there, and the next would pick them up again. He'd bet that Madame Briand was involved up to her eyebrows, and the library was the most likely place to find the plans if they were there waiting to be passed.

Jeremy would keep Jane and Kitty occupied in the garden as Nigel was carrying out his search.

Nigel frowned. Though Jeremy had grumbled when Nigel had first asked him to pretend to be courting for Lady Marchman's benefit, now his friend was all too willing. Nigel plucked a leaf thoughtfully from the ground and folded it. Kitty Davidson had formed an instant dislike for *him,* but not for Jeremy Scott. And why? Because she'd misinterpreted a perfectly innocent remark Nigel had made as some sort of improper advance? She would have to be stupid to miss Jeremy's almost-too-enthusiastic interest in her now. He was practically sniffing her and thumping his tail. It was therefore plain to see that it wasn't a man's overt interest that bothered her.

It was *Nigel's* overt interest in her that she couldn't stand, which was fine with him. He was *not* considering her romantically. Besides the fact that she appeared to wish him dead— or at least horribly maimed and doomed to searing pain for life—Nigel did not want to be the subject of the latest breakfast *on-dits* for buzzing around a nymph of eighteen. Oh, she was old enough to marry, all right. But she was the right age for a young buck of twenty-one, not a seasoned, world-weary thirty-year-old.

Nigel's father had been a childless widower when he'd married a second time, taking to wife Nigel's own mother, an eighteen-year-old beauty. The two were separated in age by twenty years. And look what had happened to them. They'd had different friends, different interests, a different perspective on almost everything. And their differences must have proved too much to maintain any sort of closeness. His father had taken a mistress close to his age. And his mother . . . how had his mother felt? By all reports she'd been intense, high-spirited, intelligent. When her husband strayed, was her heart broken? Wouldn't any young wife's heart be broken by such a betrayal?

Kitty Davidson's heart certainly would be.

Well . . . Nigel told himself that if Jeremy and Kitty got on well together, he would bloody well be glad of it. Hell, after Kitty's performance with Bankham today—pretending to fall in front of the man's carriage just so she could maneuver Bankham into an introduction to Jane—he would bloody well gift Jeremy with the blunt for a special license. Kitty would be delighted. She would have her entrée into the drawing rooms of the *ton,* and Jeremy would have a wife better than he deserved. The two of them were perfect for each other. Any fool could see that.

"Oh, my pretty Kitty." Jeremy's voice carried faintly to Nigel.

Irritation stabbed him. Why the devil was that rat using her first name? It was bloody well improper. But Nigel resisted the impulse to tell Jeremy so. It was none of his concern what liberties Miss Davidson allowed. She couldn't hope to do any better than Jeremy Scott, and if Nigel's friend were foolish enough to encourage so prickly, so capricious, so mercurial, so . . . so *frustrating* a chit, then that was his business.

Nigel closed his eyes and concentrated on emptying his aching head of everything but the ground beneath him and the wind in the trees overhead. The shadows shortened, and finally Nigel drowsed.

Then, something tickled his ear.

Nigel swatted at it, but it came back. It felt like a fluff of fur. Nigel instantly came awake, but he did not open his eyes. It was Jane, no doubt. Up to her usual tricks.

Just when he thought she had given up, he felt a wet, squirming something on the back of his hand. "Mmm . . . m'darlin'," he slurred, feigning sleep. "A lady kissing a man's hand?" The wet sensation moved to brush his neck. "M'dear . . . how daring! Mmm . . ."

"Won't you introduce us to your new lady friend, Nigel?" Jane's voice assailed him from far to his right. Nigel's eyes snapped open just as a weight came down on his chest, and

Nigel found himself staring into the moist brown eyes of a delighted mongrel puppy who dove for his face and planted an enthusiastic lick on him with her wet pink tongue.

Jane and the others exploded into gales of laughter as Nigel tried to rid himself of his unwanted company.

Suddenly, a little girl of nine or ten ran to his side and scooped up the puppy. She brushed frantically at Nigel's ruined, mud-printed cravat and waistcoat, spreading the mud and ruining his coat in the process.

"Oh, sir! I am so sorry. I tried to catch 'im, I did, but there were all o' them others an' I couldn't catch 'em all." She ran off after the other pups. "I'm that sorry, I am!" she shouted over her shoulder as she chased off, holding the sagging puppy under one arm.

"Be good lads and go help the little girl catch her puppies, won't you?" Nigel asked the tigers. Thomas and James ran after the girl, nearly colliding in their enthusiasm to be the first one to her side.

Nigel rubbed his hands together. "Well, now. Since I have dismissed the boys, I shall have to serve luncheon myself." And he did. As Nigel set out the meal, they all watched the children cavorting with the puppies, who were taking a suspiciously long time to be caught. Just when the last puppy made it into the box and the boys were walking dejectedly back, having finished their rollicking task, the little girl saw to it that her wayward puppies managed to "escape" once more, to the boys' delight.

Jeremy laughed and bounded off to help round up the rollicking pups once more and see that they stayed that way, while Nigel and Kitty shared a smile at the girl's obvious subterfuge. Their eyes locked and held for the briefest of moments, but it was enough. For in that single moment, Nigel felt a connection. There she was, just on the other side of the tentative bridge between them.

She flushed, and she looked a little scared for a moment, as though staring across a chasm she needed desperately to cross. Then she blinked and looked away. Nigel wanted to ask her if she had seen the bridge. Had she felt what he had? But of course he could not.

Even if he were inclined to wed a woman so young, he would not. It would not be fair to saddle her with a man of his years. They could have nothing in common. She had just come from the nursery, whereas he had just come from the battlefield. She was inexperienced, and he was . . . not. Besides, they were so different in temperament. Nigel was not code-named the Blue Devil in recognition of his cheerful nature. No. He was frequently bad-tempered, especially as his birthday approached each year. He was not a fit companion for a young lady like Kitty. But Jeremy? Jeremy was much closer to her age. He was irrepressibly cheerful and optimistic. And they obviously got on famously together. He would not stand in their way.

He stood at the carriage, pulling crocks and wrapped parcels out of the largest basket at random. He was making a muck of it. He didn't know what any of it was. Mrs. Farmworthy, his housekeeper, had seen to the baskets' packing.

"May I help?" a timid voice asked at his side. Kitty, timid? Nigel looked down at her and her eyes were full of apology.

"The boys are having a splendid time. Thomas seems so happy."

He nodded.

She looked down at her hands. "I . . . earlier . . . I did not mean to seem ungrateful. That is to say . . . about Thomas's employment with you, I—"

"I know. It is nothing." And indeed it was nothing.

She fidgeted with the buckle on one of the baskets.

"The boys are enjoying themselves," he said. Perhaps we should follow their lead. Don't you think?"

Kitty smiled impishly up at him. "Of course I *think.*" She was being deliberately obtuse. Then she added a little shyly, "I just do not *see* all of the time." She looked up at him through her lashes.

Nigel's heart swelled with admiration. "And I, it would seem, do not listen all of the time," he said. At her surprised expression, he laughed softly, and she joined in.

The boys came back and were encouraged to join them on the quilt.

Together, Nigel and Kathryn served the meal, improvising a comedy by pretending to be a deaf butler and a blind housekeeper. Nigel genuinely enjoyed himself, much to his surprise, and he thought Kitty enjoyed herself as well.

Much to her surprise, judging by her expression.

As they ate, the girl-child with her box of puppies sat in the sun near the drive, obviously hoping to sell the whelps. After a few moments, Nigel put his sandwich down.

He could smell the girl before he reached her. He hadn't been able to smell her over the stench of the puppies, before, but he certainly could now. She had probably never had a real bath, he thought. Nigel scanned her hands and face, which were almost—but not quite—as dirty as the rest of her. Until recent years, most people had thought regular bathing was unhealthy. Still, the hands and the face were certain to receive regular attention, if the girl had attentive parents. He was glad her hands were indeed a little cleaner than the rest of her, for he did not relish the prospect of yet another of his housekeeper's lectures on bringing home strays.

As Nigel approached, she looked up at him fearfully. Nigel thought she might run. He held out his hand. "Do not be frightened. I am not angry with you. See?" He brushed at his ruined sky blue waistcoat. "It is nothing. A few specks of dirt." The girl smiled tentatively, and Nigel peered into the box. "What are you going to do with those puppies?"

"Sell 'em, if'n I can, sir."

"No . . . ! Well . . . it is a good thing I was the first to arrive, for I have need of such fine dogs as these. Of course, the price will have to be right," he said.

The girl looked shrewdly up at Nigel. "I dunno, sir. I'm expectin' my other customers to meet me 'ere soon. Mebbe they'll want to pay more. What might you be thinkin' on payin'?'' she asked.

Mentally, Nigel calculated how much blunt he had left in his pocket after the morning's activities and named a sum. After ten minutes of intense negotiation, Nigel led the girl back to the blanket, where he traded every farthing he had with him—and his own lunch—for the splintery box of yapping puppies. After the girl's hands and face were washed—Nigel insisted—in the Serpentine, she was served her meal with all the formality the group could display, given the circumstances. Well fed and half clean, the girl promptly fell asleep. Nigel wrapped her up in the picnic blanket and ushered the party away so as not to wake her.

The six climbed aboard Nigel's carriage and rolled away as quietly as possible.

Jeremy couldn't contain his laughter any longer. ''Are you mad? What are you going to do with these mongrels?''

''I'll send them to one of my estates.''

''They'll ruin your hunting dogs. Spoil their bloodlines. And you don't even like dogs.''

''Then I'll send them to Northumberland.'' Nigel almost never visited his remote estate in the North. ''I shall send them today, without delay.''

''Oh, Nigel,'' Jane cried, ''do let me keep one of them, won't you? They are so . . .''

''Smelly?'' Nigel supplied.

''. . . so . . .''

''Flea-bitten?''

''Adorable was the word *I* had in mind,'' Kathryn said, lifting one from the box.

''Adorable and lovable,'' Jane agreed, liberating another pup.

''If it pleases you to have a pet, my pet, then of course you may have one,'' Nigel told her. *''One,''* he stressed, but by the time they had reached Baroness Marchman's School, Nigel had agreed to two, as he knew he would from the beginning. The puppy in question promptly thanked him by soiling the white leather seat of his carriage.

"Oh, Nigel, would it not be cruel to break apart a family of siblings? Only think how charming it would be to have all five running around your town house and licking your—"

"No more," Nigel told her, trying hard to keep his sense of humor but failing miserably, "or to Northumberland they go. All of them."

"Beast. Brute. Cad," Jane said happily.

Kathryn, meanwhile, looked on incredulously.

She'd been certain that when he'd rescued the kittens, he'd done it to impress Titania, who in spite of her disappearance might still have been peeking out from behind a tree. Or that he'd taken them for the more mundane purpose of mousing. But that wasn't the case this time. For all he knew, Titania was not present. And he certainly wasn't trying to impress Kitty Davidson; a man bent upon making an impression did not snooze the afternoon away beneath a tree.

A mixture of suspicion and gladness warred inside her, for she knew something was terribly wrong. How could it be possible for Nigel to be both demon and angel? For an angel is what he had shown himself to be this day. If she had been touched by his tender treatment of Thomas, she had been blown over by his kind and sensitive "bargain" with the poor little girl selling the puppies. As she watched, one of the puppies chewed happily on the blue silk tassels hanging from his mirrorlike Hessians, while another threw up into his hat. Kathryn held her breath. He eyed the pups distastefully but said nothing. The miserable, darling creatures were going to cause no end of havoc, and he had to know that.

Beside her, his empty stomach rumbled.

And, in that moment, Kathryn realized she loved him.

She closed her eyes. Dear Lord! How had she allowed

that to happen? Could it be she had been wrong about him? Had there been some terrible mix-up at Palin House that night? How Kathryn wished it might be so! But she knew what she had seen and heard upstairs on the night of the masquerade ball.

Confusion bound together her suspicion and her hope and shook them cruelly. The two sides of Nigel could not be reconciled. She didn't know whether to hate him—or to give him her heart. She loved the side of him she had seen today. He was merry and generous, intelligent and courteous. He seemed to be all that was good in men. His handsome face was quick to smile—and quick to apologize, for he had done so, with and without words, so many times that day.

She had even begun to feel apologetic for her mean treatment of him. She'd shown him her back a number of times that day. She had told herself he deserved nothing more from her. She had reminded herself why she had accompanied them to the park in the first place: to foil the demon's desire to keep his ward in isolation—and in financial thrall. But he hadn't said as much as one syllable against her outrageous performance with Lord Bankham. And he was nothing but patient, tolerant, and loving toward Jane. Was it all an elaborate game? A carefully constructed illusion? Was he trying to put them all off their guard? Or had she been terribly, terribly wrong about him from the start?

Her mind journeyed back to the beginning, to the first time she heard his richly toned voice.

Images of Lydia's anguished face, her dress torn and her hair askew flashed into Kathryn's mind. Lydia's distress had been no illusion.

She had to get hold of herself. She had to be alone. She had to think, to sort all of it out. Perhaps he still was a demon. Perhaps he'd managed to hide his true nature from everyone in London. But if that were so, Kathryn vowed, he would not deceive *her*.

A carriage approached them on the narrow street and Kathryn looked up, eager to replace in her mind the image of Nigel with the image of a stranger.

But when she looked up, it was not into the eyes of a stranger she peered, but into the eyes of her incredulous parents.

Chapter Fifteen

Kathryn froze. Her father was smiling warmly at her and her mother was positively beaming. Violet St. David raised her hand and waved enthusiastically to her daughter. Kathryn tilted her head forward so she could appear to have looked away yet still see through the open weave of her chip bonnet. As the carriages passed, Blackshire nodded politely to her parents, whose faces registered their confusion.

She watched her mother's waving hand still and wilt. "Kathryn?" she heard her father ask uncertainly as they rolled out of view in one of Auntie's fine open barouches. She could not turn to see what they would do next. She only hoped they would not come after her.

"Do you know those people?" Blackshire asked, slowing his cattle. "I can turn and catch them, if you wish."

Kathryn swallowed and tried to appear calm. "No, my lord. I do not know them. Perhaps I resemble some acquaintance of the lady's. Pray, drive on." Blackshire's carriage was soon rolling briskly along again, and the seconds ticked by as Kathryn waited for the sound of her parents' pursuit.

What were they doing in London? Did Aunt Ophelia know

they were here? What had Ophelia told them, and how was Kathryn to find out, now that Thomas was no longer able to carry messages for her? Oh dear! What a pickle! They would never approve of their daughter's shocking masquerade at the school, but that was the least of her worries. If they were to catch up to Blackshire's carriage at this moment, all would be lost. Ophelia would be ruined, and Kathryn might just be thrown into gaol. She sank back against the plush seat, willing away the swoon she could feel coming on. She was trembling. She could feel her whole body shudder with the violence of her beating heart.

When, after what seemed an eternity, Nigel's carriage rounded the corner into Silver Street, Kathryn finally relaxed. They were not being followed. Jane looked up from the puppy she was stroking and alarm claimed her features. "Kitty, whatever is the matter? You are as white as the chalk at Dover."

Across from Jane, Mr. Scott frowned. "I say, Lady Jane is quite right. You do not look at all the thing, Miss Davidson."

The marquis turned a concerned look in her direction and examined her intently. "Do you feel a swoon coming on?"

Kathryn waved her hand, dismissing their concern. "I am fine. Really. Just a little warm, is all. That is the trouble with swooning. Once it is done, everyone expects another at the least provocation. I assure you I am fine." She fanned herself with the edge of her pelisse, whereupon Jeremy had the embarrassing story of Kathryn's swoon from Jane. She was quite glad when the carriage rolled over the school's gravel drive once more. The gentlemen alighted first. Jeremy turned to hand Jane down, then Kathryn.

Kathryn's feet gained the ground, but Mr. Scott did not let go of her hand as was strictly proper. Instead, he held it a moment before tucking it firmly under his arm and setting off toward the garden. Kathryn had no choice but to follow. Back in Heathford, his behavior would be considered quite bold, but perhaps it was to be expected here in London. Not wishing to seem churlish, Kathryn trailed along helplessly, though she would much rather have been walking on Nigel's arm.

Mr. Scott led her to the small ornamental garden next to the orchard. A pair of stone benches flanked the walk, and he led her to one of them. Motioning for her to sit, he claimed the space at her side. When Blackshire and Jane followed a moment later, they had no choice but to sit on the other bench, and Kathryn was thus paired with Jeremy Scott for the rest of the afternoon, she supposed.

There were worse fates. Mr. Scott was possessed of a quick wit and a pleasing appearance. To say he was attentive to her would have been unjust, for he was not merely attentive, he was everything a willing companion could be. A pleasant hour passed in interesting conversation. Mr. Scott had travelled widely, and there seemed to be no end to his fascinating stories, which ranged from the mildly amusing to the wildly outrageous. At Kathryn's slight clearing of her throat, he retrieved a cooling drink from inside. When she commented that the roses were beautiful, he plucked one for her and tucked it behind her ear. Oh, he was very attentive. Indeed, Kathryn began to wonder if the handsome gentleman were not a little more attentive than mere politeness required. She also wondered why she was not thrilled to be the object of the dashing Jeremy's attention.

As he left to procure yet another glass of lemonade, she decided she was only being sensible. She could not, after all, enter Society. Blackshire would expose her. Or would he? Kathryn stole a glance at him.

Where was he?

A moment or two ago, he and Jane had been off in the kitchen garden, examining the herbs and the sundial. But now only Jane stood there, intent upon a pair of golden spotted fish Lady Marchman kept in a stone pond to one side of the herb garden.

Kathryn shivered, half expecting to feel his fingers brush the back of her neck. She looked behind her, but he was not there. He was nowhere in sight.

Kathryn wandered over to Jane. "Has Blackshire gone inside for lemonade?"

Jane bent over and held out her finger, trying to get a butterfly to land on it. "No. He said he was going to Berkeley Square for a short while to make some final arrangements for my ball."

"What ball?"

"*What ball?*" Jane's eye's widened. "Oh! What a bobbery-brained thing I am. Did I not tell you? Of course I did not," she answered herself. "How very thoughtless of me! Tomorrow night Nigel is holding an entertainment for young people, in my honor. It is almost a ball, but without the adults—except for the chaperons, of course, and you may be assured there will be quite too many of those!" She wrinkled her nose and rolled her eyes. "Oh, you must come. There will be music and dancing and silly games and tests of skill with favors for the winners. You simply must come. I shall introduce you as my new bosom friend. What say you?"

"I—I have nothing to wear."

"Oh, I have a dozen gowns that would look lovely on you, though they will have to be let out a bit. But I doubt you shall have need of them. La," she said, her voice chiming, "I daresay Nigel will produce yet another—" Her words came to an abrupt halt and she clapped her hand over her mouth. Above her fingers, her eyes were wide.

Kathryn put her hand on her young friend's arm. "Do you mean to say that Nigel—er . . . Lord Blackshire is the one—is the—the one who sent me this?" She brushed her hand over her walking dress.

With a pained expression, Jane answered, "No. I did not mean to say it at all. But I did, did I not?"

Kathryn nodded. "Yes."

Jane shrugged. "Do not be angry with him. You must know it was obvious you needed the gowns. And he meant to give them anonymously. I myself found out only because I . . . well . . . I was eavesdropping on Lady Marchman yesterday. Listen, Kitty, it cannot have been improper to accept them, if you did not know from whence they came, can it?''

"Mmm.'' Kathryn was finding it very difficult to focus. The robin, the girl in the park, the kittens and puppies, Thomas, and now this? Dared she hope she'd misjudged him? That she'd made a terrible mistake that night at Auntie's masquerade?

"What say you?'' Jane broke in on her thoughts.

"Hmm?''

"Please say you will attend my little entertainment.''

Kathryn would have loved to accept! But that would be madness. Wouldn't it? She had to find the diary and end her charade before it resulted in exposure and disgrace.

Oh, but the party was only one night.

An image of Blackshire pierced her thoughts, and Kathryn could feel herself blush. Surely, he would be there, at the entertainment. It was being held at his town house, after all. He would see her in one of Jane's fine gowns with her hair dressed elegantly. Perhaps they would dance. Perhaps, as they turned figures on the floor, Nigel would look into her eyes and decide that he loved her, too. Perhaps she had been wrong about him all along, and perhaps there was a reasonable explanation of what had appeared to happen upstairs at Aunt Ophelia's masquerade ball between the Marquis of Blackshire and Lydia. She heaved a sigh, hugged herself, and smiled. Perhaps he would ask her to marry him and they would hasten away to Gretna Green or marry by special license in the morning.

And perhaps pigs would sprout daisies from their arses and whistle "Greensleeves.''

She sighed. Most likely she would never have a Season at all. There would be no come-out for her. There would be no balls, no opera, no Season at all. Either the diary would be found or Blackshire would prove to be a duplicitous blackguard. Either way, her reputation would be ruined— either by Auntie's scandal or her own. Jane's ball was but a pitifully meager crumb of the Season she could never have.

She tried to summon some of her usual optimism. She would still have a choice of marriage to John or Robert back in Heathford. Or she could embrace spinsterhood.

She sighed again, and her chin quivered. Impulsively and perhaps recklessly, she decided to attend Jane's entertainment for young people. Auntie would want her to go, Kathryn was sure. She put aside her intention to decline Jane's invitation. It was only one night, a few hours at most. What could it hurt?

After a time, Jane wandered into the shade of the orchard, while Kathryn lagged behind, trying unsuccessfully to banish regret from her heart, regret that she had not accepted Nigel's offer to dance at Auntie's masquerade. She doubted John Bothwell knew or approved of the waltz, and there would not be any waltzing at tomorrow night's party, of course. As she wandered listlessly back toward the garden bench, a movement caught her eye. A shallow stone basin sat on a pedestal in the middle of the lawn next to the house. A smile came to her lips, for a pair of starlings were dipping and splashing in the basin, tossing water everywhere. Wishing to observe them more closely, Kathryn crept closer, little by little, hiding behind tree trunks and bushes.

Soon she found herself next to the house outside the library, crouched beneath the neatly trimmed rhododendron bushes once more. The birds continued to splash and play, and Kathryn watched for several moments until another movement caught her eye. A movement inside the library.

Blackshire!

The marquis was inside the school. He was supposed to be at his town house in Berkeley Square. What was he doing in the library? As she watched, her mild puzzlement turned into amazed confusion, for Blackshire was clearly searching for something. His keen eyes cast to and fro, missing nothing, and Kathryn shrank back. She was suddenly afraid, and she did not know why. Backing away from the window, she became aware that Mr. Scott and Jane were calling to her. She hurried back to them.

How silly, she told herself. What was there to be afraid of? Surely there was a simple explanation. He must be searching for his gloves or a lost cravat pin.

Cook was there in the garden, setting out tea for the foursome. She was grumbling, half in French and half in English. Kathryn understood most of what the poor, over-worked lady said and offered to assist her. Nodding her thanks, Cook motioned to the ground cover. While Kathryn helped her spread it upon the ground beneath a tree, Cook muttered, "First Madame Briand, then a messenger weeth a tremendous box I must carry up the stairs, and now thees! Do I not have enough to do to feed the hungry faces who leeve here? But no! I must now entertain guests. You would think thees was a roadside tavern. Cook do thees. Cook do that. *C'est la* disgrace. I am a famous cook, not a serving wench!

"Poor Madame Cook," Kathryn said quietly. "I am sorry to cause you such trouble."

The woman grunted, but the sound was not without a little gratitude. "I am a famous cook," she repeated, "not a delivery boy!"

"Someone asked you to make a delivery?"

"Her Higneess, Madame Briand. Heh! She was een a hurry. She was too eem-portant to stay for five minutes. She *demanded* I take Ladee Marchman a package, that I cease everything I was doing and—snap, snap—run off to Lady Marchman right away."

"Goodness," she said carefully, "it must have been an important package."

"Eet was not! Eet was just a book. *The Corsair*. Eet ees a silly title, if you ask me. What could be so eem-portant about a book with such a silly title, eh?"

What indeed? Kathryn thought.

"I put eet on the mantel over the kitchen fire, and there eet will stay—until I finish preparing dinner. Ha!"

Kathryn stood quivering. Another book! What was so important about this one? Was it a part of the strange happenings at the school? Another piece of the strange puzzle she'd discovered coming to shape around her?

Blackshire came striding around the corner.

Jane waved to him. "Nigel, you are just in time. Tea is ready. Is everything put right for tomorrow night? You did not encounter any new problems in Berkeley Square, did you?"

"Everything will be perfect, my pet."

Kathryn averted her eyes as Jane chattered happily on about their plans for the entertainment. Why had Blackshire allowed her to believe he had gone to Berkeley Square?

Did Jane believe that? Kathryn bit her lip. Jane *had* agreed to observe the goings-on at the school and report back to Nigel. . . .

She sipped her tea and nibbled on her biscuit and thought furiously. Something was going on here, and somehow Jane and Blackshire were involved, but how?

"I believe," she said, nodding at Jane, "that I shall accept your invitation to attend your ball tomorrow evening." Perhaps then she might discover some answers.

After a time, Kathryn was summoned to Lady Marchman's private salon, where the baroness handed Kathryn a sealed envelope. Her mouth was grim.

Kathryn looked at the envelope and felt her face grow white. For the missive was from Auntie—though the faked seal and direction was designed to make Lady Marchman think the missive was from Lord Arborough.

"Uh . . . m-may I be excused?" Kathryn asked.

"You'd best open it here, my dear," Lady Marchman said kindly. "We don't want you fainting alone, now do we?"

Kathryn sat.

The letter read,

My Dear Kitty,

I have need to speak with you on a matter of some importance late this evening. I will send a carriage for you.

—A

She showed the letter to Lady Marchman, who said only, "You must go where the carriage takes you."

Kathryn nodded and went silently to her chamber, but her thoughts were not silent at all. God's teeth! What was Auntie up to now? For Kathryn, the afternoon passed with nearly painful slowness.

For Nigel, the afternoon flashed by with painful swiftness. He had not found what he was looking for inside the school. Of course, it didn't help that he didn't know what he was looking for. Neither did it help that Miss Davidson had been peeping in through the library window, the tiresome vixen. She was worse than Jane! Though he did not think she had seen him, he had been forced to abandon his search. Confound Jeremy! He was supposed to have been keeping the girls busy.

When Lady Marchman came home, Nigel endured a stern lecture in her library on the almost-but-not-quite impropriety of Jeremy and Nigel having been almost-but-not-quite alone with Kitty and Jane. It was acceptable in a very public place such as the park, she told him, with their tigers in attendance, but being alone at the school was not the thing, and she hinted that Mr. Scott and the marquis might both be barred from the school altogether.

Her attitude turned about when Nigel hinted that Jeremy was courting Miss Davidson in earnest.

Nigel found himself wishing it were an outright lie.

Lady Marchman was all smiles then, agreeing easily to allowing Kitty to attend Jane's entertainment on the morrow—with the provision that she send Mary Gant as chaperon, of course.

As he left Lady Marchman's, he passed a closed coach a few doors down. Giving the barest nod as he passed, Nigel acknowledged the lone occupant, for he knew Jeremy was inside, watching. Good. The younger man would keep watch on the comings and goings while Nigel left to see to the details of Jane's ball—as long as his young friend's attention stayed focused on his duty to his country instead of on Kitty's *décolletage,* Nigel thought sourly.

Nigel made a low sound in his throat. As long as the wretch did nothing to stand in the way of the investigation, his interest in Kitty was none of Nigel's concern.

Nigel knew he should be well satisfied. Everything was going just as he'd designed it should. He knew he should be in better spirits than he was, but by the time he got home, he was in a worse mood than ever. Upon arriving home, he waved off the maid's offer of tea and sat down instead at his desk with a snifter of brandy and a salver full of the day's post. Scanning the cards and letters, he found a largish envelope addressed in a lavish, scrawling hand with scarlet ink.

Ophelia Palin.

Nigel's eyes widened, and he opened that envelope first. He was invited to another masked ball—to be held tonight, with fewer than twenty-four hours' notice. It was unheard of! But then, Ophelia Palin was known for her unpredictability, he supposed. He turned the card over and stared at the note written on the back.

Pardon the short notice, my boy, but if you attend, I shall give you what you seek.

Nigel stared at the invitation for a few moments before going upstairs to catch a couple of hours of sleep. He had not slept more than a few hours in the last several days, and it looked like he wouldn't be getting much sleep tonight, either. Bounding upstairs, he shouted an order to his valet and then dove into his bed.

The hired coach arrived at precisely eleven. The driver handed Kathryn inside and, slamming the door shut, climbed up top and whistled to his horses. The coach lurched forward.

Immediately, Kathryn noticed a large box sitting on the opposite squab. There was a card on top, and Kathryn opened it, but there was not enough light inside the coach to read it by. Kathryn moved the curtain aside to make use of the coach lamps but found that the coachman had covered them both with dark red cloth. There was not enough light to see the road, let alone enough to read by.

"Driver," she called up to him, "there is no moon, and it is quite dark. Why have you blocked out the lamplight?"

"I allus do on nights this dark, miss," he called down, "otherwise, the shadows spook me 'orses. Not to worry, though, Pattycake and Puddin' knows the way. They walked these streets so much they know 'em by smell, they does." He laughed reassuringly, and Kathryn thought no more of it as she held the card very close to the weak red glow of the lamp.

"Put these on," it read.

Inside the box, Kathryn found her fairy costume.

A masquerade? Auntie had gone to all this trouble—putting them in danger of discovery—just to secure Kathryn's attendance at another masked ball? What could she have been thinking?

Kathryn rolled her eyes, for it was all too easy to guess what Ophelia was thinking. She was planning to introduce Kathryn to Nigel Moorhaven, the Marquis of Blackshire. Formally this time, no doubt.

Kathryn rapped on the ceiling with her wand. "Driver? Turn around. Please take me back to Lady Marchman's School for Young Ladies. Driver? Sir?"

But there was no answer. The man had started to hum, and she supposed that on a chilly night like this one, he would have his scarf wrapped round his head. She would just have to make her request when they reached Grosvenor Square. There was no help for it. She settled back to wait.

But when the coach did come to a stop, it wasn't the driver who yanked the door open, but Lydia Grantham!

Kathryn gasped and reached for her mask, but Lydia stayed her hand.

"There is no need! I know who you are. Your auntie told me."

"Oh," Kathryn managed.

"She told me you were to attend her ball tonight, and I wanted to thank you personally for what you did for me at the last one." She dipped her head shyly. "It was very good of you, and I swear I will find some way to repay your kindness."

"Nonsense. I only did what any right-thinking person would have done in our situation. But I am very glad to meet you in any case, for I wanted to ask you what you have been telling people about our acquaintance."

"Later. There will be time for that later. Right now, you need to get dressed." She reached for the wings and the mask. "Here. I shall assist you, if you wish."

"I am not attending the ball."

"Oh? But you are here. Why ever not?"

"Several reasons. Not the least of which is that Blackshire knows it was I in that bedchamber. Or at least he knows it was the fairy there."

"Oh, I see. Then you are correct. You must not appear in this costume." She bit her lip. "I know! I am staying with Ophelia for the evening since my uncle is out of town and my duenna was called to a sick cousin's bedside. You can come secretly to my chamber and we shall concoct a costume he will never recognize you in."

"Your offer is kind, but truly, I would feel more comfortable returning"—she almost said, "to the school"—"returning home. I find I am not feeling well after all. Driver," she said to the man who had come down from his box and was trying to look as though he couldn't hear everything that was being said, "please take me back immediately."

"I can't do that, miss."

"Why not?"

"Because," he answered, "she as give me the fare to bring you 'ere says I wasn't to take you back." He looked uncomfortable and added, "No matter what you says, miss. Sorry."

"You shall have five guineas if you take me back now."

He shrugged. "I'm real sorry, miss, an' to be sure I'd love to help you out, but I can't. The old lady paid me more than that."

"Very well," she said, flashing a look at Lydia, who had not spoken a word during this remarkable exchange, "then I shall just have to sit here in your coach until you change your mind. For I do not wish to be here, and I am not going to climb down."

A pained expression grew on the man's face. "Beggin' your pardon, miss, but the ol' lady, she told me that if'n I had to carry you inside like a sack of potatoes, that's what I was to do." He frowned apologetically. "She gave me five guineas, miss, an' she'll give me five more tomorrow if'n I delivers the goods. I'm sorry, miss, but I got me six little ones at 'ome an' one on the way."

Kathryn sighed. "You win." She shot a look up at Palin House. "Or Auntie does, rather. I'll be but a moment or two." Swinging the door shut once more, Kathryn awkwardly donned her costume in the confined interior of the coach. Then she climbed down, beaten.

The driver smiled and climbed back up to his box. "Thank you, miss." With a flick of the reins, he was off.

Lydia's eyebrow rose at the sight of Kathryn wearing her costume. "You wish to attend the ball after all?" she said in surprise.

"No." Kathryn turned to her. "I am still not going to attend Auntie's ball, but I do not wish to be conspicuous until

I can get far away from Palin House, either. Unfortunately, I did not anticipate having to hire another coach, and I find myself with no funds. I am stuck here until other arrangements can be made, and I'd rather be recognized as the fairy than as Kathryn St. David.'' *Or as Kitty Davidson,* she added to herself. Then she laughed at the sheer absurdity of the situation, and she said, ''My dear friend Lydia, you have the opportunity to 'repay my kindness' sooner than you expected. Would you direct your coachman to take me home?''

''I should like that above all things.''

''Good.''

''But I cannot.''

''Not so good. Why not?''

''My duenna took the carriage to her cousin's home, so I have no transport to offer you.''

Kathryn rubbed the bridge of her nose. ''John,'' she muttered. ''I shall have to go in search of John.''

''Your parents' man?''

''He was employed by them for many years, yes. But he is his own person now.''

''Either way, I am afraid he will be of no help to you. Your parents did not wish to attend the ball tonight—''

''No surprise.''

''—so Mr. Robertson is escorting them to the opera.''

''Oh dear!''

''But I believe I can yet be of assistance. You cannot stay out here. Your aunt is on the lookout for you as I was. You may hide in my chamber until I summon you a coach. I shall loan you some of my pin money for your fare home.''

Kathryn sighed her relief and thanked Lydia profusely as they made their way up the dark back stairs and down a long hallway where, upon passing a footman, Lydia pulled from her reticule a folded piece of paper and directed the servant to deliver the note to Ophelia Palin without delay. Then Lydia led the way to a bedchamber not far from Kathryn's own room, where, after locking the door behind them, she lit a single wax candle. Even with the candle's glow, the room was very dark. Even if there had been any moonlight to cast a watery shadow, the heavy curtains were closed, and there was no fire in the hearth.

"You will be safe here. I am a very light sleeper, and your aunt ordered that I be given this wing to myself and that no servant should enter it from evensong to noon unless I specifically request them. So no one will discover you here."

"Thank goodness," Kathryn said. "What was in the note you gave to that footman?" Kathryn asked. "And how could you already have it written?"

Lydia's laughter trilled through the darkness. "Oh. That. I carry a half-dozen such missives with me at all times. How do you think I keep my old duenna at bay? 'Dear Cousin . . . ' " she recited, " 'I have ripped my dress and a maid is exacting repairs. I shall be absent from the ball room above a half hour.' " She coughed. " 'Dear Cousin, I have lost my brooch. Dear Cousin, I have stained my gown.' The poor woman must believe I am the most clumsy girl in England."

"But why make up those stories at all?"

"La, Kathryn, you *are* a country mouse aren't you? I tell tales to keep my duenna—your aunt, this time—from discovering what I am really doing while I am supposed to be having my dress mended, of course."

"Of course," Kathryn murmured.

"Did you not wonder how I was able to lure Blackshire upstairs without my duenna being any the wiser?"

"L—lure him?" Kathryn stammered. *"You* lured *him?"*

Lydia laughed again. "Heavens, yes! You do not imagine the Marquis of Blackshire would arrange a tryst with a girl of my age, do you? Of course not," she answered her own question. "I wanted him to kiss me, and I took matters into my own hands. I gave him one of my notes. It said I was in trouble and needed his help. I knew he would follow me." She held her palm up before her like a shield. "Oh,

I know. It was foolish of me to imagine he would succumb to temptation and kiss me. If he had, he would have had to declare for me, of course.''

Sure he would, Kathryn thought, *and I am Julius Caesar.*

Lydia sniffed. ''But Blackshire, the dratted gentleman, did not even touch me.''

''But your hair, your dress . . . and I heard the bed—''

''I ripped my dress to give him access and threw myself over the counterpane.''

Kathryn gasped, but Lydia only laughed. ''Nothing ventured, nothing gained, I say. If it had worked I could have been his marchioness by now. As it was, I gained only a ripped dress and lost nought but a little of my dignity.''

Kathryn's heart beat a pounding staccato at her temples. She moved with apparent aimlessness to a far corner of the room steeped in shadow where Lydia could not observe her trembling fingers. She was overwhelmed. Blackshire was not the devil she had thought he was! He was good. Kind. Generous.

And Kathryn had mistreated him dreadfully.

He had only been trying to rescue Lydia. Just as he had rescued the kittens and the puppies—even if he was determined to banish them to his estate in Northumberland. He spoke in the House of Lords for laws to protect the poor. And he even knew how to get a stain out of the carpet. And then there was little Thomas, to whom Blackshire had given a sense of belonging in a real home. He'd given Jane a home, too. And perhaps Bankham really was a rakehell and he was trying to rescue Jane from his clutches. And—oh!— the clothes he'd sent! He'd been trying to rescue ''Kitty Davidson'' too!

She thought about what had happened in Lady Marchman's library, when she'd shoved the tea tray and cut her finger. She thought about the tender way he had held her hand then—and about the belligerent way she had treated him.

Regret coursed through her.

"Kathryn?" Lydia asked, breaking into her thoughts. "Are you all right?"

"Yes. Yes . . . I was just considering how your poor heart must ache."

"Mine? Why, no, I am feeling quite the thing just now. Why, do I seem blue?" She put her hands on her hips and cocked her head.

"You do not love him then?"

"Who? Blackshire?" She laughed. "Heavens no! To be sure, Nigel Moorhaven is the best of men, and I daresay any woman would be lucky to have him, but matrimony was not really my aim. You see, I—"

A knock sounded at the door. Lydia squeaked in alarm and blew out the candle. Kathryn froze.

"Hello? Lydia?" A voice penetrated the door. A rich, masculine, all-too-familiar voice. Blackshire's! The doorknob rattled. "Lydia!"

"What is happening?" Kathryn whispered. "Why is he—"

"Shhhh!" In the darkness, Lydia laid a small, warm, reassuring hand on Kathryn's arm. "Everything will be as it should be," she whispered. "Stay here. I am going to the door. The room is dark. He will not see you."

"No! You mustn't open the—"

But it was too late. Kathryn heard the lock turn, and then weak light from the single sconce down the hall stabbed across the floor. To her horror, she watched the dark, massive form of Blackshire move into the chamber before the door slammed shut once more. Then Kathryn heard the lock turn again. What was Lydia up to?

"Lydia?" Blackshire said. "Who is here?"

No answer.

Kathryn heard the doorknob jiggle and then Blackshire swore. "You impudent chit!" he said, projecting his voice in the direction of the hallway outside the door. "You have locked me in!"

She did what?

He pounded on the door. "Unlock this door at once,

Lydia. I do not know what game you are playing this time, but if you do not open this door, I shall break it down.''

"No!" Kathryn cried. "Someone will hear you! We'll be found together!"

"Who are *you?*" Blackshire demanded, whirling about.

Kathryn bit her lip. "A friend of Lydia's," she said, disguising her voice as best she could. She made it softer, more hesitant, silently praying that in the darkness he would not instantly recognize her after they'd just spent most of the day together. My name is . . . Rose," she said, using her second name, "and I swear that this was not my idea. I am as surprised at what Lydia just did as you are, my . . . uh . . . *my goodness.''* She had almost addressed him as "my lord," but she was not supposed to know he was a titled gentleman!

"I am Nigel Moorhaven, the Marquis of Blackshire. Have we met?''

"Oh!" Kathryn feigned surprise. "I am certain we have not been formally introduced, *my lord.''* That much was true. Kathryn hated to lie, and did not wish to do so, and if she could only get out of this tangle with her reputation intact, she would hie off to Heathford and never, never tell so much as a fib ever again!

"Your voice seems familiar. What is your surname?''

"Oh, I . . . I am very young, my lord, and I come from the country, and I am sure you do not know of my family,'' she averred.

"I see." A bark of cynical laughter erupted from the pitch-blackness. "What am I saying? I see nothing at all. I saw light under the door when I arrived. Where is the candle? Lydia blew it out, I presume."

Kathryn's heart thudded in her chest. The candle was just beside her, but she could not let Blackshire light it! Even if he was the archangel Gabriel himself, Kathryn would not let him see her face—or her costume. "I . . . I don't know where the candle is," she told him. "I think Lydia took it with her." She groped frantically for the candlestick and, finding it, quickly tucked it under a chair. When she straightened up, she came into contact with something solid. Something warm. Something male.

Blackshire was looking for the candlestick, too. But what he found was Kathryn.

The contact surprised him, for as the girl bumped into Nigel and he reached out to steady her, his hands came into contact with an unusual contour fanning out from her shoulders in all directions. Wire, fine mesh. Rounded. Thin.

"Wings!" he said, his hands coming to rest on her bare shoulders.

He didn't know why he should have been so surprised. Hadn't Ophelia promised to give him what he sought if he came to the masquerade? Well, here he was. And here was the fairy queen. But this wasn't exactly the way he had imagined their next meeting would take place.

He'd come to rid himself of his idiotic fascination with Kitty Davidson. His attraction to the chit had to be fueled by her physical resemblance to the fairy. The attraction between Nigel and Titania had been immediate and mutual. Their kiss in Ophelia's garden had set him afire.

Like the fairy, Kitty Davidson was beautiful, clever, kind, and resourceful. Nigel had thought Kitty at sixteen was a charmer. But at eighteen, she was bloody dangerous. He hadn't had a moment's peace since he'd learned her true age. There was no way he was going to chain her, an innocent, to a man like himself. A twenty-nine-year-old soldier who had looked evil in the face—and killed it. A man who had seduced a score of women in service to his country.

Kitty Davidson might be marriageable, all right. But she wasn't marriageable to *him*.

He had to get her out of his system. And the only way he could think of to do that was to go to the source of the problem. The fairy. And here she was.

"I suppose you have a wand to go with your wings?" he drawled.

"A wand, sir? I do not know what you mean."

"Do not attempt to play me for a fool." He splayed his fingers and his hands skimmed over her shoulders and down her back. He pulled her to him and felt her tremble. "You are my Titania and no other."

"Yours, my lord?"

"Apparently that is what you are about to become whether either of us wishes it or not."

"What do you mean?"

"Though I cannot imagine why, Lydia intends to compromise us."

"I do not think so. She went out of her way to tell me no one would discover me here."

"Oh?"

"Yes. She specifically stated that no one is permitted in this wing of the house from dusk to midday, by order of Ophelia."

"Ah yes. Ophelia. She must be in on it too."

"No . . . it cannot be. She would not—"

"I received a note from the old girl today, which said that if I came to this ball, she would give me what I've been seeking."

Kathryn's mouth was suddenly dry. "Which is?" she whispered.

"You."

In the darkness, one large, strong hand found her face and cradled it reverently.

"You're beautiful."

"Nonsense, my lord. You cannot see me."

"Yes I can." He showed her what he meant, pulling off her mask and moving his fingers slowly, searchingly to the top of her head and then slowly over her face. "Since we kissed, you have invaded my waking thoughts and haunted my dreams at night." He caressed her throat and then the underside of her jaw, tilting her face upward.

"What are you doing?" Kathryn asked, though she was certain she knew what the answer would be.

"This." He kissed her lightly, once, twice. "Kissing you. I've thought of little else since the night of the ball."

She sighed. "Oh ... neither have I. Kiss me again. Please."

"As you wish," he whispered. His warm breath skittered past her ear, raising gooseflesh up and down her side. He drew her even closer to him, and his mouth descended over hers. He kissed her with a mixture of urgency and gentleness. She responded immediately, intimately, naturally.

"I've never been kissed like this before," she murmured.

It was true. This kiss was different from the kiss in Auntie's garden. That time, she had been fighting her attraction to Blackshire. She had thought he was evil. This time, she knew better.

When his lips left her mouth to trail over her jaw and down her neck, she made a small sound of protest. What he was doing to the sensitive area below and behind her ear was intoxicating—John Bothwell and Robert Brice had each stolen a peck on her lips when they were children, but now they attempted nothing more than a chaste brushing of their lips across the backs of her fingers.

She knew it was mad, she knew it was improper, but she reached for Nigel anyway and brought his lips back to her own.

Seconds ticked by, marked only by the beating of his heart. His face, where it brushed against hers, was clean-shaven, but rough. His scent rose between them, warm and masculine, inviting her to inhale more deeply. She was lost in a swirl of sensation.

Heaven help her, she didn't want to stop, for kissing—kissing this way—was lovely.

Voices sounded down the hall. Nigel forced himself to draw away from her. There was nothing to do but wait for the door to open.

"Oh dear," his fairy queen whispered in dread.

"I can think of worse fates," he said. "Marriages have been founded on less."

"You know nothing about me, my lord."

"On the contrary. I know you are kind, loyal, intelligent . . . and very pleasant to kiss. I have no regrets."

Even as he said the words, a traitorous image of Kitty Davidson flashed into his mind.

There was nothing left to do but propose.

"Will you do me the honor of becoming my wife?"

Kathryn felt tears welling in her eyes. It was all too much. She could not fathom it. She'd fallen in love with a scoundrel, torturing herself over her foolishness for days. And now she was going to be his wife. Only he wasn't a scoundrel. He was a beautiful, generous, and loving man whom she adored. She just knew her parents would love him. And of course Auntie would be in raptures.

The voices were just outside the door now. She opened her mouth to answer yes, but her breath caught in her throat.

Aunt Ophelia!

The old woman's diary was still lost at Lady Marchman's. What if she had found it this evening? Was whatever secret it contained heinous enough to bring down the powerful Marquis of Blackshire? Perhaps not, but if it was bad enough to induce Ophelia to retire for good to the country, then it was most certainly bad enough to have an effect upon Jane by association.

As plain Miss St. David, Kathryn would have escaped Lady Marchman's notice when she entered Society, but she'd never escape her notice if she became the Marchioness of Blackshire. And she doubted the lady would be able to keep Kathryn's masquerade at the school under her bonnet.

Would the scandals have a negative effect upon Nigel's influence in Parliament? Would any man look at Jane twice?

She couldn't take the chance. Too many people were counting on her. Somehow, she had to find that diary, and she could think of only one way to do that. She groped for her mask and, covering her face once more, waited by the door, ready to spring.

Nigel waited for her to answer as someone in the hall fitted a key into the lock. Any sane man would be panicked now. But it was useless to fight against the inevitable, and Nigel, though he had not come to find a wife and by all rights should have been unhappy, felt only a sense of calm anticipation. It was time he got married. His thirtieth birthday was approaching, and he had not found a woman more suited to his needs than this one. Judging from her cynicism and her demeanor, Rose, the fairy, was probably much closer to his age than—than other women of his acquaintance. She was much more suitable for a man like himself than someone like Miss Davidson. Nigel was certain Rose would make an admirable marchioness. They were obviously well suited physically; their attraction for each other had been palpable since the very moment their eyes met.

Perhaps, in time, love might even grow between them.

And perhaps, in time, he could think of Lydia Grantham and Ophelia Palin again without an accompanying urge to strangle them.

The door finally opened. Light slashed into the room, and three silhouettes appeared in the doorway. Lydia, and two shapes he thought he could identify as Lady Jersey and Princess Esterhazy. Of course. Who better to witness an indiscretion? Nigel almost laughed. Ophelia meant business.

Suddenly, a fourth shape burst from out of the deep shadow flanking the doorway. Rose! She rushed through the cluster of women at the door and ran headlong down the hall. Her mask was still on.

"Who is that?" Lady Jersey demanded?

"I do not know," Nigel lied.

"Indeed!" Princess Esterhazy huffed.

Nigel turned to Lydia. "Do you know who that young lady was?" he asked her.

Without a moment's hesitation, Lydia shook her head. "No. I do not."

Nigel didn't know if she ought to be sainted or drawn and quartered. He looked down the long hall, but there was no sign of Rose. She hadn't answered—or even acknowledged—his proposal.

"Hell and blast," he thundered. She'd escaped him again.

Chapter Sixteen

Nigel muttered a hasty apology to the ladies and, throwing Lydia a murderous stare that said they'd not seen the last of each other, he left them staring after him. He could forget about ever getting into Almack's again. Not that he cared.

Charging into Ophelia's library, he gave the bell pull a savage yank. A footman rushed in. "Inform Miss Palin that the Marquis of Blackshire is waiting for her in the library."

Nigel didn't have to wait for long. Ophelia entered in a puffed mass of silver-spangled green. "You must have made quite a muck of it, my boy." She handed him a folded sheet of paper. "She came running into the ballroom a moment ago and handed me this. I read it of course."

Nigel opened the note. It was written in a hasty scrawl with no salutation and no signature, not even so much as an initial.

> My answer is no. I will not marry you. Make no attempt to discover my identity. Ophelia will not tell you, and neither will Lydia.

"Where is she?!" Nigel snarled.

"She has gone," Ophelia answered, studying him, "and, by this time, Lydia is with her."

"Her real name is not Rose, is it?"

"No, and do not ask me what her real name is, for I will not say."

"Will you tell me nothing that will help me to find her?"

Ophelia shook her head sadly. "No, my boy. I am sorry. This is her decision to make. You can lead a mare to water, but you can't make her say 'I do.' "

Nigel turned without another word and headed home to Berkeley Square where he spent the next two hours pacing in his library. He did not want brandy. Neither did he seek his bed. Sleep would not come to him, he was certain. Not when he was fighting a sense of emptiness, a sense of loneliness so profound it made him ache.

What was wrong with him? He did not truly want to marry the fairy. Certainly, he'd journeyed to Palin House in the hope of meeting her, but he'd wanted only to rid himself of his unacceptable fascination with Kitty Davidson, which had got in the way of his investigation. He'd needed to restore balance to his mind.

But now he was more off-kilter than ever.

The fairy's touch had him reeling. Her power over him seemed almost magical. One kiss, and his desire for her had spun out of control. But that was not all the fascination she held for him. What he'd told her was true. She was clever and kind . . . and by Jove she truly wasn't interested in his fortune.

Apparently, she wasn't interested in Nigel, either.

She'd escaped. Her note to him made her feelings clear. The patronesses hadn't seen her face. Her reputation was safe. He told himself he was glad. He told himself everything turned out the way it should have. She did not want him, and he could forget her now.

He made a fist and drove it into the chair.

* * *

Blackshire's town house burst at the seams with young people.

He'd sent another gown, one made just for this occasion. Its beauty had taken Kathryn's breath away. It was a simple creation, really. Its many layers of whitest muslin were so light Kathryn hardly felt them brush and sway against her body as she moved. Seed pearls were scattered here and there. They nestled in the folds of the fabric like tiny white doves. Snowy gloves sheathed her slender arms and elegant satin slippers encased her feet. A white lace fan and a soft, matching lace shawl completed the ensemble. Jane had lent Kathryn ribbons and her lady's maid, who had fashioned Kathryn's unruly hair into a fine crown of white satin and curls. Kathryn fingered the string of perfectly matched peals at her throat. Oh, she had never dreamed of wearing such a treasure. She knew she looked lovely. She *felt* lovely.

She wanted him to see her dressed this way, just this once, even if he didn't know it was she he'd proposed to last night.

Kathryn could see little difference between Ophelia's masquerade ball and Jane's "little entertainment" but for the age of the participants, who were all under seven-and-ten, and the lack of costumes and masks.

"Is it not splendid?" Jane asked at Kathryn's elbow. "I did not realize Nigel had gone to such trouble." She indicated a shiny metal trough, festooned with garlands of flowers, which ran the length of one side of the ballroom. In it, gold and silver fish swam amid waterfalls and islands of floating water lilies. "It's said the Prince Regent is preparing a display like this for an occasion at Carlton House." The room glowed with the light of hundreds of candles. The scent of beeswax and the perfume of forced summer flowers wafted through the air, fencing with the cheerful sound of a small, yet charming orchestra. And among the young guests ran five puppies, creating a delightful melee of giggles and shrill barks. Washed and groomed, the little balls of sweet-smelling fluff were the darlings of the evening.

Kathryn gestured toward one of the puppies, which was diligently chewing, undiscovered, on an oblivious chaperon's satin hem. "I thought you were to keep only one of them," she said.

"You did not think Nigel would really banish them, did you?"

"Yes." Truth to tell, before Lydia's revelation, Kathryn had had visions of the puppies being thrown into an oubliette and forgotten.

"He is not so heartless as you imagine. In fact, Nigel has given orders for a little house to be built for them near the back door. I did not even ask him. He never had any intention of sending the little dears to Northumberland."

The puppies were helpless creatures, completely lacking in manners or usefulness, yet he had chosen to purchase them in the first place and then to keep them here in Town just to indulge Jane's whim. It was a kindness. A gentleness. A goodness.

She looked through the open doors into the ballroom. The evening was almost over, and Kathryn had yet to glimpse Nigel. She ached with disappointment.

"Oh, botheration!" Jane said at her elbow. "Here comes George Princeton. Save me, dear friend. He is even more full of himself than his regal name implies, and he thinks it a great privilege for any young lady to dance with him. Let us be off. We shall pretend to be in deep conversation." Jane looped her arm through Kathryn's and steered her away from the cluster of chaperons, whose number included, at Lady Marchman's insistence, Mary Gant. The two moved toward the open glass doors that stood at one end of the long ballroom. Kathryn's nose twitched at the sight of the young peacock George, who stood staring after them with a sour look on his face. As soon as they had gained the terrace, both of them dissolved into laughter.

"Did you see his face?" Jane asked.

"Like he had tasted a sour pickle!"

Jane snorted. "A rotten sour pickle. Oh, poor George. I have been avoiding him all evening."

Kathryn sobered. "Most of your friends have, Jane."

"Not you, though," Jane said. "I saw you dancing with him earlier. Why him? You have so favored only a few young gentlemen this night."

"I felt sorry for him," Kathryn said. "And besides . . . George is . . . not such an awful young man. He . . . he is quite good-looking, actually." Their eyes met, and Kathryn tried to keep a straight face, but Jane's incredulous look pulled from her a sudden explosion of giggles.

"Oh, Kitty! I do like you so very much. I am ever so glad we met. I've a feeling we shall be friends forever."

Kathryn's gaiety died. "I . . . am sure I shall never forget you either, Jane," she said.

"I do not know what you are thinking," Jane said, "but do stop it. Come! This was meant to be a night of happiness and adventure. Beat back the blue-devils so you can enjoy the surprise I have in store for Nigel later on."

"What surprise?"

"Today is his birthday. He thinks no one knows, but I have circled word among the guests, and they are ready to drink to his health." She bit her lip. "If he ever makes an appearance."

The marquis had disappeared soon after the guests arrived and had not been seen since. Kathryn had been late coming downstairs and had not seen him at all. "He is brooding, as he always does on his birthday, or so I have heard from the servants."

"Why?"

Jane looked around to be certain they were alone and lowered her voice. "His mother died on his birthday. The poor darling was but five years old. She was climbing a tree to retrieve a bird that had not quite fledged. She was going to give it to Nigel as his present. She fell and broke her neck." In hushed tones, Jane told Kathryn the rest of the story, about his father plummeting into a decline and virtually forgetting about his son from then on, and about young Nigel blaming himself for his parents' misfortune.

Five years old!

Kathryn's heart filled with sadness and pity for the little boy Nigel had been as well as for the man he had become. "Poor Nigel," she whispered.

Jane sighed. "In years past, the servants have let him brood alone, but I shall not. He will come back downstairs before long. I will find you when he does. I do not wish to face the lion alone when he finds out what I have done."

"Lady Jane," a handsome boy with sparkling blue eyes said from a discreet distance, "may I have the pleasure of the next dance?" Jane squeezed Kathryn's hand and walked off with the eager lad.

Not wishing to be similarly engaged, Kathryn slipped into the shadows at one end of the long terrace. Though she wanted very much to dance, the only partner she wished for was in mourning. She thought of him tenderly and lay her head against the cool stone of the outside wall of Nigel's magnificent house. Nigel had so much, but he was so poor.

Kathryn passed the time on the terrace restlessly. Sets formed, executed their figures, and reformed. The moon had risen high into the sky, and still the Marquis of Blackshire had not appeared.

Laughter spilled from the ballroom. A game of chance was under way. But Kathryn did not feel merry. It was late, and she was tired of avoiding young George Princeton and the queries of several other youngsters who entreated her to join their sets or their games. So with a silent apology to Miss Gant, Kathryn finally descended the curved terrace stair to walk among the sleeping flowerbeds and tall hedges. The moon was nearly full and its soft light illumined the carefully tended paths and boxy hedges, beckoning her deeper into the well-kept gardens. Kathryn plodded unhappily on, walking while pulling her delicate lace shawl closely about her. Coming to this ball had been a mistake. It was like being allowed to gaze upon a gloriously laden table, knowing a meal was out of the question, and she found she could not enjoy herself.

The air was chill and a heavy fog was gathering. It was quite late. She thought of her parents and Ophelia and John and wondered what they were all doing just then. She wished she were with them. Anywhere but here. She looked up to the large house, where the windows of several upstairs rooms glowed with soft lamplight. He was up there, in one of those rooms, and Kathryn was uncertain if his proximity brought her more comfort, fear, or aching loneliness. Certainly, she was confused.

Her teeth chattered, but she was unwilling to go back to the ballroom.

As she rounded a corner, an enormous glasshouse appeared on her right and she walked to it, lured by the promise of warmth. Inside, the heat, the heavy scent of hothouse flowers, and the moonlight drugged her. Daffodils, delphiniums, hyacinths, lilies, carnations, roses. The blossoms glowed in the moonlight, and Kathryn walked among them entranced, for the moment. Reaching the roses, she inhaled deeply and smiled. The glasshouse was a magical place, and for the time being Kathryn put aside all her worries to wander among the roses, her favorites.

As she bent to smell one particularly full blossom, a voice behind her said, "You're welcome to take one, if you wish."

Kathryn stilled instantly. It was him. His voice, while deep and resonant, was nearly a whisper. It was all she could do not to run to him and throw herself into his arms and tell him exactly who she was.

"There are so many varieties. I could never decide," she said over her shoulder.

"You may have as many as you wish," he told her.

She straightened, looked down, and fiddled with her fan. "I could not carry them all."

"Then you may keep them here, and visit them whenever you wish."

"I . . . I will return home soon, and . . . I do not think I shall be returning to London for a very long time. Perhaps never."

"Then you should have a glasshouse wherever you choose to live. When you marry, you must ask your husband to build one."

Kathryn gave an unladylike snort and looked up at him then. Her eyes widened. His black evening clothes were wrinkled and his hair needed combing. He had not shaved, and his snowy cravat hung limply over his neck, revealing a partially unbuttoned white shirt. Kathryn's eyes landed on the triangle of crisp, black chest hair, which managed to escape the cover of his clothing. She swallowed and dragged her eyes back to the flowers. Truth to tell, he appeared as though he had just crawled out of bed.

He looked wonderful.

"You look awful," she told him.

One sardonic eyebrow rose. "Thank you."

"I . . . I meant no offense. It is just that your . . . you—"

"Look awful. I know." He sighed. "I have not taken much notice of my appearance this evening. I have had . . . other matters to consider. Are you offended? Would you rather I left?" He started to turn away.

"No!" Kathryn cried and then more softly she said, "No. You have a perfect right to look awful." She looked away, embarrassed. She could not tell him that she thought he must look now as he had after they had been together last night. Nigel did not know who it was standing before him, who it was that had kissed him so passionately last night. There was so much he did not know about her! Or she him . . .

She coughed. "You must know, my lord, that my husband, whoever he shall be, is unlikely to be able to afford a glasshouse."

He shook his head. "You never know. With your superior education and your beauty you may surprise yourself and catch a very wealthy husband indeed."

Kathryn felt a sudden stinging at the corners of her eyes, and she turned away from him so that he would not see her sweep the budding tears away.

"Nay, my lord. I have learned to set aside dreams."

She felt the warmth of his hand then as his fingers curled under her jawline and he brought her chin around to face him.

"You lie," he said softly. "Dreams are all that sustain any of us." He brushed the back of his fingers across her cheek and then took her hand. "Come, Kitty, and dream with me." He drew her into the center of the glasshouse, where stood a bubbling fountain. The sound of it echoed off the glass around them.

"Hear the music!" he said, nodding toward the falling water. "A waltz, I believe." He dropped her hand and bowed low before her before straightening once more and asking softly, "May I have this dance?"

He stood there in the moonlight, strong, virile, and handsome, his formal black evening clothes almost fading into the shadows. His snowy shirt and cravat bespoke elegance in their stark contrast. On his inky coat, he wore a flower, a spiky delphinium. His eyes were half closed and he was holding out his hand to her. His outstretched fingers and his eyes invited her. Enticed her. Commanded her. Though her heart beat a warning, her head did not listen. Kathryn lifted her hand slowly and placed it in his. His warm fingers closed around hers, and Nigel moved closer to her. Looking into her eyes, he began humming a melody with a slow beat. Much too slow. He enfolded her in his arms and pulled her into the steps of a gentle waltz. Kathryn closed her eyes and let him guide her, as he had last night.

This was madness. She knew she should flee, but a peace had descended upon her heart and mind that she could not escape. Heaven help her, she *wanted* to be here, alone with him. She wanted to imagine for a moment that she had accepted his proposal. That he was her husband, that this was her glasshouse.

And she wanted to ease his heart.

"I . . . I am sorry to hear about your mother," she said softly. She felt him stiffen against her, and she instantly wished she had said nothing.

"Who told you about her?" he asked tightly.

"Jane."

"What did she say?"

"Only that your mother died on your fifth birthday and that you blamed yourself. Jane said she found out from your servants."

"They should not have told her. I tried to conceal from her the . . . the misery this day holds for me. She has had enough misery in her own life, enough loss, without taking on my own."

"Is that why you chose today to give her a ball?"

"I tried to make this a day for Jane to be happy, not a day for pity and sadness."

"I do not believe pity is what she intends." Kathryn gave him a tender smile and shook her head. "You and she have become a family, my lord." She paused. "Do you wish to know what I think?"

"Do I have a choice?" he asked, one glossy, dark eyebrow rising.

But Kathryn detected amusement in his carefully constructed expression. "No," she answered. "You do not." She bit her lip, pondering how to say what she felt. "I think," she said finally, "that neither of you quite knows how to behave now that you are a family. Jane doesn't know when to keep confidences, and you, it seems, do not know when to share them."

He sighed and drew her to him in a weary embrace.

"I was there," he said suddenly. "We saw a young bird hopping about in a tree. It could not yet fly, and I saw the idea to capture it blossom and spread over my mother's pretty face. She asked me if I'd like to have a baby bird for my birthday. I remember nodding eagerly. She patted my head, and I watched her climb the tree, but her skirts tangled about her feet. And then she fell. She died instantly, though I was five and did not realize . . . ." He paused for so long that Kathryn thought he would say no more, but then he spoke again. "I ran to her. She still had the baby bird clutched in her hand. It was dead. I understood that, plain enough, for it was crushed in her fingers."

Kathryn's breath caught in her throat, remembering how tenderly he had lifted the baby bird in Auntie's garden.

He continued. "It was nearly fledged, its feathers already turning blue, like its parents'. And my mother was dressed in blue as well. It was dusk, and even the sky was a deep blue. Her eyes were open, and they were more blue than I had ever seen them, staring up and reflecting the sky like that. She looked surprised, and I thought she was marveling at the beauty of the sky. I lay down on the grass, my head next to hers, so I could look at the sky too, but it was not long before I discovered—" He closed his eyes. "The entire world turned blue that day."

Kathryn put her hand to the side of his face. She looked at him with new understanding. "It is why you always wear something of that color, then." And it was also why his voice had been so choked, so gentle, when he'd lifted the baby bird in Auntie's garden back into its tree.

His hand tightened around her waist, and his feet stilled. "Yes," he said. "For me, blue is the color of loneliness. I have been alone for a long time."

Kathryn's heart thudded in her chest. She ached for him. "I am here with you, now," she said.

"Yes," he whispered. "You are. And you should not be, Kitty."

The dishonest syllables of her false name struck her forcibly, coming as they did on the heels of his admission. "Kathryn," she said, looking down. "My real name is Kathryn," she confessed, knowing she could not tell him the whole truth, but needing to tell him the basic truth about herself, "and, as you know, I am older than I appear, but"—

she swallowed and her heart fluttered in her chest—"but what you don't know is that I—"

"Whatever it is, it does not signify," he said. "I must leave now, and you must go inside. Were we to be seen together . . ."

"Of course."

He stepped away from her and hesitated, and it seemed to Kathryn he wanted to say something more. After a moment, he smiled sadly and turned to go.

"Wait!" she called. He glanced back at her, and Kathryn took a step toward him. "I . . . I love you."

Nigel's eyes softened. Slowly, he walked toward her. Kathryn's heart beat wildly as he framed her face in the palms of his hands and lowered his face toward hers. His mouth brushed hers for the barest instant, and then he drew away. "My dear Kathryn . . . I care for you. But I have seen things and done things I am not proud of . . . things I have no right ask you to share. You are still so young and I . . . I am not. If only you were—" He paused and a look came into his eyes, a look of longing.

"Yes?"

He shook his head as though to clear from it a haze. "If only things were different." He gave her a sad smile. "I must go. If I stay here . . . if I stay, I will hurt you. Good night." He turned and walked away from her, into the darkness.

She didn't have to hear his words to know what he'd wanted to say. She already knew what it was: if she were some years older, he would ask her to marry him. And what then?

She sighed, allowing her eyes to become unfocused, and tilted her head to one side. They would have a grand wedding. Aunt Ophelia would be beaming, and so would her parents, because they, of course, would love Nigel as Kathryn did. He would carry her off to his magnificent house in Berkeley Square, where they would . . . they would do what was necessary to have a child. Ah, but Blackshire would be as quick and as gentle as he could be, and then they would have a darling babe, and they would never have to do that awful thing again, and they would live happily for the rest of their days.

The urge to run after him, throw herself into his arms, and tell him she was not eighteen but twenty-two almost overcame her reason, but not quite.

She couldn't tell him the truth. Not until she found the diary.

Chapter Seventeen

Sometime in the small hours of the morning, Kathryn pulled her wrapper on and started downstairs to search the high shelves for the diary. Halfway down the long main hall of the school, she felt her stomach rumble. She'd been too much at sixes-and-sevens at the ball to eat. She hadn't had so much as a morsel. A short detour to the kitchen was in order.

The room was empty at this hour. Drawn to the warmth and the light of the banked kitchen fire, she purloined a pair of biscuits and poured herself a glass of warm milk and added a few drops of honey. Her mother had always fixed her the very same concoction whenever something was troubling her at home and she could not sleep, but Kathryn found it did her no good this night. She sat down at the long worktable and looked about her, wondering where Nigel was and what he was thinking. Standing, she wandered to the hearth, and that's when she saw the book.

It rested on the wide mantel. *The Corsair,* its spine proclaimed. Kathryn missed a breath or two. It was the title Cook had received for Lady Marchman from Madame Briand! Cook must have forgotten to deliver the book to Lady Marchman. No, Kathryn thought with a chuckle, it was more likely the grumpy woman had simply chosen not to deliver it. Why had Madame Briand been so insistent the book be delivered to Lady Marchman without delay?

Kathryn took the book down and opened it, half expecting hidden papers to tumble out, but there were none. The book appeared to be quite ordinary. Reading the first few pages as she ate, she found *The Corsair* to be engrossing. She sipped the last of her milk and read a little more, relieved to escape thoughts of Nigel Moorhaven if only for a few moments.

Nigel sat in his bedchamber, staring into the fire until he realized the flame that burned in his heart would not be ignored.

He loved her. By the devil, he loved her!

She had changed everything. Nigel had expected this night to pass just as every other birthday had since that terrible day, but Kitty—Kathryn, he amended—had changed everything. He'd been alone in the garden, alone in the world, until he'd stepped into the glasshouse and seen her there, standing in the moonlight. She'd been an enchanting sight, all dressed in Madame Vensois's pearl and muslin gown. He had danced with her to indulge her dreams, but he'd stumbled upon one of his own.

She understood about the color blue. But she didn't know how much her understanding meant to him. She didn't know she'd put an end to his reason for wearing blue in the first place, an end to his isolation. Her understanding meant he was no longer alone in the world. Nigel reached for the flower in his lapel with a half smile on his lips and tossed it into the fire, where its blue petals curled and disappeared.

He would never wear blue again.

No longer would he mourn this day each year. Kathryn had given him so much. He laughed loudly, startling his valet, who had fallen asleep on a chair in his dressing room. Nigel dismissed the man.

He remembered how she had kissed him: with an innocent passion that had shaken his very soul.

He remembered her outrage when she'd thought he'd had Thomas fired and her daring madcap scheme to bring Jane and Bankham together. She was outrageously spontaneous and rudely outspoken and maddeningly stubborn.

She was perfect.

And Nigel wanted her.

He loved her.

Dear God . . . she was so young! Eighteen . . . and yet she was so different from the other chits her age . . . she made a man wish to never let her go.

He came to a decision.

He would not let her go, by God. He would keep her by his side forever. He would do anything to ensure her happiness. Give up his service to Sir Winston, move to the country . . . give her children, have a house full of cats, whatever it took to keep her happy. Nigel pulled the bell cord. He intended to ask her to be his marchioness. She loved him. And he was certain she could help him to regain the serenity . . . the sense of wonder . . . the innocence he'd lost. Hell, she'd already begun. Nigel laughed aloud. Pure joy washed over him. He felt alive. Happy. Content.

When his sleepy-eyed butler arrived, Nigel sent the man down to fetch his mother's wedding ring from the vault below the house. It was a large, fine ruby, intricately faceted and flanked with two fiery diamonds. Whistling, Nigel went downstairs. He would have to see Lady Marchman, he supposed, but he could not—he would not—wait. He had been alone too long. He would not wait another night. By dawn, he would be betrothed. He would awaken Lady Marchman. He would rouse all of London if necessary!

He rode across town, ordering his coachman to drive neck-or-nothing. They startled a runner, several prostitutes, and two footpads—all of whom waved a greeting after Nigel's coach as it passed.

Her meal finished, Kathryn tucked the book into her wrapper, intending to take it to her room to read later. Holding the candle high, she made her way to the library.

The only shelves yet unsearched were the high ones, the ones accessible only with the tall, rolling library ladder. Kathryn climbed and, holding the candle high, scanned the topmost shelf in front of her and suddenly realized that this was the very shelf where Madame Briand had hidden her papers. Kathryn's eyes widened.

The slim volume was gone!

From the shadows at the far end of the library, Brian O'Flaugherty watched as she slowly descended the ladder. Was the girl looking for the papers? What else would she be doing up there in the middle of the night? Could she be looking for a book to read? He doubted the coincidence, but it didn't matter in any case, for she would not find the papers. He had already looked. The entire book was gone.

What if the girl *were* looking for the papers? He'd seen her peering into the library that day when she oughtn't have been. Why was she there? She was too clever . . . too watchful. And now she was up there where the papers should have been?

He watched the girl climb carefully down. He would wait until she was safely down before he moved. It would not do to have her fall and break her pretty neck. Not yet.

His superiors had hinted that the operation at this ridiculous English girls' school would soon be terminated. He had only to pass this last package, and something had gone wrong three times. They were losing their patience with him. They would not pay him if he did not deliver this time.

It wasn't his fault.

Bumbling Lady Marchman loved books, but she was not careful with them. She had lost the first book his accomplice had given her, *Childe Harold's Pilgrimage.* The second attempt to pass the package might have been witnessed by this girl, and now the papers were gone. The third book, *The Corsair,* though it had been delivered to the school, had never made it to Lady Marchman's foolish fingers. He'd asked her about it himself this afternoon when he'd come to give the day's dancing lesson. She hadn't even seen the book.

Damn Meaghan to hell! He would beat her for being so careless with the thing. Meaghan had been playing at being Madame Briand for so long she had put on airs. Madame Briand, indeed! Meaghan actually enjoyed buying fancy English gowns and riding in Hyde Park. Faith, she'd forgotten why the two of them had come to England in the first place. Puffed up with her own importance, she was. Sure, and he'd enjoy flattening the woman, damn her.

And damn this little blonde for peeking into the library at the wrong time! How his fingers shook at the thought of tightening them around her throat!

If she did have the papers, he would have to kill her as soon as he took them from her. Damn her, she'd pay for the trouble she'd caused him.

As he watched her bare feet touched the smooth, polished wood floor of the library, he thought of the pleasure he would take from her before he snapped her neck to one side, ending her life, and he laughed softly.

She heard him and gasped. "Who is there?"

He did not answer her. He would let the fear in her grow until it consumed her reason. Then he would strike.

But she surprised him. Blowing out her candle, she made a mad rush to the door. He caught her easily and pinned her with one crushing arm while he fastened his other hand over her mouth. She struggled furiously. He would enjoy her struggles when the time came, but now they only frustrated him. He twisted her arm savagely, wrenching a satisfying cry of pain from her.

"Where are ye going in such a hurry, lass?" he said, not

bothering to replace his natural Irish brogue with the thick French accent he'd been using while he played the part of Monsieur Revelet. Brian laughed. It felt good to speak properly for once. "Ye'll stay here awhile and chat wi' me. I insist," he said. "I'm going to let ye go now. If ye try to run away or scream, I'll tell Lady Marchman ye're not what ye seem to be."

She stilled instantly, and he let her go.

"I thought that would calm ye down. Sit." He placed a hand on her shoulder and with cruel pressure pushed her down onto the floor. She looked up at him with fear in her eyes. *Good.* "We'll have our chat now." He stopped in front of her and tilted her face into the moonlight that streamed in through the windows. "Ye'll look up at me now and not look away."

He sat down on a chair and looked at her through narrowed eyes. Brian was very good at seeing into people's hearts, seeing the blackness there. If she had intercepted the book and read the messages meant for him, he would know it instantly, just by looking into her eyes.

Nigel found the door of the school unlocked. Though slightly ajar, it was not gaping open. His practiced eye saw the reason immediately: it had been wedged with a stick above the jamb. Rigged so, it was unlikely the unlocked door would be noticed by anyone, yet whoever had fixed the wedge in place could escape without making a sound. Quickly, Nigel removed it, stepped inside, and carefully replaced the wedge once more.

"Where is the book?" Brian asked bluntly. After a moment, she shook her head, but her hesitation and the panicked look in her eyes suggested she was lying. "I believe you," he lied. Settling into his chair, he regarded her closely and then began to speak. He told an old Irish tale his grandmother had told him, but as he told the story, he wove in as many of the English bastards' code words as he knew, hoping to strike one or two the girl might recognize. He watched for the signs, but her smooth, round face showed nothing but her fear.

She thought he was mad. She would pay for that, too.

Growing frustrated with her continuing look of innocence and bemusement, he uttered a particularly long string of words, a pass phrase, deliberately leaving out a word. Then he ordered her to repeat it, hoping she would slip and complete the phrase.

She appeared to try, but the results did not please him. "Again!" he ordered roughly. She complied, but the phrase was even less complete than it had been the first time she tried. He caressed her jaw and neck with his gloved fingers.

As he approached the library, Nigel heard a voice, faint, but barely intelligible. It was a man's voice, with a low Irish flavor, Nigel thought. "Where is the book?" the man asked, then after a while the voice droned on. To an unenlightened ear, the man would seem to be telling a story, but Nigel immediately recognized several English code names cleverly entwined in the tale. There must be someone else in there with the man. It must be Lady Marchman and her accomplice. Nigel's heart pumped hard and he silently cursed himself. He had no weapons with him, not even the dagger that had twice saved his life and which he normally kept hidden on his person. He had taken it off when he reached Berkeley Square and, in his impatience to see Lady Marchman, he had not remembered to bring it with him. He was going to have to take them with his bare hands. Nigel stood, his hand hovering over the brass knob of the door, waiting to spring. He had only to hear Lady Marchman speak, to get a fix on her location before he burst inside, but when he did hear a woman's voice, he did not move in, for the voice he heard was heartachingly familiar.

It was Kathryn's voice, and it froze his blood.

Her voice was quaking as she repeated a phrase the Irishman had just spoken. Nigel knew the pass phrase, but she evidently did not and was trying to memorize it. She did not repeat it with any accuracy, and the man impatiently ordered her to try again.

A surge of bile rose in Nigel's throat. Fighting the urge to rush headlong into the library, he left the house as silently as he had entered it. He walked blindly past his astonished coachman, waved his hand in dismissal, and kept on walking, until the dark streets of London swallowed him up.

"I would hate to see anything . . . ugly happen to one so young as yerself. I'll give ye one more chance," Brian O'Flaugherty said almost tenderly. "Tell me where 'tis. Give it to me, and I'll forget ye took it." He put both of his leather-sheathed hands on her neck and rubbed his thumbs up and down the delicate column. Slender and almost birdlike, it would require the barest movement to break.

"Please. I do not understand," she begged him.

He smiled at the way her voice trembled. "No, ye don't understand, do ye now?" He straightened suddenly. "Ye may go." She stood shakily. "Do not," he said softly, "tell anyone about this—or I'll have to make things quite unpleasant for ye"—he touched the open hem of her wrapper with one fingertip—"and for those ye love."

She swallowed and nodded her understanding. His hand rose, his fingertips tracing higher, skimming upward over the thin cotton which clung to her high, ripe breasts.

She fled the room, and he laughed softly. She had not found the papers. He was certain of that now, though at first he had thought she was lying about not having seen the book.

Several times over the next hour, Nigel heard stealthy feet approach from behind, but always they stopped once they closed to a certain distance. He was well known among London's poor. Cutpurses and thieves knew better than to accost the man who was famous for arguing for equal treatment under the law. If Nigel were harmed, the man who had done the deed would be found dead come morning. The fog enveloped Nigel, and he knew he was safe, though part of him wished he were not. He wished someone would cut his throat, for he knew where his duty lay.

And for the first time in his life, Nigel was considering putting that duty aside.

His love was a traitor to her country. He had ignored all the evidence: Jeremy's inability to ferret out any details of her past, the unusual timing of her arrival at the school, her apparent searching of the house as reported by Jane. Then there were the people in that other carriage, who had seemed to recognize her. And always she seemed to be listening and watching—openly when she could and covertly when she could not. He should have suspected her from the beginning, but he had let his feelings for her get in the way of his duty.

Kathryn. A beautiful, strong name for a strong, beautiful woman. A good woman. A woman who bloody well cared for children and servants and stray cats! How could she be working for the French? During his years in service to his country, Nigel had run into his share of evil men and women. But on every one of Nigel's missions, he had been acutely aware that many of the people he was trying to outsmart, outrun, or even kill were people who, like him, passionately believed in the rightness of what they were doing.

Kathryn must be one of those.

She must, like him, be risking her life for her country and her people. But he couldn't let her motives, no matter how pure, influence his decisions.

If he did not capture Kathryn, then *he* was betraying England. And yet if he did capture her, he was betraying his heart. He staggered suddenly, as though a great weight had been thrust on him. Something had to be done. She was in possession of the war plans. He had clearly heard her accomplice ask, "Where is the book?" Nigel could not let the plans cross the Channel. Even if England somehow miraculously won the resulting battle, thousands would die. And if England did not win . . .

An hour later, Kathryn was still trembling. She had not heard him leave the house. Not daring to light a candle, she crept to the window. She could not see his gig, but she had hardly expected to. He would not advertise his presence so openly. He was not supposed to be there at night. How had he got inside? Had someone at the school let him in? Another accomplice, perhaps?

From her pocket, she drew forth the newly printed copy of *The Corsair* and examined it closely. Acting on a hunch, she tore open the frontispiece and then the cover. Concealed within the spine of the book were a surprisingly thick sheaf of papers. All had writing on them. The scrawls had been made tiny to conserve space, but Kathryn could see one of the papers had several maps drawn on it, maps of various places in France and Spain. The last paper she looked at shocked her. At first glance, it appeared to be a letter. It was hard to make out, for the lines had been crossed and recrossed, but as she laboriously picked out the words by the light of the moon, she recognized many parts of the letter as words the dancing master had spoken as he had told her his strange tale.

"Monsieur Revelet" was not French, and he was not a dancing master. Kathryn realized with a cold certainty that the man with the Irish brogue and cold eyes was a spy for the French, while Madame Briand and perhaps others at the school were his accomplices.

Bells in heaven! Baroness Marchman's School for Young Ladies was their medium of passing their treacherous secrets!

What should she do? She thought of going to Lady Agnes or Mary Gant. But would they believe her? She had to admit that, in their place, she would have found such a wild story hard to believe from a mere schoolgirl—especially a schoolgirl *in her condition*, who had already been suffering the vapors. Besides, how did she know she could trust them? Anyone at the school might be involved. Even sweet old Agnes Marchman or gamine Mary Gant.

Anyone.

The book lay on the floor in front of her. Kathryn stared at it. What if one of the traitors found she had it? Would that person kill her? She was certain "Monsieur Revelet" would not hesitate to do so.

And what would happen to England if the military secrets the book contained passed into the wrong hands? Taking up the book, Kathryn dashed it into the fire. Then she folded the papers carefully and cast about the room for a hiding place. She settled upon the lining of the drapery.

There was no way to contact Auntie, at least not until she saw Nigel again and contrived to be alone with Thomas and—

Nigel! Of course! He had promised Jane he would come to see her tomorrow. Kathryn had only to wait until then. She would tell him what she had found. He would believe her. He was a military man and a member of Parliament. He would know how to proceed.

The cold and the damp drove Nigel home a little before dawn. By the time the sun had burned off the fog, he was in front of a roaring fire, getting roaring drunk.

Nigel knew what he must do, but he remained motionless, staring into the fire. He had to have absolute proof.

Morgan, Nigel's elderly butler, stood at the door of the library in Berkeley Square, watching his master. He had instructed the rest of the servants to find work that needed their urgent attention elsewhere, but Morgan stayed close by. Never, since Blackshire's poor mother had died, had the young man allowed himself to lose control like this.

An empty bottle of brandy flew through the air and smashed against the wall over the hearth. His master called for another bottle, but Morgan did not answer him. No one would answer. Instead, the old butler just stood there, keeping his silent, watchful vigil.

After a time, Morgan heard the boy take in a deep, shaky breath. "It was my birthday," his master keened. Morgan left the room and closed the door behind him. Every one of the servants was aware of the terrible misfortune that had befallen their young master so many years ago. They all knew how his heart ached every year on his birthday, and they all felt sorry, but they tried never to show any sympathy, for they knew their master hated to be pitied.

Chapter Eighteen

The Thames teemed with launches of people going to Vauxhall Gardens for the evening. Kathryn was surrounded by a boatload of laughing, chattering schoolgirls, excited by the surprise outing on which the Marquis of Blackshire was taking them. He was treating the entire school—even the servants—to a night of feasting and music and fireworks at the pleasure garden. But pleasure was the last thing Kathryn was feeling. She was terribly frightened, and she had never felt more alone in her life. An entire day had passed with not one word, written or spoken, from Nigel.

He was supposed to have accompanied them to Vauxhall, but at the last moment, Lady Marchman had received word that his arrival would be delayed. He would join them there later; they were to proceed without him.

An image of Nigel's magnificent face swept through her mind and she shivered. She clung to the image and allowed it to linger, hoping it would help her keep her growing panic at bay. Lady Marchman and Mary Gant were busy getting the girls settled into the supper boxes, and Kathryn took the opportunity to jostle herself to the back of the line of girls.

She craned her neck, hoping to catch sight of him, while in her mind the image of him did not rest. In her imagination, his hauntingly intelligent black eyes swung back and forth. He was looking for something. He was looking for—

Oh, dear Lord! She was not imagining him, she was *remembering* him. Remembering how he'd looked in the library, as she'd peered at him through the window. He'd been searching for something.

Might the papers that Madame Briand deposited there have been meant for Nigel to find?

Kathryn sat quivering, the memory of Nigel's eyes casting about the library frightening her. She wrapped her arms about herself. Had he been looking for the papers? Why?

There had been so many strange occurrences since she arrived at the school, and many of them had involved Black-shire. First, there had been Lady Jane's unusual placement in the school in the middle of the term. Then his admonishing Jane that she was at the school to observe and report back to him.

And Blackshire had lied about riding to Berkeley Square when he was really searching the library. For what was he searching if not *Childe Harold's Pilgrimage, The Corsair*, or the missing papers the lilac lady had planted in the library? Most damning of all, it seemed to Kathryn, were the words he'd spoken last night. *I wish things were different,* he'd said. *I have done things I am not proud of.*

She sat, thinking furiously, putting isolated facts together. And the more she thought, the more damning the evidence seemed. Evidence that Nigel Moorhaven, Seventh Marquis of Blackshire, was a traitor to his country. The conclusion was inescapable. She pressed her fists into her eyes and moaned raggedly.

She had been ready to tell him everything she knew. If he had come to Vauxhall when he was supposed to, she would have told him everything. What would he have done? Would he have murdered her? *If I stay, I will hurt you,* he had said in the glasshouse.

It had been too late. He'd hurt her anyway.

Kathryn wiped heavy tears of grief and mortification from her cheeks, and fled from the back of the crowd. Out of the pavilion she ran and then down one of the long walks, her flight unremarked, as far as she knew.

She sobbed openly. Several people stopped to offer her their assistance, but she waved them away. Sweet summers! She was in love with a traitor.

She ran blindly toward the docks. She wanted nothing more than to flee to Grosvenor Square and thence home to Heathford. She longed to feel her parents' loving arms about her.

As she ran headlong into a crosspath, she caught sight of Blackshire, striding purposefully up a parallel path. She gasped and ducked behind a yew. Her fright cleared her mind. She stopped crying. Her heart no longer ached. A great emptiness had opened inside her, and she felt nothing. She found she could think rationally once more.

Her mind worked with crystalline clarity. She had to go back to Lady Marchman's. The school was completely empty, as even the servants were required to chaperon at Vauxhall. No one would listen to her unless she had evidence to support her claims. She would carry away the war plans and take them to the authorities. Blackshire and his French accomplices had to be stopped.

If she could finish her search for the diary while she was there, she would, but whatever happened, there must be no great delay. All it would take to find the diary were two or three good hours of uninterrupted searching. She had scoured every inch of the house except for the highest library shelves and the chambers belonging to Lady Marchman and the maids. They were all unlikely places for the diary to be. They were also the most difficult to search without fear of being discovered.

As she paid to recross the river and hired a hack to take her with all haste back to Baroness Marchman's School for Young Ladies, Kathryn's mind tried to avoid dwelling upon

Blackshire's probable fate, but her rebellious heart would not be kept in check. The tears were flowing freely as she stepped down and paid the driver. She would stand by her decision. She had no choice but to go through with her plan. She loved her country and knew where her duty lay. Blackshire would hang, and she would hate herself forever.

Taking up a rock, she made a silent apology to Lady Marchman before smashing the glass in one of the dining room windows, which were the lowest to the ground. Taking care to avoid being cut by the saw-toothed edges of the shattered glass, she unlatched the window and climbed inside.

Jane was getting worried. No sooner than he had arrived did Nigel declare he was going to pay his respects to the Prince Regent, who was dining in the Hall of Mirrors, but he had been gone too long. Neither had it escaped her attention that Kitty had disappeared. As soon as she could, she escaped the supper box.

Nigel was not in the Hall of Mirrors. The prince was not even in attendance that night, she learned. Considering that Kitty was gone as well, Jane was left with one of two possible conclusions: either Kitty and Nigel were off trysting on the Lover's Walk here at Vauxhall, or both of them had secretly gone back to the school. Goodness! If Nigel were there to catch a spy, and Kitty were skulking about in the dark looking for whatever it was she was looking for . . .

Jane crossed the Thames and found Thomas among a throng of other waiting servants. He was napping in Nigel's carriage, the reins wrapped loosely about his fingers. Jane hated to wake him, but there was no help for it. There was no time to lose. "Thomas!" she took the reins and shook him awake.

Thomas looked around him in sleepy confusion? "Wha'?"

"Did Nigel come back across the river, Thomas?"

Thomas blinked. "He . . . he s-said . . . he . . ."

"Come on, Thomas. Pull yourself out of the fog. What did Nigel say?"

Thomas sat up and rubbed his eyes. "Nothin', miss. I ain't seen 'im," he said, then he gripped the seat and looked away.

Jane could see his knuckles were white, and the tension in his little body was great. "Have you seen Kitty?"

"No, my lady."

"Thomas, listen. This is important, a matter of life and death. You must tell me the truth. Are you sure you haven't seen her?"

Thomas's eyes grew wide at the word death. "N-no, my lady," he stammered. "I 'aven't seen 'er. Just 'im." He gasped and clapped his hand over his mouth. "Crickey."

"It is all right, Thomas. You might just have saved someone's life. Where did he go?"

"I dunno, my lady. 'E just said I wasn't to tell anybody I'd seen 'im go, an' then I seen 'im get into a hackney coach. It took off like the 'orses' tails were on fire, it did. Back the way we come to get 'ere. That's all I know, my lady. Honest!"

"Good boy, Thomas!" Jane turned the carriage about and, with much trouble, managed to drive their way out of the maze of waiting carriages. She whipped up the horses and headed for Silver Street.

"Beggin' your pardon, my lady, but where are we 'eadin' to?"

"Lady Marchman's School for Young Ladies."

"Is Miss Kitty in trouble?"

"She is missing, Thomas."

Thomas held out his hands. "Then you better let me take the reins, my lady. There's somewhere else we ought to check first. It's on the way. An' if Miss Kitty is in trouble, we should tell 'im, even if'n she's not there."

"Tell who, Thomas?" Jane asked, handing over the reins.

"Mr. Ben Dullson," Thomas answered. "A bloke what lives in Grosvenor Square."

* * *

Nigel's knife was drawn and his muscles compressed to spring when the glass splintered somewhere down on the first floor of the school. Only his years of service and his rigid self-control allowed him to avoid flinching and giving his presence away. There was more than one intruder in the house. He made no move to investigate. There was a man—he was sure it was a man, just by the scent—somewhere above him on the third floor. And the man knew Nigel was there as well.

Who was he, this man who would betray England? Was he Kathryn's friend? Or her lover? The thought struck him with a force that took his breath away. Jane had told him there was a girl at the school who was expecting. Could it be Kathryn? Had the man he now stalked put a child into her belly? He tried to shrug off the thought. It did not matter, he told himself. *She* did not matter. But he knew, even as the thought crossed his mind, that he lied to himself. He had to steel his mind. He had to concentrate, or he'd get himself killed. With an effort, he turned his mind to the danger before him.

Nigel had been aware of the intruder's presence since he had arrived. The dastard was taking no care to hide himself. He was bold as a miller's shirt. He'd left the door unlocked, and he was carrying a candle around to light his way. Nigel had lain in wait downstairs for his enemy to come down, but the traitor did not show. Nigel could not wait any longer, so he crept slowly upstairs. When one of the treads creaked, the candlelight disappeared. The intruder was no longer bold. He was cautious, expertly stealthy, and almost silent.

But not as silent as Nigel. Nigel almost had him when the sound of shattering glass broke the stillness. Nigel's attention wavered for a split second, and his opponent escaped, but Nigel doubted he would leave. There was something in this house that the spy wanted enough to kill for, Nigel was sure.

It was also enough for Nigel to die for.

The war plans were in the house. England's security. And proof of Kathryn's innocence—or guilt. He continued his hunt, even though the odds against him had just multiplied with the arrival of the second intruder.

The second man would either run or he would be upon Nigel as soon as the first man screamed. With a blow at just the right angle, Nigel knew he could render the man unconscious instantly, but it would be impossible to deliver the blow with the needed accuracy in total darkness. Nigel knew he could kill them both, but Sir Winston thought it vital that the spies be brought in unharmed or at least still able to speak.

Nigel wasn't going to let either of them escape. England was depending upon him. Thoughts of Jane flashed through his mind. He hoped she was not alarmed about his prolonged absence from the supper-box back at Vauxhall. It could not be helped. If he had told her where he was going, he had no doubt she would have found a way to follow him.

Nigel crept through the house, his senses alert for any movement, any odor, current, or sound that would allow him to strike. He would not fail—except in one regard.

He was going to let Kathryn go.

Hell, he would *force* her to go. He knew certain parties who would deliver human cargo anywhere in the world. When he found her, he'd probably have to knock the hellcat out. She'd wake up on a ship bound for America.

And Nigel would have to live with the terrible knowledge that he'd betrayed his country.

There was another English pig-dog in the house, and a foolish one by the sound of it, Brian O'Flaugherty thought as he listened to the glass breaking downstairs. He used the opportunity to slip away from the other English bastard. He, damn him, was not the oaf the one downstairs evidently was. Perhaps the clumsy one would serve to distract the other one long enough for Brian to kill him. Or perhaps Brian should kill the clumsy one first. Painfully, if possible.

Screams would certainly serve as a distraction to the clever one.

Brian wanted nothing more than to retrieve the plans and collect his reward, a portion of gold the French had promised would see him safely back to Ireland and living in comfort for the rest of his days. No longer would he be at the mercy of an English landlord. He would be free. And no more playing the part of the mincing, sniveling dancing master. He was even willing to give up on taking his pleasure from one of the girls at the school. Meaghan would serve well as the receptacle of his anger. She was the cause of this delay. She was the one responsible for placing the plans into Lady Marchman's hands. Though he did not intend to kill her, he would make sure she knew how much trouble she had been to him.

On the other hand, if Meaghan were dead, then there would be no one demanding a share of the gold. . . .

Suddenly, he heard a loud thump downstairs and just below him. A piece of heavy furniture toppled, crashing to the floor, and a high-pitched wail welled up from the second floor.

"Owee-me . . . owee-me . . . oweeeeeeeee!"

Chapter Nineteen

A cruel smile sharply curved the hard planes of Brian O'Flaugherty's mouth. So . . . it was the wee blonde. That was the only person it could be. Foolish little pea-brain. Didn't she realize what she was doing was dangerous? Hadn't he shown her last night he was dangerous? The senseless chit, didn't she know he wanted to kill her? It was her own fault. He would take care of her first, and then he would kill the other one. But he could not rush. No, he had to take his time, be silent. The other one was not senseless. He was cunning, and adept. Probably a government agent. Yes, he would have to be careful. Mustn't hurry. Slowly, he made his way to the back stairs.

When he heard the woman cry out, Nigel recognized the sound instantly, for he had heard it twice before. It was Titania, his fairy queen. Rose. And there was only one explanation for her being here.

Titania and Kitty Davidson . . . Kathryn . . . Rose . . . They were all the same woman.

He was stunned.

What kind of fool was he? How could he have been so blind? He ground his teeth together to stop himself from issuing an oath. He had noted the resemblance between the fairy and Kitty/Kathryn. Kathryn had Titania's same halo of golden curls, the flashing blue eyes . . . and angry words which stung like a magic wand applied to one's backside. Why had he never considered they were one and the same? He cursed himself.

And yet, even now that his knowledge was certain, now that he *knew* who she was—who she'd been—he still found it nearly impossible to reconcile her different personas into one being. She was a schoolgirl and a woman grown, a spy and Ophelia Palin's close friend. A gallant rescuer, and a traitor to her country. She was a tiny, fiery bundle of contradiction, and he had a hard time believing both sides of her could coexist.

Perhaps they could not. Perhaps she was somehow being coerced into passing the secrets. She was not a very practiced spy. The front door was unlocked and open when she arrived, yet she had loudly broken a window to gain entry. Why?

Did it mean she did not know her accomplice was already in the house? Or did it mean she was entirely innocent? That she was here for some other reason?

He had to find out. If she were taking part in all of this against her will, he must save her. But he had to find her first—find her, silence her without killing her, interrogate her . . . and still deal with the other spy. Swearing silently, Nigel hid his pistol under the cushion of the couch and then moved off toward the front stairway. He could not afford for the gun to go off during a struggle.

And his fairy turned hellcat would struggle like a demon, he was sure.

Kathryn's toe was definitely broken this time. "Damn it to bloody, deuced, devilish hell!" Her parents would be shocked at her language, but then her parents would be shocked at most of what she had done since she came to

London, and why shouldn't they be? Kathryn herself was shocked at all she had done.

When she had run into the heavy dining chair and knocked the thing over, she had tumbled with it. She tried to stand, but pain shot up her leg. How could a thing as small as a toe cause such big trouble? She pulled off her shoe and yelped with agony. Gingerly, she felt her toe. Her fingers came away wet, for her stocking was soaked with blood from her lower leg downward. It was more than a toe this time.

The school was completely dark. Because all of the servants were at Vauxhall, every hint of flame had been extinguished for fear of fire. There was no way, barring flint and steel, for Kathryn to light a candle except for the lamp, which by law burned at the front door and lighted the street.

Slowly and painfully, Kathryn made her way to the front door, a candle in hand. The door was slightly ajar. The light of the moon shone through. She was certain she remembered Lady Marchman locking the door with her great ring of keys before they left for Vauxhall.

Which meant someone else was in the house.

Monsieur Revelet's fiendish features came to mind. Madame Briand had visited the school that day. If she had left something for him today, why of course he would take advantage of the vacant house in order to retrieve whatever it was. Or perhaps she had left nothing at all. Perhaps he was still looking for the plans Kathryn found and hid last night. Suddenly, Kathryn heard a nail squeak in a loose tread on the front stairs. Step number ten. After traversing them several times at night, she knew them by heart. Number ten was just inches from her head.

Kathryn's heart pounded in her ears, and she shrank back into the deep shadows under the staircase.

What was she going to do now? If he saw her, he would kill her, she was certain. She could not run on her injured foot, and how could she even think of leaving when all of England depended upon her? She could not let him seize those plans. She had to do something, but what? What could she do when she could not see her own hand held six inches in front of her face?

Carefully, slowly, she backed against the wall and moved toward the small hall tree that stood under the stairs. Kathryn reached it just as she sensed a stealthy movement directly in front of her.

Groping wildly, she grabbed the first solid object she came to and brought it down upon what she hoped would be the villain's head. The heavy brass candleholder made solid contact and, to her amazement and joy, a large, heavy body fell at her feet. She had done it!

Kneeling, she reached for the man. Her hands made contact with his wide torso, and she patted her way up to his neck. Untying his cravat might have been much more trouble, but the loose mail-coach knot was not as much of a challenge as an Oriental or a Mathematical would have been, she thought. Her fingers stilled. Blackshire wore a mail-coach. Her fingers flew to his hair and face. She knew every contour. She had dreamed of touching him this way, in the dark. She snatched her hands away as though they had been burned. "Oh, my . . ." she said aloud. "You are not Monsieur Revelet, are you?" Had she killed him? Had she killed the only man she would ever love? She cradled his head in her lap, and leaning over him, caressed his cheek. "Do not die. Do not die, my love, for I could not bear it."

Laughter welled up from the darkness down the hall. "He is not 'Monsieur Revelet'—and, come to think of it, neither am I," the Irishman's voice piped with an uncanny cheerfulness into the night. "Ye're between me and the front door. I can see your silhouette. If ye move, I'll kill him. If ye haven't done the job yerself already, that is." He laughed again.

Kathryn's arms tightened reflexively about Nigel's broad shoulders. The Irishman must not know it was his accomplice who lay inert on the floor. "Monsieur Revelet, this is Nigel

Moorhaven,'' she said before a notion struck her. "Are you not working together?"

"I wish we were," the dancing master answered. "He works for England, and he is a worthy opponent. To think he was felled by such a puny chit! I can't wait to tell 'im. The knowledge will prick his puffed-up English ego. It'll be amusing. And don't call me 'Monsieur.' The French are no better than you filthy English. My name is O'Flaugherty. Brian O'Flaugherty."

A thrill of dread coursed through Kathryn as she realized he intended to kill them both. Otherwise, he would not have told her his name. She had to stall him somehow. Perhaps someone would discover them both missing and come looking for them. Sure, and a mackerel would be crowned Lord Mayor tomorrow. No one would come.

"I . . . I don't understand," she said to keep him talking as she tried to formulate a plan. "I thought you were working for France."

"I work for meself. No one else. I am free, as all of Ireland will be someday. Don't move. My gun is pointed right at yer head." He moved past her to the front stoop, where he held a candle to the outside lamp. He did indeed have a pistol. Kathryn did not dare to move. She dared not provoke him into shooting Nigel. Nigel . . . who was not a spy for France after all, but a true English hero! Her hero. Kathryn's heart soared and then plunged. He would be a dead hero unless she could do something about O'Flaugherty.

O'Flaugherty motioned her aside with his gun and then ripped Nigel's waistcoat and shirt open. He took two knives from Nigel's person. One was quite large and not very well concealed in a small, narrow scabbard Nigel had sewn inside his boot. The other was much smaller. Nigel had worn it strapped to his waist underneath his shirt. O'Flaugherty backed away, tucking the knives into a leather pouch that hung about his waist. He waved the gun at Kathryn again. "Untie his cravat."

"I beg your pardon?"

"Do it!" he cried, and Kathryn moved to comply, but when she tried to kneel, pain streaked through her injured leg and she fell. When the length of white linen was undone, O'Flaugherty ordered Kathryn to bind Nigel's hands and feet, directing her movements as she did so. When she tried to roll Nigel's inert body over in order to gather his hands behind his back, Kathryn did not have the strength. O'Flaugherty drew back his arm and backhanded her across her cheekbone, knocking her over. With his heavy boot, he savagely kicked Nigel's ribs, turning him over onto his belly. She crawled back to Nigel and bound his hands, then O'Flaugherty tied her hands. Leaving her feet unbound, he disappeared into the gloom. Returning with a large pitcher of water and a kitchen towel, he gagged Nigel and then threw the water onto his head.

Nigel gasped and sputtered. He came to, shaking himself and looking wildly around him. "It is all right," Kathryn said, wanting to reassure him. He looked pointedly about them and then back over at her before grunting and rolling his eyes. Everything was clearly *not* all right. "Yes. I know," she said quietly.

"Enough!" roared O'Flaugherty. "You will now tell me where the books are—all of them—or I will begin cutting off his fingers."

"Go ahead," Kathryn said blithely. "I do not care a fig about him. Hand me the knife and I will do it myself." She spared a glance at Nigel and a part of her died, for his eyes were full of shock and pain at her words—the pain of unrequited love. He did love her, after all!

O'Flaugherty sneered. "Oh, come. Do not insult my intelligence." In a high-pitched voice he mocked Kathryn's words to Blackshire: " 'Do not die, my love, for I could not bear it!' " He laughed and Kathryn threw him a venomous look and clamped her mouth shut.

"Very well then." He shrugged. "If you do not care about his fingers, perhaps you care about your own." He pulled the longer of Nigel's knives from his pouch and twirled it expertly in his hands. Nigel growled low in his throat and lunged upward, trying to free himself. He struggled for a moment, then a moan escaped him and he collapsed, his head rolling limply to one side. His breath issued from his throat in a weak hiss, and then he was still.

The candlelight glinted off the cold, smooth metal of the dagger and Kathryn felt her stomach lurch. She looked away. "Please, Mr. O'Flaugherty, I . . . I don't know what books you are talking about. I told you that before."

He approached her, his mouth shaping itself into a grin. "I grow impatient."

"If it is money you want, I have almost ten guineas upstairs, in my valise. It is yours."

He shook his head and took a step closer to Kathryn and Nigel, caressing the handle of the dagger. "Sorry, me girl, but it isn't enough. I've been promised a lot more, ye see, upon completion of me job. Now, where are the books?"

Kathryn watched him approach. She feared him, but she would not tell him where the plans were no matter what he did to her. O'Flaugherty knelt beside her and reached for her. His bare fingers caressed her neck before trailing down her arm and grasping the linen that bound her wrists together. Kathryn tried to be brave as he brought the knife down and laughed, an unearthly sound that echoed through the house.

Just before the steel touched her skin, movement exploded beside her as Nigel propelled his powerful legs upward with deadly accuracy, kicking O'Flaugherty in the face and knocking him to the floor. The knife flew through the air and skidded across the floor just out of Nigel's reach. Kathryn dove for the blade, but O'Flaugherty was upon her in seconds, and the other knife he had taken from Nigel appeared at her throat.

"Another move and I'll kill her!" O'Flaugherty cried.

Nigel stilled, his fingers just touching the long dagger. O'Flaugherty pushed Kathryn roughly aside and kicked the second dagger, which spun away across the floor from

Nigel's bound hands. O'Flaugherty approached Nigel and raised the dagger he still held.

Time seemed to stretch crazily as he brought the dagger down and stabbed Nigel with it. The blade entered Nigel's chest just under his shoulder. Kathryn heard herself scream as Nigel's body jerked convulsively back and his face contorted in pain.

O'Flaugherty wrenched the blade out of Nigel, who grunted and gasped for air through clenched teeth. "Now then," O'Flaugherty said to Kathryn with menacing civility, "ye'll tell me where the plans are or I'll kill him."

Nigel shook his head violently. His eyes implored Kathryn not to comply. She looked away from him. Steadily holding O'Flaugherty's gaze, she said, "The first room on the right on the second floor. The papers are in the hem of the drapery. I burned the book I found them in. I do not know where the other books are."

Without a word, O'Flaugherty scooped up the long knife and calmly climbed the stairs, taking the candlelight with him. Kathryn watched Nigel close his eyes and, exhaling forcibly, let his head drop to the floor, as the circle of light receded upward. Before they were plunged into darkness, she saw a great fall of blood gush from the gaping wound in his shoulder. "Oh! Nigel, do not move. You are bleeding profusely."

Nigel mumbled something and strained against his gag. The light disappeared completely, and they were plunged into darkness once more. Kathryn scooted along the floor toward Nigel and leaned over as far as she could. "Hold still. I'm going to get that gag off you." She leaned a little further and toppled on top of him as she knew she would. He was warm and solid, and it was hard to believe he was going to be dead soon. But Kathryn did believe that. They were both going to die.

Walking her way upward with her chin, she maneuverd her face next to his, and with her teeth pulled the gag free. "You should not have told him where the plans were."

"I am sorry," Kathryn whispered. "I could not let him kill you."

"He will kill me anyway. He will kill us both."

Kathryn shivered. She knew it was true, but she did not wish to frighten him with her hopelessness. She grumbled. "You are a pessimist."

"And you are a nuisance."

"You didn't seem to think so last night in the glasshouse."

"I did not say I did not like you. I simply said you are bothersome. You cannot deny it, now can you? Even more so than Jane. How can one eighteen-year-old cause so much havoc?"

"You like me?"

"I did not say that either. You have much explaining to do before I'll admit to liking you."

"And so do you."

"Men do not have to explain things to their women."

"Not all men feel like that. Just the self-centered, bad-tempered men like you. Especially you, you ... 'their women'?" Kathryn asked, her mind just then realizing the significance of his words. "I am yours?" she asked softly.

"No, you are not, for I do not like nuisances," Nigel said. He grunted and Kathryn felt him twist his body to one side. He stifled a groan of pain. "Damn it to hell! I cannot get to my knife. You'll have to extract it for me."

"You have a knife?! Why did you not tell me sooner? We have wasted precious seconds. Extract it? Extract it from where?"

"You are not going to like this," Nigel said, and he told her where.

Minutes later, Kathryn felt the knife's handle against her hesitant fingers. "Why," she asked, "do you keep your knife there?"

"At least the metal is nice and warm," he said.

"You are grinning," she accused.

"How can you tell?"

Kathryn did not know how she knew, but she was certain

of it nevertheless. He was smiling broadly. "I am guessing, you beast," she said. "You cad . . . you . . . you . . . man!"

"How pleased I am you noticed my gender. Do have a care when removing the blade from the scabbard, Miss Davidson."

"I ought to yank it free and attempt to conduct an orchestra on the way."

He laughed softly, then fell into a spate of coughing.

Kathryn said no more, and continued to move slowly and carefully. As she worked, the silence of the house bore down upon Kathryn and her hands stilled. "Listen!" she whispered. "I don't hear anything."

"You are not likely to. O'Flaugherty left by the back door two minutes ago."

"I did not hear him," Kathryn said, skeptically, "and I have excellent hearing."

"Nor did I, dear heart. Nevertheless, I am certain he is gone, for the back door has created a draft, which has carried the smell of smoke to my nostrils. O'Flaugherty has set the school afire."

A tide of dread licked at Kathryn's remaining courage. "Then this is how it is to end?"

"Who is a pessimist now? You have almost worked the knife free."

Just then, the front door burst open, and Jane's clear voice came to them. "Nigel? Kitty?"

"Her name is really Kathryn, dear," a gravely, tremulous voice corrected her.

"Aunt Ophelia?" Kathryn called, frantically trying to work her hands free of Nigel's breeches. "Are Mama and Papa with you?"

John's baritone boomed through the entry hall. "Your mama and papa remain blessedly ignorant of your adventures, Miss Kathryn. They are still asleep in Grosvenor Square. The old dragon here has told them you are visiting friends of hers in Scotland."

"John!" Kathryn sang out joyously.

"John?" Nigel muttered. "Mama and Papa? Aunt Ophelia! You have a great deal of explaining to do," he told Kathryn.

Kathryn groaned and continued to struggle. "She is my great-aunt, actually. And *why,*" she whispered fiercely, "do you wear your blasted breeches so tight?"

Ophelia's voice wailed into the darkness, "Oh, Kathryn, I am so sorry. I was mistaken about the diary. I did not leave it here at the school at all. I would have sent you word as soon as I found out, but little Thomas stopped coming to Grosvenor Square with your messages."

Nigel put his head to Kathryn's. "Diary?" he asked. "That is why you are here? To find Ophelia Palin's lost diary?"

"Yes," Kathryn said. "Did you think I was a spy?"

"For a time, yes. But you thought the same of me, did you not?"

Kathryn knew he felt her head nod, for he chuckled softly.

With a lantern held high, Jane approached. Upon seeing their forms stretched out side by side on the floor, she exclaimed, "Oh, poor dears! Are you hurt?" Then she reached them and held the lantern over them, illuminating them completely. "Oh!" she said, her eyebrows raised.

Ophelia puffed up beside Jane, with John close behind. "I was mistaken. The diary was never . . . oh!" Her eyes widened as she, too, absorbed the sight in front of her. A ghost of a smile traced her lips and she clapped her hands together, but she lowered them almost immediately and then she gasped—a little too dramatically, Kathryn thought. "Blackshire," she said sternly, "I shall expect an announcement to appear in the newspapers on the morrow."

"Aye, and if'n it doesn't, I'll expect to see you at Bethnel Green at dawn the very next day," John said, his voice menacing.

Kathryn sputtered and tugged at her hands, frantically shaking her head. "No. You do not understand. It is not how it looks. I am just—"

Blackshire cut her off. "Yes ma'am. Yes sir. Now, if you will be so kind as to untie me—"

"Ladies first," Jane said and pulled from a carefully concealed slit in her dress a dagger with a jeweled handle. With a flick of her wrist, she had freed Kathryn. She moved on to Nigel next.

Kathryn said, "Give me your dagger, Jane. The school is on fire. Help Auntie outside, and I will cut Nigel loose. Then alert the neighbors and send someone for a physician." Jane and the slow-moving Ophelia hastened to comply.

"Mr. Robertson," Nigel ordered, "make haste to the War Offices and insist on speaking to Sir Winston. Tell them that the Blue Devil sent you. They will understand. Tell them what you know. Tell them the name Brian O'Flaugherty."

"Yes sir. Anything for Kathryn's fiancé," he said meaningfully and quit the school.

"There is something I wish to say to you, away from the others," Kathryn said when they were alone again.

"Kathryn, listen to me. There is no time for words. O'Flaugherty is getting away, and if he does, all of England is in peril. You must believe me. I promise you complete truth as soon as I return. Cut me loose."

"As soon as you return? From where?" But Kathryn knew the answer, and she was afraid.

She refused to cut the clean linen cravat restraining his hands. She unwound it instead and used it to bind his wound.

Nigel protested. "Hurry. Losing time is bad, Kathryn."

She kept on working. "Losing blood is worse. You'll be no good to anyone if you collapse. And, if you are dead"— she cinched the knot tight and he winced—"then you shall not be able to tell me the truth. All of the truth," she said meaningfully.

Nodding his understanding, he freed his feet with an expert flip of the dagger and Kathryn shivered. Lifting her with his one good arm, he helped her to the street. Ophelia and Jane were already out of sight.

Kathryn bowed her head toward him and pressed her face

into his chest. She inhaled, taking in the scent of him, and
then she spoke softly. "And, Nigel—" She pushed down
a sob. "Nigel, if you die you shall not be able to show me
how differently from an eighteen-year-old a man kisses a
twenty-two-year-old."

"Twenty-two," Nigel repeated. He took her by the shoulders then and kissed Kathryn. Roughly, hastily, yet gently
and with an urgency that had nothing to do with time. "I
promise you truth," he said. Then he was gone.

"But you did not promise me love," she whispered.

When Nigel limped back into Silver Street an hour later,
he carried several more wounds. A light rain had begun.
Nigel's clothes were covered in half-dried blood, though he
was unsure of whose it was. Baroness Marchman's School
was a blackened skeleton of glowing timbers against the
cloudy sky. He pushed his way through the sea of people
who had come to watch the fire consume the old house or
to take part in the fire brigade. Their faces glowed orange
against the remaining pockets of fire, and some of the poor
were already braving the heat and the danger from falling
debris to scavenge through the perimeter of the burned hulk.
Seeing Nigel, many of them offered whatever meager assistance they could provide, but he waved them away. The
only salve he needed was Kathryn. Suddenly, a small hand
touched his shoulder and Nigel turned. It was Kathryn.

"The plans?" she asked.

"Safe," he answered. "Some men . . . friends of mine,"
he whispered enigmatically, with a meaningful glance at the
crowd that was gathering around them, "are looking for Mr.
O'Flaugherty's acquaintances."

Kathryn nodded her understanding.

"Everything will be taken care of by morning." Nigel's
eyes flicked over her shoulder. "There is your aunt."

Ophelia emerged from the crowd. Kathryn took her hand
and asked after Jane and John. Ophelia explained the two
had gone back to Grosvenor Square to tell the entire story

to Kathryn's parents. "Good," Kathryn said with a glance at Nigel. "I cannot bear to keep secrets from those I love."

"Poor Agnes," Ophelia said, staring at the burned-out school. "She will have no place to live." Tears of genuine sympathy brimmed in her eyes.

"My dear lady," Nigel said, lowering his voice and shielding his words from the ears of the crowd with his body, "you needn't worry about where Lady Marchman will sleep. There is a bed waiting for her at Ludgate, though I am sure it will not be to her liking."

Kathryn's eyes widened? "Lady Marchman? A spy?"

Nigel nodded gravely. "She has been receiving large payments for forty years from an unknown source. It is very likely she was a French sympathizer all those years."

"Oh, my!" Ophelia said. "You . . . you may want to tell your friends to hold off on arresting her, my boy." Her face reddened, and she looked embarrassed. "You see," she explained, "I am afraid *I* am Agnes Marchman's unknown benefactor."

"Auntie! I thought you disliked Lady Marchman."

Ophelia gave a sheepish half grin and a shrug. "We have been great rivals," she said as though that explained everything. She suddenly appeared to find something of intense interest on the ground several paces away and knelt there.

Nigel smiled after her. "The old shammer." He turned back to Kathryn and looked deeply into her eyes. "I see love in your heart," he said as he took her head in his hands. "But I also see mistrust. It is time to answer your questions. Ask them."

Kathryn chuckled. "There is little need. Jane told me what she knows, and of course—"

"Of course Jane knows everything," he finished wryly and sighed. "That girl is a sneak."

Kathryn grinned. "At least she comes by the trait honestly." She stepped closer to him and looked into his eyes.

"Aw, go on . . . kiss 'er!" someone called from the crowd.

Though they could not hear Nigel and Kathryn's private words to each other, they could easily see the love that moved back and forth between the two like leaves swirling in the wind.

Nigel smiled. "These people"—he made a sweeping gesture toward the crowd—"are my friends."

"I know," Kathryn said. "I have spoken with many of them. The children, especially, seem to love you. It is no wonder you do not travel to your estate in Northumberland. It must be overrun with animals."

Nigel shrugged.

" 'At ain't no way to treat a lai-dee, me lord! Kiss 'er! She wants you to. Any bloody fool kin see 'at!' "

"Kiss 'er . . . kiss 'er . . . kiss 'er . . . !" The gathering crowd took up the chant and pressed closer. Nigel and Kathryn no longer had any privacy, even for words. Kathryn lowered her eyes. He did not need to see her face to know she was blushing.

"Well then," he said loudly, "I mustn't disappoint her, right?"

"Right!" "Right-o!" Whistles and catcalls broke out spontaneously as the crowd realized he was playing into their hands and the pretty lady was obviously embarrassed—but willing. The rain was coming down much harder now, but the crowd continued to swell, and Nigel's heart with it. These people were his friends. He had fought for them in France. He had fought for them in Parliament. They protected him on the streets, they cheered him when he passed. They had been his family. It was fitting that they should be here with him on this occasion.

Nigel spotted Ophelia Palin at the edge of the mob.

"Kiss her," she mouthed silently, her eyes sparkling.

Nigel smiled broadly. "Well now . . . I cannot kiss her," he said. The crowd booed and moaned, then quieted, sensing he was only jesting. "After all," Nigel said, allowing his deep voice to boom over the crowd. "I cannot kiss a lady to whom I am not betrothed."

Kathryn watched him, her gaze as soft as a caress as she waited for what she knew must follow. He did not want to disappoint her. Slowly, carefully—and somewhat painfully—Nigel removed his coat, then his azure brocade waistcoat. As he held her gaze, her eyes never wavered, but they had taken on a teary sheen.

The crowd fell to an expectant silence.

"The color blue," Nigel said in a voice designed to carry, "has always meant pain and loneliness to me," he announced. "If this lady will do me the honor of becoming my wife, I know I shall never be lonely again, and my pain will be a thing of the past." There on the street, in front of a hundred witnesses, with water streaming down his face, Nigel knelt. He held out to her his blue waistcoat, now stained dark with blood. "Will you, beautiful Kathryn, be my wife and make me the happiest of men?"

Kathryn took the waistcoat from him. She swallowed. All eyes were on her as the crowd waited breathlessly for her answer. The only sound was the rain pattering on clothing, oilskin, and cobblestones, and the pop and hiss of the steam that rose as the drops fell on the coals. She hugged the waistcoat to her breast and then walked over to the glowing rubble. She stood there for a moment as time stood still, and then she threw the garment onto the coals and turned. Her gaze flicked across his, and then, to his surprise, she let her eyes play across the crowd, feigning to seek their approval.

She had it.

The men waved their caps in the air, and the ladies were nearly all dabbing at their cheeks as they wished them both happy. She smiled at them and nodded, before turning slowly to him and winking. He took her hands and squeezed them lightly. Stepping closer to her, he whispered "Thank you."

Her smile grew sweet and wistful, and when she spoke at last, he knew she had forgotten the burned hulk of the school, the crowd, the rain. He was the only thing in her world as she looked into his eyes. "Yes," she whispered.

Kathryn was surprised to find she did, after all, have a blush left in her, for she felt her skin burning crimson as Nigel enfolded her in his arms and she became aware of the crowd once more.

"What did she say?" one old lady asked.

"What did she say . . . what did she say . . . ?" The rest of the crowd took up the chant.

"Yes!" Kathryn called out, laughing. "I said yes!"

The crowd roared. "Kiss 'er!" And Nigel did.

Epilogue

The last ball guest had left an hour before, and the sun was beginning to rise in the east. Still, Kathryn was unable to tear herself away from the window. She could not stop worrying over the absence of Ophelia and John. Coming up behind her, Nigel pulled her into the comfort of his strong embrace.

"Do not worry," he said, nuzzling her ear. "They are probably together."

"Oh, Nigel, that is exactly why I *am* worried. You know they detest each other. If they are together, it is probably because they are plotting to do harm to each other as we speak. Or perhaps the harm is already done, and the victor has cheerfully paused to dig a shallow grave."

Kathryn and Nigel had come home from their wedding trip the previous day. Ophelia had given them a welcome-home ball as a surprise, but the biggest surprise of all was that the old lady had not been in attendance. During the late supper after the ball, John was discovered missing, too.

Kathryn was truly worried. For as long as she could

remember, the two had been swapping insults. Had their forced company finally allowed their mutual hatred to simmer into violence? What else could explain their absence?

Kathryn was so tired she was close to weeping. The ball had been merry. Nigel had so many friends. The ladies had been openly envious of her, though pleasantly so, and they all wanted to know how she had snared the Marquis of Blackshire, while the gentlemen all wanted to dance with her. Kathryn hated to disappoint them all, but her husband had been quite unwilling to share her. They had danced until, laughing, Kathryn had begged to sit down, whereupon a throng of well-wishers surrounded her and Nigel—including a smiling Lord Arborough, whom Kathryn had informed of his unwitting role in her adventure.

Even her parents had abandoned their country ways for the evening. Declaring themselves charmed by Nigel, they had danced and drunk champagne with as much enthusiasm as anyone. They were truly happy for their daughter. The ball had been delightful.

Except for Ophelia and John's absence.

"Dear heart," Nigel said, rubbing his thumb across her shoulders, "you need not worry about Ophelia and John. Jeremy Scott took me aside a few moments ago. He told me the Home Office has finished its investigation."

"I do not know why they had to pry into my aunt's past. She was most upset about it, and she is no more a spy than I am."

"I know, love, but Sir Winston leaves no stone unturned. That is why he has remained in his post for so many years. He is very good at keeping England safe."

She nodded and smiled ruefully. She was still worried. "What has the end of the investigation to do with Auntie's disappearance?"

"The investigation uncovered a secret—something she has kept hidden for many years."

"Oh, yes. I already know about it, Nigel. She was secretly helping her 'rival' Lady Marchman for many years. That was the 'terrible scandal' she'd written of in her diary. Can you imagine? I went through all of that just to keep that one fact hidden!''

"Mmm . . . not exactly."

Kathryn crooked an eyebrow at him. "Oh?"

Nigel smiled. "It seems that was only one of the dear lady's secrets. The other concerns John."

"John?"

Nigel nodded. "Dearest, Ophelia and John were married thirty years ago tonight." His eyes sparkled with laughter.

Kathryn opened her mouth to reply, but she was interrupted by the sound of carriage wheels and horse's hooves. Nigel and Kathryn emerged onto the wide front stoop as Auntie's black lacquered coach pulled to a halt on the circular drive, and John stepped down to help Ophelia alight. Seeing Kathryn, the old lady blushed like a schoolroom miss.

John tucked her arm in his and bowed slightly to Kathryn and Nigel. "May I present Mrs. Ophelia Robertson!" he said proudly.

"We . . . we have eloped," Ophelia said. "We went to Gretna Green." Nigel and Kathryn traded conspiratorial smiles. "We meant to be back sooner, but . . ." Her words trailed off into an embarrassed sigh.

John put his arm around Ophelia's shoulders. "What the old dragon means to say is that we would ha' been back fer the ball, but I insisted on stoppin' fer some weddin' night capers." Ophelia batted at him with her fan, but she was giggling girlishly. "She can't get enough of me, you know," John said, ushering Ophelia inside and right up the stairs with a spate of loving pinches and tickles.

"Oh, and, Kathryn dearling," Ophelia called from the landing, "I . . . I hardly know how to say this, but . . . since we're all family now—" She patted John's cheek and whispered the rest. "Well . . . since I am a national heroine for rescuing you and catching the spy and all—"

Kathryn spared a glance for Nigel, who was doing very

well—much better than she—at concealing a grin, but his eyes were dancing nonetheless, for Ophelia was not the only one who had been commended by the Prince Regent. John and Kathryn had also been named in the official proclamation, though Nigel, of course, had not been publicly recognized.

"—and since Agnes and I are not . . . not equal anymore . . ." Ophelia stammered to a halt.

"Yes, Auntie?"

"Well . . . life just won't be the same without . . . I just cannot imagine life without . . . without . . ."

"Without Agnes breathin' fire up your skirts?" John supplied helpfully.

Ophelia swatted him playfully, but it was clear her rivalry with Lady Marchman would be missed. "I think you can help me, Kathryn," Ophelia said.

"Anything, Auntie."

"Oh, good. Just good." Ophelia turned to leave.

"Auntie?" Kathryn called after her. "What do you want me to do?"

"Return the diary to Lady Marchman's school, of course. Can you think of another way?"

Nigel grinned. "You are correct, Ophelia. It is the only way. I'm sure Kathryn will think of something." He smiled mischievously down at his wife.

"Call me 'Auntie,' my boy."

"Quit yer yammerin' ye old hag, and get movin'."

"Watch yourself, John. Do not forget I am your old hag, now." She smiled sweetly, and John resumed his pinching and tickling as she preceded him up the stairs.

Kathryn looked after them, her heart full of happiness for them—and for herself.

"Well," Nigel said at her side and scooped her up into his arms. "I suppose it is time, once again, for us to perform our sacred duty to our country!" He sighed dramatically and trudged up the stairs.

Kathryn echoed his sigh. ''I shall try to lie still and think of my Queen.''

''Liar,'' Nigel whispered.

Kathryn only laughed, happy to have been wrong about a great number of things.

ACKNOWLEDGMENTS

This, my first book, could not have happened without the love and support of many people. I must thank authors Adrienne Hardie, Ann Bair, Terri Lynn Wilhelm, and the late Carol Quinto for their kind patience with a pesky and clueless greenhorn; Mary Louise Wells, Debra Barr, and my brother (my very own St. David!), who were present at the birthing of this story; my kind editor, Amy Garvey, who plucked me from obscurity; my trusty and tigery literary agent, Jennifer Jackson; the 99ers, my life-line; my test-readers Erica, Jude, Stephanie, a lovely lady whose name I have lost (I'm so sorry!), and my own dear mama; my little girls, who love videos and PB&J's, bless them; too many overworked librarians and teachers to name; and my Golden Heart judges.

Thank you all.

And thanks also to you, dear reader. I do hope you enjoyed this tale!

ABOUT THE AUTHOR

Melynda Beth Skinner was born in 1963 in Florida, where she still lives with her husband of ten years and their two charming hellions, little girls who could easily be mistaken for angels, from time to time. The author enjoys hearing from readers, and you may write to her at 7259 Aloma Avenue, Suite 2, Box 31, Winter Park, FL 32792. Please enclose a SASE if you wish a reply. Or visit her online at *www.melyndabethskinner.com.*

If you enjoyed this story, you may also enjoy the forthcoming *Miss Grantham's One True Sin,* which is connected to *The Blue Devil* in some surprising ways. The author would love to hear what you think about either or both stories.